SNAKEBIRD

SNAKEBIRD

Marilyn Dungan

*To Ramona and that guy
she is married to, Howard
Best wishes,*

Marilyn Dungan

Arcane Books
Paris, Kentucky

Published by Arcane Books
P.O. Box 5102
Paris, Kentucky 40362

ISBN 0-9666478-5-8

Library of Congress Catalog Card Number 98-73589

First Edition 1999

Printed in the United States of America

For Claude

Acknowledgments

To say this book was an individual work would be an untruth. If I could, I would list on the cover all the people who contributed in some way to the writing of *Snakebird*.

I was constantly amazed at the willingness and kindness of friends, relatives and strangers to answer my many questions while writing this novel. Special thanks to Hardy Dungan, D.V.M., for his veterinary input, to Chief Conner "Buddy" Fletcher of the Bourbon County Fire and Rescue Department and Bruce H. Forsythe, director of the Hinton-Turner Funeral Home, for technical information. Thank you, Lalie Dick, for your honest appraisal of the publishing process.

Many thanks to my sister, Doris Hamilton, who probably doesn't remember the Christmas day that she suggested that I write a novel and sparked the process. To my other sister, Linda Hertz, I offer my gratitude and admiration for the time and creativity involved in designing the cover of *Snakebird*.

To Ruth Elvove, who read my earliest draft and gave me ongoing insight and support every Wednesday evening, I am especially grateful.

Thanks to Patty Adams for her excellent camera-ready text and to John King for his meticulous copy editing and the extreme patience he must have endured while correcting my manuscript.

Love and thanks to Claude, Julie, Hardy and Kenny for their unwavering confidence in my ability to write *Snakebird*.

Finally, love to my mother–if only you could know.

Prologue

Cutty settled on the Jig 'n' Pig. "One more cast and I'm outta here," he said, baiting his hook with the number eleven pork rind. "Already lost a Bushwacker and my best Hot Spot. Goin through my whole damn tackle box."

He cast his line toward the bank and drew the jig slowly through the muddy water until he sensed the hook. Yanking the rod, he felt the snap and his line waggled a couple passes before coming to rest on the surface.

"Shit! That's it." He threw his rod into the boat, pulled the collar of his worn denim jacket up around his neck and dragged in his stringer. He glared at the two small bass with disgust. "Whatta bitch. Nothin but fish bait. The big ones are probably laughin their gills off under a rock somewhere."

From beneath the johnboat, he heard a thump followed by a killing rasp that ripped at a nerve. "Shoulda known better than to put in after all this rain. The crap washin downstream is tearin my gal up."

Slamming the lever of the trolling motor to the right, he began the wide turnaround. With his hand steady on the throttle, he took a final swallow from his beer then crumpled the can and tossed it into the creek.

Midway through the turn, Cutty spotted white water to his right and heard it spilling over the riffle. Storm debris hung on the crossing and a hulk of a log was caught at dead center.

Lurking behind gray clouds all morning, the sun suddenly slithered free.

Below, a glint of silver.

"What the . . . ain't no damn log."

He pulled out of the turn and headed upstream. As he drove toward the crossing, the motor whined and kicked against the current. He cut to the bank. Reaching calmer water, he trolled to a massive hollow sycamore. Tossing the towline, he drew it tight against a gnarled root, misshapen by years of pounding floodwaters.

He killed the motor and stretched his stubby legs to their limits. By grasping handfuls of weeds and bluebells, he scrabbled sloppily up the embankment on all fours, his lumpish body rolling and heaving with the effort.

When he reached level ground, he hiked his soggy jeans over the crack in his butt and huffed along the sodden bankside toward the crossing. As he trudged through the viscous, plate-size sycamore leaves, his army issue combat boots slicked like catfish. He could almost imagine he was back in 'Nam, emerging from the jungle.

When Cutty broke out of the trees, he could see the object clearly. A canoe–at least what was left of one–lay upside-down and wedged between two rocks. Its aluminum skin had been pummeled into a dimpled and pitted acne, some of the craters twisted into sharp shards of metal.

"Jesus! This one went over the dam."

Something black and white bobbed behind the canoe. Cutty tugged at his camouflage cap and waded into the crossing. He balanced alternately on rocks that jutted out of the swirling water. Eventually, he splashed down between the slick stones. With each ensuing step, the mocha colored water seeped slowly down into his boots, soaking higher and higher on his jeans until settling at knee level.

Then, he saw her. A Border collie lay on her belly in a deep pool, her head and front paws resting on the partly submerged bow of the canoe. Her shivering body churned the murky water.

Cutty caught his breath, "Blackberry . . . that you? Girl, you caught?" Cutty reached beneath the canoe and with a long guttural grunt, heaved it over. As it rolled aside, he heard a sloshing noise. Then slowly, a ghostly mass rose to the surface of the water like a hideous mermaid, golden hair undulating around a battered face. An opened hand, stiffened in death, floundered about like it was grasping for help. With a whimper, Blackberry splashed forward and clawed at the broken form.

"No, Blackberry!" Cutty yelled, his eyes disbelieving, his guts convulsing. He spun, vomited, then watched, transfixed, as his breakfast floated down the creek.

Trying hard not to look at Cara, he lifted Blackberry into his arms. From somewhere above him, Cutty heard a heavy flapping of wings. The serpentine shadow of a snakebird glided ominously across the surface of the water. As Cutty struggled toward the bank, the awkward, primeval bird swung across the riffle and perched clumsily on a limb of a sycamore tree, just like it was any other morning on Stoney Creek.

1

Wednesday, May 1

Drumming her nails on the sill, Laney McVey watched the planes take off and land through the viewing window of concourse 3C. She checked her watch for the fourth time. Where was her sister? She had been waiting for forty-five minutes, time to go to the restroom, collect her luggage from the baggage claim area, and choke down a cup of coffee from a vending machine. Car trouble. That's it, Laney thought to herself. The Whooptie must have finally given up the ghost.

Laney dragged her carry-on, stacked with her laptop and large cardboard box, to the row of public phones, punched in her calling card numbers, and dialed the farm number. She was surprised when she heard a familiar, soft, "Hello." The voice sounded far away.

"Mother, is that you?" Laney asked.

A hand reached around Laney and abruptly broke the connection. "Laney," she heard behind her, then the hand gently pried the phone from hers and hung it up. She spun. It was a moment before she recognized the man standing there.

"Jackson? Jackson Burns! Oh, you handsome thing." She rushed into his arms and gave him a staggering hug. "I was beginning to think I would have to spend my vacation at the airport. God, you look great." Laney bestowed another crushing squeeze, then suddenly pulled back. "Jackson, you disconnected Mother. She'll think I hung up on her. No one hangs up on Mother," she giggled, in mock horror.

Jackson stood silently, letting her rattle on. His dramatic, brown eyes with pupils like black diamonds stared into hers. His jaw clinched, setting his dimple in motion. It appeared and vanished in his left cheek like magic. His hand rested on her shoulder and Laney thought she felt it tremble.

"Jackson, did you hear me? Where's Cara? Is she waiting in the Range Rover?"

Jackson swallowed and looked away. Shuffling his feet, he removed his felt outback hat and raked his fingers through straight, black hair that fell thickly to below his earlobes. When his eyes swung back to Laney, she saw that they had darkened and that he was in some terrible kind of anguish.

Laney's legs began to shake. "Oh God, Jackson . . . something's wrong . . . tell me."

"Laney, not here," he said, his fingers kneading the soft brim of his hat.

With growing alarm, she studied Jackson while he searched with desperate eyes about the terminal. Suddenly, he seized her arm and attempted to lead her toward a door with a sign that read "Conference Room," but Laney dug in, as though bracing for a shock. She stood frozen to the spot, grasping the carry-on handle with white knuckles. With wild eyes riveted on Jackson's face and an out of control thrashing in her chest, she pleaded, "Tell me! My God, Jackson, tell me now!"

With impulsive resignation, he blurted, "Laney, it's Cara. There's been a canoeing accident. Cutty Bell found her this morning . . . below the dam." His lips quivered the words, his eyes darting away from her face. "Laney, I hate telling you this."

As Jackson spoke, Laney felt as though he were turning a cruel dimming switch inside of her, extinguishing her very soul.

"Not Cara," Laney whispered, her body beginning to sway. "Not my Cara."

Images blurred, faded. The carry-on crashed to the floor. Jackson caught her as she pitched forward.

As they drove away from Bluegrass Airport, Laney sat motionless, staring through the windshield with unseeing eyes. Weak and unsteady, she had leaned heavily on Jackson as he had guided her to the Rover. When told about the situation, airport officials had been sympathetic and had loaded all her things into the back of the farm vehicle. She hadn't spoken since Jackson had broken the news, and he looked surprised when she asked in a small and strained voice that didn't seem to belong to her, "How did it happen?"

Jackson cleared his throat. "The police believe she took the canoe out yesterday morning like she always did before breakfast. Stoney Creek was swift and full of debris from our recent rains." He paused in his explanation as though giving her time to swallow the grave account gradually. His expression was grim as he continued. "Somehow, the canoe capsized in the current and she hit her head, either on the canoe or on a floating log. Cutty found her at the crossing below the dam."

"Enough!" Laney shivered, and covered her face with her hands. She pictured Cara plunging into the cold violent creek. A few seconds later, she whispered, "Was she wearing a life jacket?" knowing full well the answer. This was something the two sisters had disagreed about last spring when they'd taken the canoe to "Old Hickory" and back. When she had handed the life jacket to Cara, her sister had rolled her eyes and had tossed it into the bottom of the canoe.

Jackson reached inside his shirt pocket, removed a toothpick and placed it between his teeth. "Laney, you know how fearless your sister was."

Heat suffused her face as though she were feverish. She turned her head and pressed her forehead against the cool window. Jackson's hand reached over and covered hers and she began to cry quietly. Pulling over to the shoulder of the road, he gathered her into his arms. She felt the comforting softness of his chamois shirt upon her cheek.

"Laney, it will be all right," he said. "I'll help you get over this. I swear."

Laney awakened as they were driving through Hickory. For a moment, she didn't remember, but then like a sudden deep thrust to her heart, it all crashed back. How will she ever get over this? Her sister, the one person who was always there for her, was gone.

It began to rain again. The wipers clicked back and forth in a haunting rhythm. Jackson plucked the mangled toothpick from his mouth and stuffed it into an already full ashtray.

The short nap had not revived her. Laney gazed dully at the wet, narrow street–its sloppy and gray dreariness. At the light at Fourth and Main, Laney recognized Nancy Mastin as she splashed across the intersection under a black umbrella. Thomas Castle, a loan officer at Hickory Bank, dashed next door to Max's Barber Shop, a suspended newspaper over his head. Cara had dated him in high school. In fact, Laney had thought that they might get married, but then Cara had met Jay–what's his name–at Western Kentucky University.

"Cara," she whispered, and Jackson's strong hand shot out and enveloped hers again.

The sodden derby banners slapping on every light pole reminded Laney that the Kentucky Derby and the opening of Cara's bed and breakfast were why she had come to Kentucky. Though it was to be a working vacation because of a May thirteenth deadline for an article she had to write for *Three Rivers Magazine*, she'd hardly slept the night before in anticipation of seeing Cara and her mother again. She closed her eyes and prayed for sleep. None of it mattered anymore. Cara was gone.

"Laney, we're here," Jackson announced fifteen minutes later as the Range Rover made a right off Hickory Pike onto the long blacktop lane. A freshly painted sign with "Stoney Creek Bed & Breakfast" printed in Old English lettering, swayed from a black wooden post at the entrance.

"Oh God," she choked, recognizing it as one of the two signs she had mailed to Cara for her thirty-second birthday in March. Her eyes blurred.

To her left, she spotted the black tobacco barn perched on a small rise not far from Hickory Pike. It was empty now. Last year's tobacco was sold long before Christmas, and this year's new plants would not yet be large enough to set out.

The Rover passed under a canopy of mature scarlet maples lining the narrow lane on both sides. The living, green tunnel tossed and shuddered in the driving rain.

As they emerged from the trees, a gray mare in the left paddock reached up and cribbed the top plank with her teeth. Crescent-shaped bites scalloped much of the fence enclosing her pasture. Cara had told her only yesterday, that because Unreasonable was getting so old, this would be the last year that the mare would be bred. Laney could not believe that it was only yesterday morning that she had talked with Cara.

Two fieldstone pilasters topped with coach lights announced the entrance to the yard and in a clump of yews to the right, the second bed and breakfast sign swung recklessly. As Jackson drove through the opening, Laney's eyes traveled immediately to the grand limestone house that stood behind the circular drive.

The house was a solid five-bay, two-story structure with twin chimneys, one on either end, and a promise of a couple more peaking over the wet slate roof. The massive gray walls seemed to rise out of the yard as if they had always been there. The two-over-two wavy glass windows were accented by stone arches with raised keystone, and they dropped to stone sills at floor level on the ground floor. Lending whimsicality to the house, a sparkling white wooden front porch with its small touches of Victorian gingerbread, stretched across the entire width of the house.

The midday rain had dwindled to a misty shower and the swishing branches of the maples and wild cherry trees stilled. Closer to the house, small trios of dogwoods and redbuds dripped raindrops and their delicate blooms softened the cragginess of the rock structure. Beginning at the end of the porch and reaching around and up the chimney wall, tentacles of English ivy felt their way over the shaped stone. They reminded Laney of grasping fingers, clutching at the rock. Two bicycles–one red and one black–rested in a wrought-iron stand to the left of the curved brick walk.

Jackson parked behind the St. Clair County sheriff's car. A gray Chevy station wagon that Laney didn't recognize and her stepfather's green Ford pickup were also parked in the drive.

"Jackson . . . my mother!" she cried. "How could I have forgotten? This will kill her."

Jackson switched off the engine and tucked her icy fingers inside his two warm hands. "Your mother was told this morning. She's waiting for you on the porch."

Reluctantly, Laney tore her hand from Jackson's and stepped from the vehicle. As hot tears intermingled with the chilling drizzle, she ran into her mother's open arms.

2

Wednesday Afternoon, May 1

Laney watched from inside the screen door as Deputy Freddie Rudd balanced his considerable bulk on the narrow wicker stool. Every time Freddie moved, the antique shifted and creaked as though its legs were spreading apart. He braced his feet and tried not to relax, intermittently uttering a short grunt from the isometric exertion. From time to time, he wiped beads of sweat off his upper lip with the back of his hand. It was his job to take notes while Sheriff Gordon Powell questioned Laney's mother and stepfather.

Gordon turned to the Websters. "Mrs. Webster, I know how difficult this is for you so soon after your daughter's death."

Maddy didn't speak and barely nodded. Karl and Maddy were sitting together on the porch swing. The rain had stopped and the sun was trying to escape from behind a fast moving cloud. Maddy shivered and her freckled hand buttoned her pink woolen sweater at the neck, then fluttered and picked at a small snag on the sleeve. She stared at the sheriff with desolate swollen eyes which looked like heavily lashed buckeyes streaked with amber. Her faded red hair was brushed back and secured with a black ribbon that had become untied and trailed over her left shoulder.

Everyone thought she favored her mother, Laney thought. Both of them had freckles and the same thick unruly crimped hair, although Maddy's hair had paled to a beautiful warm redwood and hers was the jolting color of cayenne pepper.

Karl's deep voice interrupted her thoughts. "We'll answer any questions you have, Sheriff," he said, as he nervously pushed off with his feet. The swing rocked backwards. Maddy heeled in and the swing stopped. Karl shot her a contemptuous glance and she lowered her eyes.

Gordon lifted his cap and scratched his head, briefly exposing a band imprint like a halo in his graying blond crewcut.

"When was the last time you spoke with your daughter, Maddy?" Gordon asked, slipping into her given name. Laney remembered that they had known each other since they were small children and in fact, had gone through all twelve grades together.

"Saturday mornin . . . the mornin after she got back from the workshop," Maddy said, drawing a quivering breath.

"What workshop was that, Maddy?" Gordon rearranged his lean buttocks on the porch railing.

"I think it was the one on creative marketin or somethin. She'd gone to so many since she decided to open this bed and breakfast. Anyways, it was in Frankfort. She was gone a couple days."

"Where were you yesterday morning between seven and eight o'clock?" Gordon asked. Maddy brushed back a corkscrew of her hair and rubbed her right eye before she answered. Her hand trembled.

"Home, bakin. Cara's first guests were comin on Friday. She was payin me to do all the bakin for her business. I was makin all my rolls and muffins and this, that, and the other. You know, freezin them ahead. Cara couldn't bake worth a fig . . . but she makes the best homemade jam and herb butter you ever put in your mouth." Maddy's voice raised in pitch and her right hand squeezed and twisted around the chain that supported the swing. Realizing her mother was talking as though Cara were still alive, Laney's face crumpled and a tear rolled down to her chin.

"Damn it, Maddy, the sheriff doesn't want to know your life history. He doesn't have all day," Karl said.

"It's all right, Maddy. I have plenty of time." Gordon smiled at Maddy, then flashed daggers at Karl.

Maddy slumped in the swing with fatigue and grief.

"I think that's all the questions right now," Gordon said. "Why don't you go in and get some rest or something to eat?"

Maddy and Karl stood up to leave.

"Mr. Webster, if you don't mind, I'd like to ask you a few questions," Gordon said.

"What are all these questions for, Sheriff?" Karl whined. "This was an accident pure and simple. That crazy girl went out in a canoe when the creek was deadly. No one had been on that creek for three days at my boat dock. Even "shit for brains" didn't take his boat out until this mornin when he found Cara." Karl gave the chain a shove and the swing swiveled sideways. "Damn weather is costin me an arm and a leg. There are usually so many boaters out there, you can't stir em with a stick."

Freddie struggled to his feet and opened the screen door for Maddy. Her mother's hand caressed Laney's arm as she disappeared into the dark foyer. Karl settled back into the swing and Freddie opted for the larger and more comfortable wicker rocking chair.

"These questions are just routine in any death, Mr. Webster," Gordon said, glaring at Karl with stony eyes. "Everything points to an unfortunate accident, but the coroner in Frankfort has the last say as to cause of death. His results should be in some time tomorrow."

Laney was surprised that Gordon didn't try to hide the disgust that he felt for the man. Indeed, she felt much the same way about her stepfather. Cara had hinted to her that Karl slapped their mother around, but whenever Laney had probed her mother, Maddy denied it.

Karl was a neat little man with a hard body that owed some of his fitness to the physical work of running a boat dock. He had shiny blue-black hair, and Laney suspected that if it were touched, the color would come off on your hand. His small eyes were callous, black shiny beads that slid around in their sockets like ball bearings. The nostrils of his slightly hooked nose had the odd quirk of flaring when he spoke, reminding Laney of fish gills. He wore a plaid long-sleeved shirt and blue jeans that were tucked into his oiled cowboy boots–his year round wardrobe.

Karl and her mother had been married for almost eight years–three years longer than the combined length of his two previous marriages. Laney often wondered about the circumstances behind his two divorces. She had her suspicions.

"Mr. Webster, where were you yesterday morning?" Gordon asked.

Karl shoved off again on the swing.

"I was on my way to Florence to see about buyin a couple paddle boats for the dock. There's a warehouse up there that holds an auction once a month and a buddy of mine in Cincy told me he saw a couple good ones that'll probably go cheap." Karl squirmed in the swing and chewed on a cheek. "Jake said he'd bid for me since I won't be able to go Saturday cause of the Derby. Derby week's a bitch in this business."

Gordon spotted Laney standing inside the door.

"Mr. Webster, will you give the names and addresses of the warehouse and your buddy in Cincinnati to my deputy here?"

Freddie rocked forward and took the information while Gordon stood, crossed the porch and opened the screen door.

"Laney, may I ask you a few questions?" Gordon asked, gently.

Jackson materialized at her side. "Couldn't this wait until tomorrow?"

"It's all right, Jackson," Laney said. "I'd rather get this over with. And there are some questions I'd like to ask Gordon, too." Laney stepped down to the painted wooden surface and settled on the small stool that Freddie had abandoned.

Jackson stood protectively by her side, his hand resting on her shoulder while Karl walked a few steps into the yard and lit a cigarette. Blackberry appeared unexpectedly from behind a clump of hostas edging the wooded hillside beside the house. Walking stiffly across the yard, she climbed the three steps onto the porch and eased her body down under a gigantic Boston fern that hung in a corner. She dropped her head to her paws and was asleep, instantly.

"Could I get you a cup of coffee, Gordon? Jesse made some fresh and there are some of Maddy's ginger muffins in the kitchen," Jackson said.

"Thanks, but no. I need to be leaving in a few minutes," Gordon said. Jackson squeezed Laney's shoulder and disappeared into the house.

"Laney, I believe you were the last person to speak with Cara before she took the canoe out yesterday morning. Could you tell me what you and Cara talked about on the phone?" Gordon asked.

Remembering the call, tears sprung into her eyes once more. "I called her before I left for work to tell her my flight number and arrival time at Bluegrass Airport this morning." She wiped her nose with a tissue. "I knew I would be tied up all day yesterday and I never can reach her in the evening."

"Did she say she was going to take the canoe out?"

"Yes, she seemed to be a little breathless, as though she were in a hurry."

"What time did you call her?"

"It was a little before seven . . . maybe six-fifty or so."

"Did she say she was going canoeing alone?"

"She didn't say, but she hardly ever went with anyone . . . except Blackberry, of course."

"Blackberry always went with her?"

"Always. Cara would paddle from the back seat of the canoe and Blackberry would sit upright in the front as though she were a regular person." Laney's voice caught as she pictured them and she glanced at Blackberry sleeping in the corner.

"How long had she had this ritual of canoeing every morning?" Gordon asked.

"Ever since she married Joe Collins and moved to the farm . . . let's see . . . seven years, I think. Joe gave her Blackberry for their first anniversary. When Joe died two years ago, I thought maybe she would sell the farm and that would be the end of the canoeing, but then Cara decided to make the place into a bed and breakfast. She started taking Blackberry because the day after Cara got the dog, Blackberry jumped off the dock and swam behind the canoe until Cara pulled her in. She was only a puppy."

"Did you ever canoe with your sister when you visited?" Gordon asked.

"Yes. The few times Cara and I canoed together, Blackberry either followed us along the bank or sat in the bottom of the boat in the center. I sometimes thought she resented that I took her spot. Laney shot a quick look at Blackberry before she spoke again. "Gordon . . . did she go over the dam with Cara?"

"We have no way of knowing that for sure, but she didn't have any injuries that we could see. Dr. Prescott checked her over this morning when Cutty Bell brought her in and he said she was close to exhaustion, but no treatment other than rest and nourishment was needed. I think she must have made it to the bank instead of going over the dam when the canoe capsized. She probably followed the canoe down the bank to the crossing. At some point, she must have attempted the crossing and stayed with Cara until Cutty found her." Gordon paused and smiled at Blackberry. "Animals have an eerie sense of loyalty."

"Gordon, these questions . . . is there some reason to think she wasn't alone?" Laney asked.

Gordon shook his head. "Only one paddle was found and of course only Blackberry was at the crossing. We found three paddles in the springhouse with the life jackets and other canoe. Do you remember how many jackets there were?"

"I remember four adult and two children's."

"That checks," Freddie piped in.

Gordon stood. "Guess we'll be on our way. Jackson gave us his statement before he left for the airport this morning. I'll call you tomorrow when the results of the autopsy come in. Again, our condolences on the death of your sister. Please give your mother my sympathy."

Laney walked to the police car with Gordon and Freddie. Gordon ignored Karl who was smoking a second cigarette in the grassy circle formed by the drive.

"Scum," Gordon mumbled under his breath.

Laney, at the round oak table, watched as Jesse fluttered about, wiping off the Italian ceramic tile counter tops. "Jesse, that's the third time you've done that counter."

Jessica Mills was a tall, thin, rather ordinary looking woman with mousy colored hair cut in a short springy bob and pretty gray eyes. She was about the same age as Cara. In fact, they had gone to school together, but Jesse had dropped out her senior year to marry some fast talking salesman from Lexington who was fifteen years older than she. The marriage had lasted about six months and then he'd dropped her like a stone for another sweet thing just out of high school, but not before Jesse had found herself three months pregnant. Laney had thought that perhaps it had been for the best when she'd lost the baby a few weeks after he left. Jesse had no skills to support herself, let alone a child, too. She'd worked at a few bars in Lexington until she found a job at the Finish Line, a popular restaurant in Hickory. She'd worked hard and was now assistant manager for the owner, Maury Morrow. Jesse had been Cara's dearest friend for as long as Laney could remember. Laney, who was six years older, had always thought it an odd coupling.

"I can't help it, Laney. I'm afraid if I think about what happened,

I'll have a go-to-pieces right here in the middle of the kitchen." Jesse's eyes threatened to spill over. She rubbed her nose with the back of her sweatshirt sleeve and opened the pie safe. Removing a plate of Maddy's ginger muffins, she placed them in front of Laney. Next, she retrieved the whipped vanilla cream cheese spread from the refrigerator. "Eat something, Laney. You haven't had a thing."

Laney looked dully at the food and turned her head away. "I have to go to Chase's Funeral Home. Where's Mother?"

"While you were on the phone dictating the obituary to the newspaper, Maddy and Karl left to make the arrangements."

Laney was hurt that her mother hadn't asked her to go with them. On second thought, she figured Karl had something to do with the way they had slipped out without her knowing. She sensed he disliked her as much as she disliked him.

She watched absently, while Jesse started on the short back splash behind the porcelain sink. Laney's gaze traveled upward to the bright red and white chintz framing the window that overlooked the screen porch and to the matching paper on the soffit and walls. Dark polished oak cabinets inset with leaded glass, hung around the U-shaped kitchen. A drop-in range set in the counter top separated the kitchen from the breakfast room. To Laney's left, a wood-framed eighteenth century clock said five-forty and next to it, colorful old tin boxes teetered on the top of the antique pie safe.

Laney sometimes amazed herself at how well she could tune things out when she tried. Out of the blue, she asked, "Where's Jackson?"

"He had to get Unreasonable up to be checked by Dr. Prescott. She was bred yesterday morning."

"You mean Gray is coming to the farm?" Laney asked, as she squirmed uncomfortably in her chair. She picked at her muffin.

"You still care for Gray, don't you?"

"Of course not. It ended last year when I was here," Laney said a little too quickly.

"Cara told me that she told you about Gray dating her a long time ago."

"I don't want to talk about it."

"He dumped her," Jesse said, as she pulled out a chair and collapsed, her energy finally depleted. "Is that why you stopped seeing him?"

"Jesse, I live in Pittsburgh and he's a vet in this embryonic town."

Jesse smiled a knowing little smile and said, "You didn't answer my question."

"Listen, I caught that look and this is none of your damn business," Laney said. She stood so abruptly that her chair almost toppled as she charged out the French doors onto the screened porch. She didn't stop there. She continued out to the kitchen garden, banging the screen door behind her.

Laney followed the damp stepping stones to a iron bench under a wild cherry tree and sat down on the wet seat. She fought the tears but they came anyway–hot rivulets of pain that slid down her face and soaked into inky stains on her dark skirt. They poured silently from some bottomless reservoir near her heart. As though looking through a waterfall, Laney caught a sudden movement and Blackberry appeared from behind the short rock wall surrounding the garden. Laney wiped her eyes with her sleeve and reached out her hand. When she heard her name, Blackberry turned her handsome face toward her. Then, with a wary look, she painfully crept away, her full white-tipped tail tucked under her body.

Laney shrugged. "Put it all out of your mind, Laney. Don't think about it. Don't think about Cara. Don't think about Gray. Tune it out. It's worked before. Get through this funeral and go back to your peaceful apartment in Pittsburgh."

"Jesse, I just called to apologize for my outburst earlier this evening. I'm so tired. I guess my temper got the best of me." Laney forced the words into the phone.

"Laney, it's okay. No apology necessary. Should have minded my own business. Is there something I can do for you?" Jesse asked.

"Actually, there is. I'm in the library looking for the name of the family that was coming this Friday as Cara's first guests. I have to cancel their reservations right away."

"Look in the file drawer next to the desk. Cara kept a folder with all the reservations for the month of May in there," Jesse said.

"Hold on, Jesse." Laney pulled the drawer open and began to search. "Here it is. As Laney pulled out the reservation file, the contents spilled out onto the floor. "Damn! This looks like a bunch of letters." Holding the phone against her ear with her shoulder, Laney shuffled through the envelopes. "This can't be it . . . wait . . . here it is. Some mail must have gotten into the wrong file." Laney placed the sheet of paper on the desk and scanned the page. "The name for Friday, May third, is Mr. and Mrs. Charles Baldwin from St. Louis."

"That's it, Laney. Give me the phone number and I'll call them for you and tomorrow, I'll get the list and cancel the rest of the names."

"Oh Jesse, would you? That would be such a help." Laney quickly gave Jesse the number and sighed to herself. One more problem taken care of.

Laney heard a faint tap at the front door and Blackberry began to bark. "I have to go, Jesse. Someone's at the door." Laney hung up the phone, abruptly.

Laney turned out the desk lamp and stepped out into the hall, shutting the door behind her. As she passed the hall-tree, she glanced at her reflection in the beveled mirror inset. A pallid face with deep ashy smudges under red-rimmed brown eyes stared back at her. Her curly red pepper hair sprang out around her freckled face like it had a soul of its own. Laney rushed away from the reflection and pulled at the dark, wood-paneled front door. As the massive door swung open, Laney could see Jackson through the screen leaning against the porch rail. She turned on the porch light and stepped out. The night air was cold and Laney hugged her arms and felt goose bumps.

"I hope I didn't waken you, Laney. I didn't want you to think I had deserted you this afternoon. I wanted to stay, but there's the farm to run, you know."

"I appreciate all you've done, Jackson, and no, I hadn't gone to bed yet. There's so much to do . . . think about. I don't think I could sleep anyway. Did Unreasonable check out all right?"

"She ovulated, and that's good. She was bred yesterday morning and you want the mare to ovulate within forty-eight hours."

"Is that where you were when Cara? . . ." Laney forced the words out, wondering why she really needed to know, anyway.

"I'm sure Cara was already out on the creek when I left. Unreasonable was booked for the eight-thirty breeding and I left a little after seven. It's about an hour to Wilmere Stud."

"Didn't you usually see Cara during the day?" Laney asked, softly. It was an effort for her to speak.

"Not necessarily. It wasn't unusual for a couple days to pass without touching base with her, especially lately when she was getting the house ready for the opening." Jackson reached out and touched Laney's bare arm. "You're cold." He stepped forward and his arms closed around her. "Let me warm you."

"Jackson, I feel like I'm in a fog . . . in a bad dream."

He didn't speak but she knew he understood her pain.

Laney watched as the Rover's lights faded into the darkness on the farm road to Jackson's little house by the creek. Thank God for Jackson, she thought. What would the farm would do without him? Jackson had learned all about horses and their care from his father who had managed the farm before him until his death. When Paul Carson had retired, Joe and Cara had bought the place and Jackson had kind of come with the farm. Joe Collins, who had been twenty-two years older than Cara, and a successful bloodstock agent, knew a good horseman when he saw one and had hired Jackson even before closing on the property. What would become of the farm now, she pondered. Would Jackson have to leave when it sold? She couldn't imagine Stoney Creek Farm without him.

Laney closed the heavy front door behind her. With the latch's solid click, a dark and sheltering silence whispered through the old limestone house. Even the grandfather clock in the front hall ticked with a hushed, cathedral-like softness. Laney crossed the rich silk Persian rug that covered the polished wooden floor and as she climbed the staircase, she noticed that the scarlet runner was held in place by brass rods. She felt the lustrous smoothness of the cherry wood balustrade under her hand and breathed in the woody scent of furniture polish.

Above the mahogany wainscoting, an emerald green wall covering framed a succession of oval photos of her family. Laney's grandmother, Charlotte, was first, her hair the color of claret and twisted severely into a tight knot. Two steps further up was Laney's favorite picture of her father holding three year old Cara in his lap. Her heart-shaped face looked up at Poppy adoringly. Golden curls spilled down her forehead and framed her blue eyes. Because her father was gazing down at his youngest daughter, Laney couldn't see the color of his eyes, but she knew that they were the same clear sapphire blue, like the sky on a brilliant sunny day. Grandmother, Cara, and Poppy, all gone now. Laney didn't stop to look at the last two pictures. The memories were too real and the agony of Cara's death too raw.

The first bedroom at the top of the stairs was the room she usually stayed in when she was at her sister's home, so she turned right and reached for the light switch on the wall. The room exploded with light. She saw that the room was totally redecorated for the bed and breakfast, dramatically different from the bold, rich, glowing rooms of the main floor. She wondered if the other five bedrooms were this gay. There was color, but it was softer, lighter. The walls were covered with a delicate pink and gray-green floral pattern–almost impressionistic–and all the woodwork, including the wide crown molding, was painted a slightly deeper tone of pink. Over the queen size bed, hung half canopied drapes that were swagged and secured with lavish satin bows. A pure white lace curtain hung behind. The bed was covered simply with one of her mother's beautiful quilts. Layers of crisp white pillows trimmed in lace completed the effect.

Laney spotted her luggage, laptop, and the large carton she had brought for Cara next to the wicker chaise. She carried the box to the closet and deposited it on the top shelf. It was to have been her gift to her sister on the opening of the bed and breakfast. Her jaws clinched painfully, as she unpacked her suitcase. She hung a few items in the closet, then stuffed the rest of her clothes into dresser drawers. After arranging her toiletries in the bathroom, she reached down into the bottom of her luggage and retrieved her copy of *The World Life List of Birds*, a bird identification book that she never traveled without. Kicking off her shoes, she sank into the downy cushions of the chaise longue.

The room had a serene old-fashioned air, reminding her of her apartment bedroom in Pittsburgh. Cara's personal touches were in evidence everywhere, from the small crystal vase filled with sunny lemon colored tulips on the bureau, to the oval-framed photo on the tiny table next to the chaise. Laney touched the glass over the photo, wishing she could somehow travel through it to touch her sister. Cara and she were holding hands, she with untamed hair flying about her freckled face, and Cara with her free hand poised on her hip and curled tongue thrust out at the photographer.

"Cara."

As Laney placed the bird book next to the frame, she moved aside a tiny pink pincushion trimmed in lace. No doubt her sister had been the one who had studded it with the bead-topped pins. Laney ran her fingers over the colorful beads, then quickly grabbed the cushion up and held it to the light. This time, she couldn't stop the broken whimper that grew to wracking sobs. The pins spelled out her name.

3

Thursday, May 2

"Whatta you think?" Freddie asked, in a muffled voice. He had an annoying habit of talking with his mouth full. Gordon thought he always seemed to have his mouth full. Gordon and his deputy were having lunch at the Finish Line Restaurant, and Freddie had just chomped off a huge bite of a meatball sandwich.

Gordon took a deep swallow of iced tea before answering. "Everything checks out. According to Jake Rudnik, the guy that's supposed to bid on those paddle boats for Karl, Karl was seen at Bailey's Warehouse in Florence about nine a.m. Tuesday. Ben Smith from the PD up there checked it out for me. He owed me one and it saved me a trip."

"What about Jackson's story?" Freddie slurped the last of his pop and swallowed a burp.

"I just got back from Wilmere Stud. Jackson brought the mare for a eight-thirty a.m. breeding the morning Cara died. The farm showed me the breeding record for Captain Jim and Jackson's signature on the breeding papers. Guess the autopsy report will sew it up."

"I still can't believe that girl took that canoe out on that creek without a life jacket," Freddie said, sopping up the drippings on his plate with the last hunk of Italian roll and popping it into his mouth.

"You never met her, did you?" Gordon asked.

"Nope. She some kind of a free spirit or just nuts?"

"She was . . . well, maybe outrageous is the word I'm searching for. She marched in fast time, at least until she married Joe. She did everything fast. Talked fast. Walked fast. Drove fast. I'd given her three speeding tickets before she even got out of high school. Poor Maddy bit her nails to the quick over that one. Marriage seemed to settle her down some and ever since Joe died, she'd been too busy fixing up the place to do much damage."

"Was she dating anyone?" Freddie munched on a cracker that had come with Gordon's chef salad.

"I don't think there was anyone special. I remember she dated Doc Prescott for a while before she married Joe, but something happened there and they split. Speak of the devil." "Hey Doc," he called to a tall man who had just entered the restaurant.

Graham Prescott approached the table with his secretary, Natine Sullivan, a jolly girl who had worked for Gray ever since he had bought the practice ten years before.

"What's going on?" Gray said, tucking his hands under his armpits as though he were embarrassed by their size. His khaki pants were spattered with blood from an early morning cow prolapse and a suspicious brown ring around the right shoulder of his green surgery scrubs revealed a possible pregnancy check on a mare or two during his horse farm rounds. Gordon caught a whiff of manure originating from his Wellingtons.

"Grab a seat, you two. We have room," Gordon said. Gray and Natine pulled out chairs and sat down. "I've finished, but Freddie here is contemplating dessert."

The waitress, dressed in a red jockey silk with a matching cap, took their orders and left.

"Nice tan, Doc. How's your mother?" Gordon asked.

"Great . . . still loves Florida. Wanted me to stay longer but spring's my busiest time." A frown suddenly crowded his features. "Gordon, heard about Cara's death when Cutty brought Blackberry in. Can't believe it. Laney and her mother must be devastated."

"They're taking it pretty hard. Even the dog seems depressed. She won't go to anyone and Maddy said she won't eat."

Gray looked concerned, "Maybe I should stop out there and look at her again. Was going to stop in yesterday but felt it wouldn't be a good time."

The waitress brought their lunches and Freddie plunged into a piece of cherry topped cheesecake.

"When Cutty brought Blackberry to the clinic yesterday morning, she was shivering so badly, I thought she had hypothermia," Natine said while plopping some catsup on her plate. "Cutty said Cara looked pretty beat up . . . like she had gone over the dam with the canoe." Natine shook her head as though picturing Cara. "She was such a beautiful woman . . . and so full of life."

At that moment, Gordon's walkie-talkie squawked and he went outside to the squad car. When he returned, he motioned to Freddie to join him at the cash register. Gordon threw a quick wave to Gray and Natine.

"That confirms it," Gordon said, as they walked to the car. "The coroner's report's in. Death by drowning. The blow on her head was consistent with a fall against the canoe or debris. It may have knocked her unconscious, but it didn't kill her. Plenty of creek water in her lungs. When she was swept over the dam, the undertow probably beat her against the dam, released her, then washed her downstream to the riffle with the canoe. That would explain the cuts and contusions all over her body."

Freddie moaned as he climbed into the police car.

"Did you eat too much?" Gordon laughed.

"Nope, I didn't get to finish my cheesecake."

"Lose your appetite ?" Natine asked, as she nibbled a French fry.

Gray took a sip of coffee and played with his bowl of chili. Finally, he just pushed it aside.

"Don't know what's wrong with me. Take that back. Do know. It's Cara's death."

"I didn't know that you still cared for her. I'm really sorry . . . or is it Laney you are concerned about?" Natine added.

"Sometimes you know me better than I know myself."

"I've worked for you for ten years. Occasionally, your cloaked emotions do infiltrate this clairvoyant overworked brain of mine." Natine grinned a dazzling smile that burnished her bronze cheeks.

Gray had shared numerous failed romances with his secretary and at different times she was mother, Dear Abby, or big sister to him.

"Okay. Been avoiding Laney and feel guilty as hell about it. Think

I'll go to see her this evening after my last call. How's that, 'Oh Mystic One?'" Gray slid his bowl of chili back in front of him and plowed in. "Hungry, all of a sudden."

Sounds outside Laney's window awakened her. At first, she thought she was in her city apartment and morning traffic was passing under her window. Gradually though, she recognized the sound of a tractor and mower out in the paddock. She opened her eyes and squinted at the sun streaming through the lace curtains covering the open window beside her bed. She stretched and for a sweet moment, absorbed the sounds and smells of the spring morning on the farm. The strong aroma of rich coffee and luscious yeasty cinnamon drifted up from the kitchen. Then, the staggering jolt of reality hit hard.

"Laney," a voice said, from outside the door to her bedroom. The door opened and her mother walked in carrying a wicker tray.

"Mother," Laney struggled to a sitting position in the large bed. "How did you get in?"

Maddy laid the tray in front of Laney and sat on the edge of the bed.

"Cara gave me a key so I could put my baked goods in the freezer if she wasn't here. Have some hot coffee and one of my cinnamon rolls. It's past noon."

Laney reached over the tray and caught one of Maddy's hands. They were like ice. With her touch, a veil of heartache dropped over Maddy's face, then quickly lifted as she gave Laney one of her artificial smiles. Awe Mother, Laney thought. You deal with pain the same way I do. You emotionally disconnect.

The phone and the doorbell rang all day long. Everyone offered their condolences and wanted to know what they could do to help. Neighbors and friends dropped off casseroles, roasts, desserts, breads, and salads. By supper time both refrigerators were full. Maddy labeled every offering with the person's name written in ink on masking tape which she stuck to the dish. She faithfully remained at the house even though Karl called twice, asking her to hurry home to help with the boat dock. He called one last time to tell her he had hired a college boy to help him with the boats throughout the weekend. Laney had taken the call and had listened with distaste to his peevish voice.

Laney made a pot of freshly brewed tea and set out Cara's blue and white china teapot and two matching cups and saucers. Earlier, they had eaten a light supper of a savory lamb stew that Dory Beale, from the Hickory Christian Church, had brought over.

Maddy let Blackberry in for the night and she slunk into the pantry where she curled up on her rug. Laney and Maddy were drinking their tea in detached silence when the phone rang. They both startled. When Laney returned to the table, her hands fumbled at her teacup, making tiny clinking noises as she replaced it in the saucer.

"That was Gordon. He said the autopsy report was in and that the cause of death was drowning. They're officially ruling her death an accident." Laney looked away for a moment, then finished her tea. She stood and carried her cup and saucer to the sink.

"Mother, I'm really tired. Would you mind if I go on to bed?"

Her mother looked disappointed but said, "I'll see you in the mornin, honey. The service is at eleven."

Laney bent down and kissed her mother on the cheek. When she rested her hand on Maddy's shoulder she could feel her bones through the thin blouse. The fine cobweb wrinkles around her eyes had deepened and her lips were narrow and pinched. Quickly, Laney disappeared into the back hall and climbed the narrow back stairs to her room.

When Laney stepped out of the bathroom, she heard voices downstairs. "God, who could that be so late? Surely it's not someone with more food." She heard a light step outside her room and her mother opened the door and peeked in.

"Laney, I'm leaving. Gray's downstairs checking Blackberry. He said not to disturb you and that he would let himself out." Maddy shut the door before she could respond.

Laney stiffened. Her stomach was a rubber band pulled taut. She wiped her palms on her gown and rubbed the back of her neck.

"I won't go down there," she swore to herself, and crossed the room to her bed. When she clicked off the bedside light and pulled the quilt up under her chin, the moonlight swept over the room, its white light merging, shaping, and transforming it into a mysterious place. She heard the slightest tap on the door and she knew he was there.

"Laney," he whispered. "Please don't be frightened. I needed to come."

Then he was standing there in the moonlight, a luminous form by the bedside. Laney's heart thumped against her ribs and her breath came short and shallow.

"Gray, don't–"

"Laney, let it be. There are no words. Just let me comfort you now." Gray reached out and touched the side of her face and she heard him catch his breath, almost like a sob. She fumbled for his hand and covered it against her cheek. He sat by her side and gathered her to his chest and cradled her, rocking gently, his breath a whisper against her hair. She felt his fingers brush her lips like a passing breeze. She wanted him to hold her forever.

When she finally slept, she dreamed Gray lowered her to the pillow, pressed his lips against her palm, then vanished as the moon slid behind a silvery cloud.

4

Friday, May 3

For Laney, the day of the funeral never existed. May third was as lost to her as if it had been torn away from the world's calendars forever. She was physically present but like a sleepwalker, she was unfocused and undefined–like someone who looks at the sky on a clear night and doesn't see the stars.

The graveside services were held at St. Clair County Cemetery under an ancient black oak with gigantic spreading limbs. Laney sat next to her mother and on her left, Jackson pressed her hand tightly throughout the service. Laney didn't hear the words of Reverend Dunbar, only the endless sing-song drone of the scriptures he read. A yellow butterfly lit briefly on the spray of yellow roses on the casket, then fluttered away like it had better things to do. Then it was over and friends gathered around them, expressing their sorrow and wiping their eyes and noses with sodden handkerchiefs. Laney thought she recognized Gray standing next to Karl with the other pallbearers, but she wasn't sure. All seemed just a blur but she did catch bits of Carolyn Hendrick's remark to her sister, Jesse, that Laney "appeared spacy . . . a million miles away." If only she were, Laney thought. Jackson clutched her arm possessively, and finally propelled her away from the tent to the waiting limousine. All that Laney could think of was that her sister was finally put to rest and that she could soon leave for Pittsburgh.

But it wasn't yet over. The house filled with friends and neighbors, everyone talking, eating, and commenting on the funeral and the beautiful house. Jesse and Carolyn kept the dining table replenished with food and drink from the kitchen and pantry.

Jackson, Laney, and Maddy sat in the parlor on the red damask covered sofa. Laney looked down at her black suit and thought how odd the three of them looked–three pairs of black covered knees–like ebony piano keys, neatly together. Across the room, Karl, also dressed in black with a string tie tipped in silver, stood in front of the marble topped center table talking with several unsavory looking characters that he had invited to the house after the funeral.

Maddy broke the silence. "Karl looks like he's holdin court," she said and looked away. A bony little man with thinning gray hair and wearing unbuckled black rubber galoshes entered the room and galumphed toward the sofa. Karl followed him with his eyes. Marshall Knight introduced himself to Laney as her sister's attorney. He offered his sympathy to her and Maddy, and he shook hands with Jackson.

Turning to Maddy and Laney, Mr. Knight said, "Miss McVey, there are some legal matters that must be attended to before you return to Pittsburgh. Could I see both you and Mrs. Webster in my office on Monday morning, say about ten o'clock?"

"I guess that–" Maddy began.

"Mr. Knight, I was planning to leave on Sunday," Laney interrupted.

Her mother turned to her quickly and said, "Would you stay a few days and help me pack up Cara's personal belongings?" She rubbed her right eye.

Laney's whole body screamed to refuse but the thought of her mother going through all of Cara's things alone was just was too cruel. Laney nodded and said, "Yes."

Marshall turned to Jackson, "May I speak to you in private? Perhaps on the back porch?"

Jackson stood and followed Marshall out of the room.

The screened porch off the kitchen was deserted. Marshall followed Jackson through the French doors, and Jackson's eyes immediately focused upon the creek below the house.

Marshall offered Jackson a cigarette. "No thanks," Jackson said, as he stuck a toothpick into his mouth.

"Jackson, I don't know what your plans are, but as executor, I would appreciate it if you could at least stay on here until the estate is settled. I would continue to pay you at the same salary. You do an outstanding job and it would be a relief to know that you were still in charge."

Jackson looked over to the buggy house that was used as a garage. When he turned back to Marshall, he was smiling.

"Thank you for the compliment, Marshall. I'll be glad to stay on as long as you want." Jackson shifted the toothpick to the other side of his mouth.

"Damn, you're an agreeable fellow. What a relief. I don't know what I'd have done if you had refused." Marshall looked out at four wood ducks leaving rings on the water below. "God, this is a beautiful place. You've lived here all your life, haven't you?"

"Yes, you can see my little house from here in the winter when the leaves are off the trees. It also overlooks the creek."

"I understand your father was the farm manager until he died some years ago." Marshall opened the screen door and flicked his cigarette butt into the yard. Jackson frowned at the thoughtless littering and didn't answer.

"Jackson, let me know if there is anything you need to keep this farm operating smoothly. I sure appreciate your cooperation." He shook Jackson's hand vigorously and clumped through the French doors. Jackson continued to gaze at the creek. He never got tired of looking at it.

The day was almost over. Laney lingered on the screened porch and watched the shadows gradually inch down beneath the trees to the dark water below. The evening sun dipped behind the house, its final glow mottling the new leaves on the treetops with molten gold. Someone called her name and she turned to see Gray in the daylight for the first time. Blackberry stood by his side. He reached down and scratched her ear, and she didn't sulk away.

"I think she's coming out of it, Laney. She is depressed. She lost someone she loved, too."

Blackberry's brown eyes looked up at Gray and she sat down at his heel.

"It seems you have a way with her. She won't come to me," Laney said.

"Give her time. Touch her. Talk to her. She'll come around."

Just like I did last night, Laney thought. "About last night, Gray. Thank you for–"

"No reason for thanks, Laney. I know how much you loved your sister," Gray said, while tucking his hands under his armpits.

Laney remembered his self-conscious gesture from last spring. He looked almost the same–perhaps a little heavier. He had removed the jacket to his navy suit and his striped tie lay slightly askew against his oxford cloth shirt. The button down collar was frayed. The same turquoise eyes leaped out of his tan face and the smile lines traveled long from the corner of his eyes to well below his mouth. That mouth. Laney could remember its sweet softness upon her lips last spring. The memories were too vivid. She shifted her feet and tore her eyes away.

"Laney, why didn't you answer my phone calls? I left messages on your voice mail at least a dozen times and even sent e-mail to *Three Rivers Magazine*. Maddy gave me your address."

"I don't want to talk about it, Gray. It's in the past." Laney strode abruptly to the screen door. Blackberry bolted under the white iron porch table and curled up with her head on her paws.

"Damn it! Some things have to be faced, spoken about." Gray took hold of her arms and turned her around. Motionless, like a mannequin in a store window with movable limbs that could be worked into any position, she gazed at him. Her arms dangled at her side under his grip. Suddenly, he crushed her to his chest. "Laney, how can I restore your sparkle?"

"Gray, leave me be." She twisted away.

Gray dropped his arms. "Forgive me. This isn't the time. Like Blackberry, you need time to heal."

Discouraged, but not defeated, he opened the screen door. "Would you take a walk with me before it gets dark? Everyone has left."

Laney hesitated, then nodded, and they stepped out into the yard.

They followed the flagstone walk toward the buggy house. Laney glanced back at the porch as though she didn't want to leave the security of the house. Blackberry sat on her haunches, peering at them through the screen.

"Laney, this is a wonderful old building. Look at that crumbling shake roof. Let's go inside." Gray turned the white porcelain doorknob and they stepped inside. Laney gasped.

"Laney, what is it?" Gray asked.

"The Whooptie. I knew it was in here but it's still a shock to suddenly see Cara's car." The dusty, 1989 white Nissan Sentra was parked on two tracks in the center of the floor. A dent in the passenger's side door, a couple scrapes on the right fender, and some rust around the wheel wells indicated a long and perilous life.

"Why did she call it the Whooptie?" Gray asked.

"I'm not sure, but I suppose it was after her expression for exuberance. You know, 'whoop-de-do.'" Laney raised a forefinger in the air and twirled it around while she looked upwards with a wry look on her face.

Gray laughed, relieved to see that Laney saw a little humor in something. "Where do the trap doors lead to?" Gray pointed to double wooden doors in the floor in front of the car.

"There's a stone ice house under the buggy house. Before electricity, landowners cut blocks of ice out of the creek and hauled them up the hill. Then they would carry the blocks down the steps and layer them with straw. The ice would keep all summer."

"Let's go look," Gray said excitedly.

"Not me. The cellar is about fifteen feet deep and full of snakes." Laney had a quick chill.

"Snakes? On second thought, maybe another time. I admit I'm a weenie when Mr. Snake is around."

His head rolled upwards. "Look at those old tobacco cottons." Gray pointed upward to the thick braids of dirty gray gauze hanging from the rafters. "You don't see those anymore. Most farmers are cultivating the plants in greenhouses. Gray walked over to one of the six foot high windows and rubbed a peephole in the grimy, wavy glass. "What's that building, Laney?"

She crossed the wooden floor and peered down at a rock building on a slope near the creek.

"That's where Cara kept the canoes. Years ago, it was used as a springhouse. Laney turned and looked at Gray. "Let's go back." Then she was gone, her heels clicking on the flagstones as she dashed to the screened porch.

They sat in the breakfast room drinking hot tea. Gray cut himself a piece of hummingbird cake and licked the cream cheese icing off his fingers. "Want a piece?"

Laney shook her head. "That has to be the most fattening cake in the world."

"Maddy claims it's calorie free," Gray said, as he forked a moist bite into his mouth. "She made one of these for my birthday. Think I ate the whole cake by myself—with a little help from Puccini."

"How is Puccini? The last time I saw him, he was up in a tree."

"Thanks to Blackberry. Sure learned a lesson there. Don't let him out of the truck when Blackberry's outside."

Laney pictured the gray tabby, named for the Italian operatic composer, stretched out below the windshield of Gray's Grand Cherokee like some kind of furry dashboard ornament.

"How's the publishing business these days? Still doing the "Pittsburgh After Dark" feature for *Three Rivers Magazine*?" Gray asked, as he pressed his fork down on the few remaining crumbs on his plate.

Laney sighed, "Yes, in fact I have to write one by next Monday."

"Have you started your novel yet?"

Laney waved the dream away with her hand. "Novel writing takes a commitment I just can't seem to make. Working full time for *Three Rivers* and squeezing that feature in every two weeks is all I can handle right now. I'd have to set up a regular writing schedule and not let anything get in its way."

Blackberry walked over to Gray and sat looking up at him. Her tail pumped away, begging for attention. Laney reached down instead and stroked between her ears. Blackberry didn't move away. "Well, that's a start, I guess," Laney said.

"When are you going back to Pittsburgh?" Gray asked with lowered eyes.

"I'll begin packing Cara's things tomorrow. That should take a couple days, then Mother and I will see Cara's lawyer on Monday. Shortly after that, I imagine. In fact, tomorrow I'd better call and change my flight."

"Laney, will you let me know before you leave this time?" Gray blinked a couple times and Laney watched his jaw muscles work.

Laney stood and crossed to the French doors. She tried to see through the darkness to the creek but only her reflection in the glass stared back. Behind her she caught Gray's hand brush across his eyes.

"Yes, Gray, I promise."

5

Saturday, May 4

It seemed as though Laney had just fallen asleep when harsh ringing startled her awake. Moaning, she fumbled for the phone.

"Laney," said the tight, tired voice of her mother. "I won't be able to help you today. Karl needs me to help with the boat dock." Struggling to clear her head, Laney opened her eyes and was surprised to see light filtering through the lace curtains.

"He has to haul a boat to Frankfort for someone and the boaters are standing in line to put in. That college kid he hired for the weekend isn't worth much. He can do some of the grunt work but I have to keep an eye on things so I'm afraid to leave."

"Mother," Laney said, yawning, "I can handle it. If it gets too much, I can call Jesse. She offered to help." There was a commotion in the background and Laney heard her mother tell someone she would be right there.

"I've got to go, Laney," her mother said and hung up.

Laney dressed in a pair of jeans and a oversized T-shirt with "Pittsburgh Pirates" in black and yellow letters printed under a colorful picture of a snarly pirate. When she reached the bottom of the stairs, Blackberry waited by the front door. As Laney opened the door and bent to pet her, Blackberry bolted past her in pursuit of a red squirrel that was flapping his bristling tail on the porch railing. Laney fixed a pot of coffee and heated the last cinnamon roll in the microwave. She carried her breakfast out to the screened porch on a wicker tray.

The day was gray and still. Through the buckeye trees, Laney saw ominous clouds quietly forming. As she sat at the round table, once again her eyes were drawn to the shadowy creek. Some obscure and unsettling energy seemed to ascend from its calm surface. Laney jerked her head away and attempted to erase the compelling creek from her mind.

As she took a last sip of her coffee, Laney became aware of someone watching her through the screen door. "God, Jackson, you startled me!"

"I'm sorry, Laney. I knocked at the front door but I guess you didn't hear me." He opened the door and stepped onto the porch. "I brought the boxes you wanted." He handed her the morning newspaper.

"Thanks," Laney said, thinking of the job ahead. "I really need to get started, but I keep dragging my feet. All Cara's things . . . how will I bear to see it all again?"

"I wish I could help you get through this." Jackson put his arm around her and squeezed a shoulder. Bending, he kissed her on the forehead. "Why not postpone the packing and go to a derby party with me this afternoon?"

Laney looked at Jackson in surprise, "I couldn't possibly . . . but thank you."

Jackson opened the screen door and turned, "Laney, you know I'm always here for you. I care very much. Please don't forget that. I'll put the boxes on the front porch."

He left as silently as he had appeared.

Laney hurried down the hall to the library to look up the number of the Bluegrass Airport so she could change her reservations. On the way, she searched her purse for her return ticket to Pittsburgh.

When she opened the door, she was assaulted by the musty odor of old books. The dark shuttered room came to life in the soft glow of the fringed desk lamp. Strange how she hadn't noticed the wall of beautifully bound books the other night when she had called Jesse. Last spring when she had been here, the bookcases had been empty and layered with dust from the newly sanded floors.

She crossed the room and skimmed over the titles. Some of the well-thumbed volumes had belonged to her father: Mark Twain's complete works, Walt Whitman's *Leaves of Grass*, the poems and plays of Robert Browning, and the fifty volume set of the *Harvard Classics* in their blue leather bindings. Laney hadn't seen them for years. Cara must have salvaged the books from Maddy's damp basement, where they'd been stored when Karl had displaced them with his sleazy paperbacks.

Laney turned toward the double pedestal flat-top desk and was admiring its black walnut finish with burl-veneer details, when she spotted the reservation list that she had forgotten to give to Jesse the day before. *Damn, these people have to be called.* As she reached for the desk phone, she stepped on some papers lying on the floor. The contents of the file she had dropped the night she had arrived were just as she had left them. Laney gathered the envelopes together and began to stuff them back into the file folder. A photograph slipped out of one of the envelopes, and as she retrieved it, she paused and studied the picture. It was of a mustached young man standing next to black convertible. Laney wasn't sure why she pulled the accompanying letter out of the envelope. If she felt a pang of guilt for reading her sister's mail, it didn't prevent her from reading the complete note:

> *Dear L-P Box 12H,*
> *Your ad caught my eye. I've never done this before, but there is a first time for everything.*
> *I'll begin by introducing myself. My name is Tony. I am 38, divorced, no dependents. I'm 5'11" tall, brown eyes, auburn hair, and about 170 pounds. I love cooking (pretty good, too), flying (I have a pilot's license), and boating (I own a boat and a RV dealership). I majored in business in college and would enjoy someone like you that likes dining out, good conversation, dancing, and the outdoors. I hope my photo doesn't scare you off.*
> *If you are interested in meeting sometime, call me at the number below.*
> *Tony*

Laney's mouth dropped open in disbelief. Surely her sister hadn't placed an personal ad in a classified newspaper. Laney plopped down on the oriental carpet. She rummaged through the rest of the envelopes, pulling out the letters and reading them. Only two others included photographs but several had business cards enclosed. There must be a couple dozen letters here from guys, Laney concluded.

As she stared down at the mail, she noticed one large manila envelope from the *Lexington Post* that had Cara's address on the front. Evidently, the newspaper had collected the responses and had sent them to Cara in this envelope, she reasoned. Peering inside, she saw what appeared to be a newspaper clipping. She plunged in her hand and extracted the partial page that had been ripped out of a classified section. A penciled red circle enclosed a small personal ad:

> *Pretty, intelligent female, 32, interested in meeting a mature, professional, sincere male with a sense of humor for dining, dancing, outdoor activities, and conversation. L-P Box 12H, Lexington, Ky. 40510.*

Laney leaned back on the wooden file cabinet next to the desk. She wiped her flushed face. Why would Cara do this?

Suddenly, Laney heard Blackberry barking in the front yard, followed by a light step in the hall. Before she could jump up, Jesse poked her head in the library. "The front door was open so I let myself in. I saw the light on in here."

"Jesse, don't you ever knock before you enter a house?" Laney scrambled around on the floor gathering up all the letters and cramming them into the folder. Her face burned hot and her hands shook. And when she glanced up briefly, she realized that Jesse knew just how rattled she was.

They spent most of the afternoon in Cara's bedroom that was part of the new section of the house that Cara and Joe had built on to the back. Laney didn't mention the letters nor did Jesse ask about her strange behavior. Laney was sure Jesse could sense her disquiet, but couldn't bring herself to admit to Jesse that her sister had placed the ad. Surely, her sister hadn't told anyone about the ad. She would have been too embarrassed.

The master suite off the kitchen and behind the back staircase was light and spacious. Laney saw that it was the perfect private quarters for the bed and breakfast. Like her own room upstairs, the colors were delicate and simple. Pale gray painted walls softly set off the antique lace coverlet, threaded with ribbons, that covered the dusky blue bedspread. Several antique lace pillows spilled over the top of the bed and more lace covered the blue, softly draped dressing table.

Because of Laney's upbraiding, Jesse was unusually silent and obediently did whatever Laney asked. She assigned Jesse to the bureau while she tackled the huge walk-in closet. Laney grabbed at the garments that hung on covered hangers and flung them into a large box positioned behind her. At one point, Laney looked behind her at Jesse and watched while she carefully folded Cara's clothes from the bureau, patting and smoothing each piece lovingly. Jesse's large, gray eyes were brimming pools of sadness and immediately, Laney realized how much Jesse had truly loved her sister.

"Jesse, would you like any of these things? I was going to give them to the church to distribute," Laney said, as she carried an armful of hangers over to Jesse.

"Oh, I couldn't. I would think of Cara every time I wore . . . ." Jesse's tears overflowed and cascaded down her cheeks.

Laney wrapped her free arm around Jesse's shoulders. "Just store them awhile and see how you feel about them later. I think Cara would want you to have them."

Laney sat in an ornate wicker chair in the corner of Cara's room. She was taking a break from the packing while Jesse called the names on the reservation list in the kitchen. Laney couldn't get her sister's ad out of her mind. Just when she was beginning to get Cara's death behind her, there was something else to nag at her. Why was it bothering her so much? Cara placed an ad in the personals. So what? She wasn't the first person to ever place such an ad. Calm down, Laney. Don't think about Cara's past. She's gone. It doesn't matter.

Jesse entered the room. "I couldn't get hold of a single person on the list, but I wouldn't worry about it yet. I've already called the couple booked for this weekend and the next reservation isn't until the thirty-first. The month of June is full, but I'll get them called in plenty of time." Jesse's usually springy bobbed hair was in disarray and her eyes, her best feature, were puffy and red.

"Let's call it a day, Jesse. You look exhausted and I know I am." Laney helped her carry the four boxes of clothing to her station wagon. As Jesse drove away, Laney felt relieved to see her go.

Blackberry followed her into the house and Laney was feeding her when Gray called. "What's going on? Could I come over? Maybe we could watch the Derby together."

"Gray, please, not tonight. I think I'm going to eat a bite and go to bed. It's been a long day. I hope you understand," Laney said.

"Sure, talk at you later," Gray said. For the longest time she could hear him breathing on the line, as though he didn't want to break the connection. Laney finally did it for him.

Laney stared at all the food crammed into the refrigerator, but nothing appealed to her. She was about to shut the door when she saw a bottle of red wine on the bottom shelf. Without a thought, she uncorked it, grabbed a wineglass hanging from the glass rack in the pantry, and climbed the stairs to her room. She sat in the chaise and clicked on the remote. She drank glass after glass of the wine while mindlessly flipping channels until she saw the horses in the post parade. When the band played "My Old Kentucky Home," Laney felt a little drunk, and by the time the horses were loaded in the gate, she had sunk among the cushions and was asleep.

6

Sunday, May 5

Laney awakened in the middle of the night to a pounding downpour that matched the pounding in her head. She moaned and hauled herself out of the chaise and staggered to the window. Lightning blinked, then flashed through the room and the answering thunder crashed and shook the house. The window rattled in her hands. When she flipped the light switch, nothing happened. Undressing in the dark, she felt for her gown on the back of the chaise. Slipping it over her head, she groped her way to the bathroom where she fumbled for her bottle of aspirin. She popped a couple with water cupped in her hands. Feeling her way to the bed, Laney crawled beneath the quilt and covered her head.

Unexpectedly, something large and probing jumped upon the bed, pushed aside the corner of the quilt and burrowed down beside her. Blackberry's quaking body nuzzled her neck and she felt her rough tongue place a slurpy kiss.

Pure fear had replaced Blackberry's depression.

The rain ended some time toward morning but the day broke damp and gloomy. Laney spent another afternoon in Cara's room. This time, Laney whisked photographs in nineteenth-century silver frames and Cara's silver backed hairbrush and comb into a cardboard box. She worked frantically, scooping up toiletries, personal memorabilia–anything that reminded her of her sister. Out of sight, out of mind, she thought. Even the tiny lavender sachets that she knew Cara had individually tied–gone.

Blackberry lay on the hearth, her head resting on a pair of pink slippers that Cara must have kicked off, perhaps that final morning, Laney thought with a stab of anguish. She ripped them away and into the box. Blackberry shot under the bed.

By late afternoon, her sister's quarters were transformed into a cold clinical space, like a motel room with all the amenities but none of the warmth that Cara had given it. Laney scanned the bedroom one final time. She was satisfied. She whirled and walked out the door.

7

Monday, May 6

Early the next morning, Laney called her mother and arranged to meet her at Marshall Knight's office across from the courthouse. The phone rang just as she was going out the door. Gray's voice sounded hollow.

"What's going on?" he asked. When Laney didn't answer, he went on, "I apologize for not calling yesterday like I promised, but I have a cold and I spent most of the day on the couch with Puccini and a box of tissues. I made myself one-too-many hot toddies and they knocked me out. If Natine hadn't banged on the door at eight o'clock last night with some soul food, I'd still be asleep . . . and probably a few pounds lighter, I might add. Laney, how are you?"

Laney smiled, picturing Gray and Puccini lolling on the sofa together, "I'm all right. I was just leaving. Mother and I have an appointment with Cara's attorney at ten."

Laney heard a sneeze and then Gray said in a nasal tone, "You'd better go. Talk at you later."

Laney lifted the wooden plank from its cradles and placed it against the side of the buggy house. She pushed and grunted and was breathing hard by the time the large barn-like doors slid aside exposing the

Whooptie. She dreaded driving Cara's car, not only because it reminded her of her sister, but also because the Nissan didn't have an automatic transmission. She had a terrible time with standard shift. The few times she had driven it, she had stalled it when she had stopped on a hill. Laney opened the door and slid behind the wheel. She turned the key and blinked in surprise when the car immediately came to life. The morning was warm and humid from the rains but at least the sun was shining. As she pulled out of the buggy house, she stopped for a moment to wind down her window so she could hear the spring warblers at the thistle feeder in the kitchen garden. The birds flashed yellow as they played musical chairs for the six perches. She must remember to refill the plastic tube, she thought. Reluctantly, she put the car in gear and drove through the rock pilasters.

The drive to Hickory took about fifteen minutes, but finding a place to park on Main Street took almost as long. Her mother was already pacing back and forth outside the lawyer's office when Laney ran up to her.

Maddy grabbed her arm and ushered her through a door between two storefronts and up a flight of narrow steps. She turned right and Laney followed her down a dingy hallway to a door with a frosted window. "Marshall U. Knight, Attorney," was printed in chipped black lettering on the glass. Laney wondered what the "U" stood for. A bell tinkled as Maddy opened the door to the reception area. The room was sparsely furnished with what looked to Laney like yard sale outcasts. A battered green linoleum-covered steel desk stood against a grimy wall sporting a picture of the current county judge, Raymond Perry. Laney didn't recognize the secretary who was typing furiously on a prehistoric Underwood typewriter, but she appeared as ancient as the typewriter.

"Mr. Knight will be with you in a moment," she said, without looking up or missing a beat on the keyboard. Maddy and Laney sat down in a pair of blond wooden chairs from the fifties. Laney had read two articles in a two-year-old *Smithsonian* magazine before Mr. Knight stepped out of an inner office and approached with his hand extended. Although the weather was clear, he once again wore the unfastened galoshes.

"Please come in," he said, as he shook hands with both of them.

Marshall Knight's office was a larger version of the waiting room. Papers and law books competed for space on his desk, and those that had lost lay scattered on the threadbare oriental carpet. Cigarette smoke drifted upward from a smoldering, overflowing ashtray on top of a pile of documents. Mr. Knight gestured to a couple chairs that matched the two in the reception area. Maddy removed a man's straw hat from her seat and sat down. She placed the hat on her lap.

Mr. Knight reached under the mound of papers and miraculously pulled out a blue, official-looking document and read: "I, Cara Collins, a resident of the state of Kentucky, being of sound, disposing mind and memory, and of legal age, do hereby make, publish and declare this instrument to be my Last Will and Testament . . . ."

Obviously, Mr. Marshall Knight doesn't fool around, Laney thought. She watched as Mr. Knight read away, really not hearing or understanding all the legalese. As he droned on, the forefinger of his left hand played with a tuft of cotton stuffing that protruded from a crack in the leather arm of his desk chair. A repetitious creak and rasp emitted from the vintage chair as Mr. Knight rocked back and forth, and Laney found herself rocking along with the lawyer.

". . . I give and bequeath to my sister, Laney Lea McVey, all my tangible personal property, including, but not limited to, my automobile, furniture, jewelry, and clothing. I also give and bequeath to my sister, Laney Lea McVey, all the rest and residue of my estate, both real and personal, including my farm and residence at 1326 Hickory Hill Pike, Hickory, Kentucky.

Laney's head snapped up and she jerked forward in her chair and grasped the edge of Knight's desk.

"What did you say?" Laney choked. "Would you repeat that?"

Mr. Knight struggled to remove his finger from a deepening hole in the leather arm and it finally popped free along with a small amount of filling. He cleared his throat and laid the will on the stack of documents.

"What the will states in item three, Laney, is that your sister has left you the bulk of her estate, including the house and farm. If you were listening to item one and two of the will, you would have heard that your mother was left all of Cara's stocks and bonds, which add up to a considerable sum. Joe Collins was an only child and was left quite a inheritance when his father died. Apparently, Joe invested wisely and since he had no heirs himself, he left it all to Cara."

Through all this, Maddy sat mesmerized, turning the straw hat in her lap round and round by its rim.

"But I thought everything would have to be sold to pay the debts on the farm–the taxes, the mortgage, the improvements, the remodeling of the inside of the house for the bed and breakfast. Are you saying–" Laney sputtered.

Mr. Knight interrupted her. "The last mortgage payment was made when Joe Collins died two years ago. The remodeling and improvements have been paid in full and the taxes prepaid. Laney, I don't know what your sister ever told you about her situation, but she was very well off financially."

Laney's wide eyes were riveted on Marshall's face, looking for some sign that this was some sleazy lawyer's prank or tasteless joke, but he only smiled warmly at them both.

Maddy spoke for the first time. Her voice was steady. "Marshall, is everything that's said in this office private-like?"

Marshall's chair creaked as he leaned forward. "Of course, Maddy. What is it?"

"I want my inheritance to be kept quiet for a time. Can this be done?" Maddy glanced at Laney. "What Laney says about the farm is her business. I just don't want anyone to know about the money that I'll get . . . say . . . for a couple weeks?"

"No one needs to know for a while, Maddy. Probate takes time. However, once probated, it will become public knowledge," Marshall said.

What is this all about, Laney thought. Then instantly, she knew. Karl! Mother didn't want Karl to know she was getting the money.

"Laney, will you keep this a secret for a while?" Maddy asked.

"Mother, I won't breathe a word about the money. But I will eventually have to make arrangements to sell the farm, so I can't keep that a secret."

Marshall leaned back in his chair and put his hands behind his head and stretched. Laney heard the chair groan. A popping noise followed.

"Laney, I think you should know that I spoke with Jackson the day of the funeral and he agreed to stay on at the farm as long as needed. What a fine young man! You can't find a more outstanding horseman," Marshall said.

"Cara always said she was lucky to have him," Maddy added. She placed the rather crumpled straw hat on a teetering stack of state statutes on the corner of the desk.

"Unless there is anything else, I guess that's it for now. If either of you have any questions, don't hesitate to call me." Marshall foraged into the mountain of documents and magically produced two business cards.

Maddy asked Laney to have lunch with her at the dock, and as Laney drove through the stone gateway, her childhood rushed back. In her mind, her early years seemed idyllic, almost carefree. Poppy often took her on the fishing boat with him and baited her line when she squealed about hooking the wiggly worms. She recalled how his fine blond hair fell over his laughing blue eyes when he'd grab his Maddy around the waist and dandle her neck. She remembered how, when Cara was about four months old, Poppy would put his mouth on the baby's belly and blow raspberries until Cara would get the hiccups from giggling so much.

The sign over the office brought Laney down. She had been twelve, and Cara six years old when Poppy had decided their fishing dock needed a name. Little Cara was singing her favorite nursery song, "Hickory Dickory Dock" when Laney chirped up, "That's it, Poppy—Hickory Dock!" It was just after he and Maddy had hung the sign that, as they all stood admiring it, Poppy suddenly clutched at his chest and without a word, collapsed and was gone.

Laney pulled up to the little frame house adjacent to the office and parked behind her mother's blue Chevy Cavalier. She could see Karl collecting money from a fisherman who had just put in his boat. Evil little man, Laney thought. She wondered again why her mother had married him. He wasn't anything like Poppy and she was sure her mother was afraid of him.

Maddy bustled around her small kitchen fixing lunch. Laney emptied a couple ice trays into a pitcher of fresh tea, placed it on the table, and sat down. Every few minutes, Maddy glanced out the window toward the boat slip.

"Don't forget, Laney, don't say anything to Karl about the money. I need time to think about this." Maddy placed a huge plate of her cashew chicken salad in front of Laney and a smaller plate on the other side of the table. The salads, circled with quartered hard-boiled eggs and tomatoes, nested on leaves of garden lettuce.

"Mother, I can't eat all this," Laney protested, but her mouth watered with the thought of attempting it. "But back to Karl. Sooner or later, he's bound to find out and he'll be mad as hell that you kept it from him."

"I can't go into it right now. Here he comes." Maddy stepped quickly from the window and sat across from Laney. Maddy lifted her fork and picked at her salad as though she had been eating.

The screen door banged behind Karl. "Well, what did Marshall say?" His little eyes shifted back and forth from Maddy to Laney.

Maddy looked down at her salad, "Cara left the house and farm to Laney." Maddy's hand trembled as she stabbed at a chunk of chicken.

Karl's eyes shot from Maddy to Laney. "You're shittin me!"

"That's right, Karl. I'm just as surprised as you are," Laney said.

Karl's eyes seemed to turn even blacker against his flushing face. "What the hell you goin to do with a damn horse farm?"

"Sell it," Laney said, and noticed that with her words, the intense color receded from Karl's face and he exhaled sharply.

"I think you should keep the farm," Maddy said meekly. She avoided Karl's eyes as she spoke.

"Maddy, you butt out of this! Laney knows what she's doin. No woman needs to own no damn horse farm." Karl's face had turned crimson once again and he slammed his fist down on the table. Maddy grabbed the stack of paper napkins and mopped up a puddle of iced tea.

Laney squirmed uncomfortably and raised her hand, palm outward. "Karl, please. Mother meant no harm. I have no intention of keeping the farm. I've already told Marshall."

Karl glared at Maddy, turned his trim little body and marched out the door with a smirk on his lips.

When Laney was sure that Karl was out of hearing range, she asked, "Mother, did Karl think that you would get the farm?"

"What? I can't imagine why he would think that. He probably thought like you did–that it would have to be sold to pay debts and the mortgage. I'm glad you got it, Laney. I meant what I said in front of Karl. I think you should keep it."

"Mother, I live in Pittsburgh. My home is there. My job is there. I left Hickory eighteen years ago. I'm a city girl now and I love it."

But Maddy persisted. "But you could keep the farm and still live in Pittsburgh. Jackson could run it for you. Think about it. You could still visit here several times a year."

"What makes you think I ever want to set my eyes on that place again? It kills me every minute I'm there. I can only think of Cara and what happened to her. Can't you understand?" Laney jumped to her feet. Her arms thrust outwards–her fists, angry pistons pumping out her frustration.

Maddy stood and tried to hold her but Laney only shook her away.

"Just leave me alone!" she cried, banging the door open and running to the Whooptie without looking back at her mother.

8

Tuesday, May 7

Rivulets of condensation trailed down the door screen like branches of a south flowing river. The morning fog permeated the morning so thoroughly that Laney felt the dampness seeping into her cotton blouse beneath her sweater. She wiped the seat of a wrought iron chair with her hand and it came away cold and dripping. No matter how she strained to see the creek below the screened porch, the mist obscured everything beyond the closest trees.

Blackberry sat by the door. Ever since the thunderstorm, she would hardly leave her side. But now she thumped her tail and looked up with her brown eyes that begged Laney to open the door. When she did, Blackberry jumped down the step, turned and sat expectantly.

"All right, girl. But you'll have to lead the way 'cause I can hardly see my hand in front of me." Laney followed the stepping stones through the kitchen herb garden and behind the buggy house. Blackberry stayed a little ahead, never getting completely out of her sight. A brightness in the eastern sky promised that the sun would burn away the fog before long. When the steps began to run down-hill, Laney knew they were approaching the springhouse.

"Blackberry, not here." But the dog bounded ahead. She doesn't understand, Laney thought. She and Cara had always walked to the springhouse in the mornings for their canoe ride.

The building suddenly appeared in front of her, its damp rock walls and cedar shake roof from another place and time. A galvanized pipe protruding from a rock wall still dripped the clear spring water into a concrete stock tank set deeply in the ground. Blackberry stretched her neck and drank from the algae covered water. As Laney passed by the wooden door where the canoes and paddles were stored, Blackberry hesitated, then scurried to catch up with Laney. The dog turned onto the footpath that followed the creek toward the crossing.

Laney wished she had worn her rubbers and shorts. The cuffs of her wet jeans slapped about her ankles and with every step, her canvas sneakers sloshed from the heavy dew that saturated the grass and weeds. As the overgrown path led them on, Laney heard a cow bawl somewhere through the fog, and the pungent odor of manure filled her nostrils.

They had walked for nearly thirty minutes when they reached "Old Hickory." In the fog, the massive shape hovered like a demonic apparition, filling the tiny clearing. Laney had only seen the tree from the canoe before. The gray shaggy bark split from the trunk in long flakes and some of the branches with their new yellowish-green leaves almost touched the ground. Then, through the lifting mist, Laney saw Stoney Creek for the first time that morning. Like a gray-brown bolt of satin, it flowed downstream–sleek and lustrous in the nebulous light. Vapor stroked the surface like cloudy fingers.

Laney walked faster, knowing where the unfurling bolt would take her and she could hear the crashing water ahead. "A little further," the voice in her mind prodded, so she followed the bank until unexpectedly, the sun broke through the mist and highlighted the fine line of the dam.

Oh God, Laney thought, why did I come here? Did Cara see that frightening edge as she approached the dam or was she already unconscious in the water or the canoe? She pictured Cara fighting the strong pull of the current as it pulled her over the brim, along with the canoe and debris.

Blackberry abruptly scooted left and disappeared in the high weeds. Like some crazed competitor, Laney followed her down the steep bank, the sound of falling water drowning out her call, "Blackberry, stop!"

When Laney finally broke through the brush, she stood downstream looking back and up at the dam. The water was up a couple of feet and its free-fall descent over the dam made Laney gasp at its power. The water plunged in a massive sheet and seemed to explode all at once in a huge upsweep of crashing and tumbling. Once, a giant limb swept over the top, and Laney stared in horror as it disappeared under the surface and didn't pop up again for several seconds. She watched, hypnotized as logs and branches–and what looked like a barrel–hurtled over the stone dam to be swallowed up below. Prying her eyes away, she looked behind her as though it might relieve her anguish. Perched on the hill above her, Jackson's little cottage was barely visible. She yearned to go to him, to allow him to soothe her but she knew he would be out on the farm. She compelled herself to go on.

Blackberry continued along the bank, occasionally plunging into the water hemlock along the path to explore. This must be the route she took to the crossing that day, Laney thought.

By the time they reached the riffle, Laney was exhausted and her mouth was parched. Blackberry waded into the water and swam out from the rocks. Laney heard the hum of a motor and spotted a johnboat gliding from behind some tall weeds and purring towards her. She recognized Cutty Bell. One time when she and Cara were just climbing out of the canoe at the floating dock below the house, he had suddenly appeared and had given them enough freshly caught bass for dinner that night.

"Say, Laney," he called. He trolled to the crossing and shut off the motor. The ripples spanked and rocked the boat.

Laney waved. "I want to thank you for everything you did for Blackberry that morning–taking her to the vet and all," Laney said, trying not to mention her sister.

"Ain't nothin. Wish I coulda helped your sister but ain't nothin coulda done her no good."

Cutty watched as Blackberry swam in a small pool near the boat.

"Looks like Blackberry ain't any worse the wear. Now, that's one fine dog. Stayed with her." Cutty's navel peeked out below his T-shirt and danced around on his blubbery belly. He put a forefinger up to his nose and pressed on a nostril. He snorted and snot flew into the creek. Blackberry, back from her swim, sniffed around a large rock.

"Look at that, will ya," Cutty said. "That's just where your sister and the canoe ended up. She still remembers . . . one smart dog, that Blackberry . . . and I seen lotsa dogs." Blackberry heard her name and waded over to the johnboat. Cutty reached over and scratched her ear.

There was a splash to the left of the crossing and Laney, who was sitting on a rock, bolted.

"A snake!" she screamed, scrambling and stumbling as she backed off the crossing. She clambered up the gravel slope.

"Ain't no snake," Cutty yelled, laughing. "It's a snakebird. See his long neck? Crooks like a snake when goin through the water."

Laney looked back at the bird swimming through the water with only his small head and long slender neck showing. The neck was curved in a serpentine S. That's one to look up in my bird book, Laney thought. Abruptly, the bird rose vertically, his wings pumping. He sat down on a limb of a sycamore farther upstream. Balancing awkwardly on yellowish webbed feet, he spread his enormous black wings to dry, revealing beautiful silver patches that shimmered in the sun.

Fascinated, Laney stared at the immense bird and inched back to the crossing.

"I seen him that mornin I found her. Bet he seen it happen, too. Wish I coulda known what he seen. Just can't figure it. That sister of yours was one smart gal. I seen her upstream on this here creek when it was high like today, but why she went out early of a mornin when the creek was wild as a deer . . . can't figure it."

Cutty shook his head and started up the motor. A black widow spider tattoo, centered on a web, crawled around on his right elbow. He dug down in his cooler, pulled out a beer and snapped the top. With a salute, he turned the boat and hummed back down the creek.

Laney remained at the crossing for a while. Something was tugging, nagging at her. What really happened on the creek that morning? It all seemed so impossible to her. Cara took chances–yes–but she always seemed to know her limits. Stop it, Laney. Let it go, an internal voice scolded her.

The walk back to the house by the blacktop lane almost got the best of her. Sun and humidity had replaced the fog and she continuously wiped sweat from her temples and the back of her neck. She removed her sweater and tied it around her waist and before long, her wet sneakers began to rub a blister on her left heel.

Laney headed for the foaling barn and office, about the halfway point to the house. Blackberry, with her endless energy, zigzagged her way up the lane. She took a harmless barking dash at the black quarter horse teaser, Applejack, who pranced about his paddock tossing his large head.

When Laney peered in the door of the office, Jackson was busy at his desk updating his teasing records.

"Laney, your face . . ." He jumped up and poured a paper cup of water from the utility sink and smiled as she gulped it down and refilled it three times. She put the last cup down on the floor for Blackberry.

Laney plopped onto the vinyl couch in front of the desk. "We took a walk and I guess I forgot just how far it was to the crossing."

Jackson frowned. "You walked to the crossing? Laney, it's so soon."

"Well, I didn't plan to go. Blackberry just seemed to lead me there," Laney said.

"You followed the creek? That is quite a ways."

"I saw Cutty Bell at the crossing. He seemed perplexed that Cara went out that morning," Laney said, while she watched Jackson fish a toothpick out of his shirt pocket and begin to chew. He seemed thoughtful.

"Any mares due to foal this week?" Laney changed the subject.

Jackson smiled his beautiful smile. The dimple surfaced in his left cheek and Laney felt her heart do a little hop. Damn, he's good looking, she thought, and remembered her sister's droll expression when she saw a handsome man: "He can put his shoes under my bed anytime."

Jackson crossed to the window. "Red Dust is due today." He nodded in her direction. "She's waxed and ready to go, so I have to stay pretty close to home."

Laney groaned as she struggled to her feet. She refilled the cup for Blackberry but she didn't drink.

"In all the times I've been here, I've never seen a foaling," she said. Stepping to the window, she admired the chestnut mare near the gate who was heavy with foal.

"I'll try to call you in time, but they really go fast when they start labor. Usually twenty minutes and it's all over. Laney, can I take you to the house? You look beat." Jackson touched her cheek gently. "I think you have some new freckles."

Laney groaned. "I felt them popping as I walked up the lane. Thanks for the offer, but I started this trek and I'm going to finish it."

Laney opened the door and let Blackberry out. As an afterthought, she sat on the stoop and removed her sneakers. After tying the laces together, she flung one shoe over her shoulder, bent down, and rolled up her soggy jeans.

"I haven't done this since I was a kid," she giggled, and with a little wave, she and Blackberry started up the lane toward the house.

Laney felt Jackson watching her from the door. Why didn't I tell him about inheriting the farm, she asked herself. Damn it. He would only encourage me to keep it, too. After all, his job here could depend on it. Maybe he could buy it himself, she considered, but instantly realized that would be impossible. The place was worth a fortune. Jackson didn't have that kind of money. With a sigh, she dismissed it all. She just wanted the extra burden of owning the farm to go away. As soon as the estate was settled, she'd put it on the market. Someone would buy it.

When Laney arrived at the house, the red light was flashing on the answering machine. The cool dark library soothed her as she played through the messages. Gray stammered a bit at the beginning of his message, then he cleared his voice and said, "Would you go to dinner with me this evening?" Click. Laney frowned. His cold sounded better.

The second message was from Jesse. "I just wanted to thank you again for the lovely clothes. That's all."

Jesse's call reminded her again about Cara's classified ad. Laney settled into the desk chair and dialed Jesse's number.

"Jesse, don't you work today? I thought maybe I wouldn't find you at home."

"Laney?" Jesse sounded sleepy. "No, I go back to work tomorrow night. Maury gave me the whole week off. Did you get my message?"

"Yes. I'm glad you like the clothes. C . . . Cara was heavier and shorter than you. You may have to let out some of the hems and take in the seams." It was still difficult to say Cara's name. Would she ever get over this?

"Jesse, do you remember the other day when you came into the library and found me on the floor, picking up some letters?" Laney heard Jesse inhale, then pause before answering.

"I remember you seemed upset about something," Jesse said.

"Cara took out an ad in the personal classified section of the

Lexington Post. When you interrupted me, I was gathering up the responses to the ad." Laney could have heard a pin drop.

"They were letters from men, Jesse. There must have been a couple dozen of them—all introducing themselves and asking to set up a date with her." Still, Jesse didn't say anything.

"What I want to know," Laney went on, "did Cara ever mention placing this ad or did she ever say whether or not she had had a date with any of these men?"

"No . . . of course not . . . she probably did it on a lark . . . you knew Cara . . . always joking around." Her answer was hurried—sentences running together.

Laney stretched to her right, opened the file drawer, and retrieved the reservation file with all the letters.

"Jesse, are you sure? I know how close you and Cara were. If she did this on a lark, as you say, wouldn't she have confided in you? You were her best friend, for heaven's sake."

"Cara didn't tell me everything, Laney. She had lots of secrets. I don't know anything about the ad and I've gotta go." She immediately hung up.

Laney was surprised at Jesse's ill humor. Why was she so ruffled? Laney sat back in the desk chair and shuffled through the letters. Exasperated, she scooped them up and jammed them into the envelope. I'll burn them, she thought. Then I can forget about it. She put her head down on her hands and rubbed her temples. Staring at the envelope, she realized that Jesse was right about one thing. Cara had had secrets. But she also knew now, that Jesse had secrets too.

Laney sank down in the hot bubbly water. Every muscle and bone regretted the long morning hike. She propped her blistered heel over the edge of the porcelain claw-foot tub, hoping its gradual submersion might be possible after the rest of her body relaxed enough. Peering over the edge of the tub, she could see Blackberry curled up on the small pink and blue fringed rug. She doesn't seem any worse for wear, Laney thought, thinking of Cutty's comment.

Across the room, Laney saw her reflection in the heavily framed bevel mirror hung over the creamy marble vanity. Her nose was a blooming poppy and the still-sprouting freckles were green against her sunburned face and jarring wildfire hair. Turning away from her image, she studied the transformation Cara had made to the room. Last year, when she visited, the workmen were repairing the broken plaster and the white hexagon floor tile. They also had cut a new entrance into the guest room that she was using. Cara had carried over the same floral paper and painted crown molding into the bath. A long walnut shelf beside the tub held a brass soap dish, a stack of crochet trimmed towels, and an open bowl of sweet smelling dried fragrances–lavender, lilac, and orange peel.

Laney turned the white porcelain four-spoke faucet with the toes of her left foot and a stream of hot water warmed the cooling bath. God, this is heaven, she thought, sinking lower into the tub.

At that moment, the telephone rang, causing Laney to drop her blistered foot into the water. "Yow!" she cried, as she reached for the portable phone on the shelf.

Wincing and splashing upright, she said, "Hello."

"What's going on?" Gray's soft voice asked.

"I'm taking a bath," Laney said, but suddenly embarrassed by her admission of nakedness, she added, "I mean, I just finished taking a bath, hoping he hadn't heard the water pouring into the tub. Blackberry and I took a long walk this morning and wore ourselves out. At least I did. She's sitting here raring to go again." Blackberry waggled her tail at the mention of her name.

"I called earlier. Guess you didn't check your messages. Wanted to see if you would go to dinner with me tonight. My cold is about gone and Puccini is dying to see Blackberry again."

"She has a tree all picked out," Laney said, smiling in spite of herself. What would it hurt, she thought. I'll be gone in a few days. "Okay, what time?"

"You'll go?" Gray sputtered. "Seven o'clock?"

"That's perfect. That will give me time for a nap. I'll see you then."

Laney clicked the off button on the phone and stared at her rosy reflection again. "This is going to be a challenge," she groaned.

Laney slept as though drugged. She had known she would and had set the little travel alarm by her bed. When it went off, she moaned. I must begin some sort of exercise, she thought. Abruptly, she recalled her sister's daily canoe trip. Although Cara had exercised every day, she had battled her weight all her short life. Her sister had been rounder than she–almost chubby. Laney still could see her beautiful heart-shaped face. People had been attracted to her, stimulated by her. Laney stepped to the window and gazed across the front yard to the paddock beyond that held five mares and their foals. Cara had been just like them, she thought–lively, energetic, and rambunctious–just like one of those healthy foals frisking in the sunlight. She let the lace curtain fall back over the window and felt the tears well up. A toss of her head and a swallow kept them from overflowing again.

Laney was waiting on the front porch when Gray pulled into the circle drive in his restored 1958 Buick Special. God, the pink monstrosity had to be the ugliest car in automobile history, she thought. Everything that wasn't baby-bottom pink was shining chrome, from the chrome-wrapped tail fins to the one hundred sixty squares inside its colossal grille. Gray had told her he had counted them once while polishing every single one. The car glided to a stop, its outrageous grid gleaming in the evening sun.

Laney stepped off the porch and immediately knew that Puccini was on the dash. Blackberry bounced and barked as Gray opened the massive door and stepped out. Puccini raised his great barred head and narrowed his copper eyes. His frown marks formed a perfect M,–M for malice, Laney thought, her mouth twitching. After lengthening his handsome body with a flagrant stretch of his legs, Puccini snapped back into a tight curl. Tucking his ringed tail under his chin, he went back to doing what he did best–sleep.

"Laney, you look absolutely fabulous." Gray stood with his mouth agape. She had dressed in an emerald green silk dress that skimmed her small waist and fell softly to just above her knees. Her freckles and red nose had receded behind a skillful application of make-up. She had done her best with her unruly hair by restraining its bulk with two strategically placed combs, one behind each ear. On her feet, she wore a pair of soft, low-heeled T-straps that she hoped wouldn't rub against the Band-Aid covered blister.

"Thanks . . . but Gray, look at you," Laney said admiringly as she checked him out.

He wore an obviously new blue and burgundy tattersall button-down shirt and blue background tie. A lightweight burgundy sport jacket made his shoulders look as broad as a linebacker's. Her eyes swept down his dress khakis to his cordovan penny-loafers. Unusual, she thought. Socks.

His blue-green eyes smiled at her like they were stuck in stare. He tucked his tan hands under his muscular arms. Only when Blackberry stormed towards the front seat, did Gray tear his eyes from Laney and shut the driver's side door. "Shall we go?" he asked. Giving Blackberry a pat, he escorted Laney to the passenger door.

As they pulled away, the Border collie watched from the driveway, a "been abandoned" droop to her body. Puccini smugly elongated his body across the dash, flexing one paw and then the other.

Gray dropped in a CD, and Luciano Pavarotti burst forth with "Che gelida manina" from the opera, *La Bohéme*. Laney sat back and enjoyed the aria, glad that Gray had sacrificed the Buick's authenticity for the CD player. Gray's cold seemed to have spent itself. Only an occasional tickling cough remained.

Maury met them at the door of the Finish Line. It had been a year since Laney had eaten at the trendy restaurant that catered equally to the locals, tourists, and the horsy set. "Miss McVey, I'm so sorry about your sister," Maury said. He had the palest blue eyes Laney had ever seen–the color of opals–and his bald head shone like a polished pink planet. Laney thought he had shrunk a few inches from last year, but she realized it was because of his bent arthritic knees. Maury grabbed one of her hands and held it tightly until he seated them at Gray's favorite corner table. He handed out the menus and took their drink order. Laney knew he was hosting for Jesse. He usually spent most of his time in the kitchen badgering his wife, Jewel.

Laney's eyes moved around the restaurant. Most of the tables were occupied. Probably leftover derby visitors, she thought. The waitress, dressed in a yellow cap and jockey silk tucked into black slacks, brought Gray a bourbon and water and a Bloody Mary for Laney. They ordered their meals and relaxed, sipping their drinks.

"Gray, I don't think you know this yet, but Mother and I saw Cara's lawyer yesterday," Laney said. "I don't want this advertised, but she left the house and farm to me."

Gray sat to attention. "Laney, you're moving back?" He seized her hand, his eyes bright and expectant.

"No, I'm going to sell it all."

Gray's smile wilted and his body sagged. "I thought . . . I hoped . . . . "

"Join the club, Gray. Mother is already a member. I haven't told

Jackson yet but I'm sure he'll join, too. The only one who thinks I should sell is Karl, and for the life of me, I don't know why Karl wants me to sell."

"Your dream, Laney . . . this could be your opportunity to fulfill your dream."

Laney's brows pulled together and a deep ridge formed between her eyes.

Gray went on, "Your dream to write full time. You could run the bed and breakfast and write at the same time. Think of it. Your mother could do all the baking and cooking like she was going to do for Cara, and Jackson could continue to run the farm. I bet he would jump at the chance. Laney, the house is ready to go." Gray wiggled in his chair, his face flushed and elated with the thought.

"I hate to bring you down, Gray, but you don't understand any more than Mother does."

The waitress approached the table with their salads. Laney was ravenous. The sliced melon, laced with a ruby port and mint dressing, teased her palate, making her long for the entree.

Laney continued while she ate. "Gray, I don't belong in this town. Pittsburgh's been my home for so long, I can't imagine life in Hickory again. The house only reminds me of Cara. How do I get over that?" The pain was so deep, Laney lowered her fork.

Gray studied her face for a long time, then spoke. "Time will heal you, Laney. But you have to help yourself to face the pain head on. You can't run away or it will follow you the rest of your life."

Laney knew Gray's words came from his own deep and personal pain when his twin brother, Bart, died in an automobile accident when he was only seventeen. The tragedy ultimately destroyed his parent's marriage and they divorced. When, after three years of college, Gray was accepted in vet school, he left Hickory but returned when he graduated from Auburn. Two years before, his mother had moved in with her widowed sister, Martha, in Florida.

Laney squeezed Gray's hand and didn't speak for a moment, then said, "Let's not spoil the rest of the evening."

Their dinners arrived and they dug into the wonderful food. Laney had ordered grilled rosemary lamb chops with garlic and parsleyed baby red potatoes. Gray, who usually ate fast food for dinner, suffered through a thick, grilled, T-bone steak with a fresh mushroom wine sauce. Maury poured a lightly chilled Beaujolais. For dessert, they each had the restaurant's specialty, a strawberry and chocolate tart with a walnut crust.

After Gray parked in the circle drive, Laney ushered Blackberry into the house so Gray could let Puccini out of the car. He had to wrench the cat from the dash and place him on the ground. He left the driver's side window open so the cat could leap to his resting place when it suited him.

Laney fixed coffee and they sat in the library sipping the hot brew. Blackberry lay curled at Gray's feet with her nose resting on one shoe. Gray leaned back on the tan leather sofa.

"This is the best room in the whole house. Your sister really did a job of it," Gray said, with a great sigh of content.

Impulsively, Laney jumped to her feet. "I want to show you something." She opened the file cabinet and removed the reservation file. She held the newspaper clipping out to Gray. "Read this," she said.

He tried to read Laney's expression as he took the clipping, then lowered his eyes and scanned it.

"What is this? Who placed this ad?"

"According to the newspaper date, Cara placed it about three months ago. But that's not all . . . look." Laney sat across from Gray and spread out the letters like she was holding out a hand of playing cards. Gray drew one envelope and read the letter inside.

"Laney, are all these responses from men?" When she nodded, he said, "Did Cara go out with any of them?"

"I have no idea. I asked Jesse about it but she denied knowing anything."

Gray handed the letter back to Laney and picked up his coffee cup and sipped. "Why are you telling me this?"

"I'm not sure, Gray. Something really bothers me about it and it's not just the embarrassment of knowing that my sister would do something like this."

"What are you saying, Laney?"

"I know the water patrol officer, police, and coroner all believe Cara's death to be an accident, but . . . ." Laney began to breathe rapidly and her face felt on fire.

"You don't think it was?" Gray was incredulous. He leaned forward.

"Laney, if it wasn't an accident, then it can only be one other thing."

Laney grasped the arms of her chair and kneaded the cushiony red velvet. Her mouth trembled but her eyes were steady when she answered softly, "I know."

Gray stood up and Blackberry moved under the desk. "What you're really saying is that you believe Cara met one of these men and he did her in."

"Gray, tell me I have a screw loose or something."

"I don't think you're off, Laney. I just think you're angry because you lost your sister in a senseless accident. I remember feeling much the same way when Bart was killed . . . such a waste. I wanted to strike out at someone . . . blame someone." Gray knelt in front of her. His arms enclosed her body and he pressed her head to his shoulder. "If only I could take the pain away." Laney felt his hand catch her hair, his fingers combing, separating. He pulled back and placed his large hands on either side of her face and his mouth came slowly toward hers. That sensuous mouth brushed hers ever so slightly. His lips opened and whispered her name. He covered her mouth with his, pressing the softness, enfolding. Laney dissolved in a raw and flowing weakness that went to her very center.

Gray abruptly straightened. "Laney I can't do this. It's not right . . . for you or for me. You will leave. I can't go through that again." He stood and turned to go, his face as pale as though he were ill. "Thank you for the wonderful evening. I'll never forget it. Please call me before you go."

Laney didn't stop him, and after she heard the door close, she sat very still on the plush chair. The letters stared at her from her lap. The clock in the front hall struck twelve and this time she knew that Gray, like a prince in some twisted fairy tale, would not return.

9

Wednesday, May 8

Laney opened the paneled front door and saw that the morning sun was already painting the crowns of the wild cherry trees in the far side of the front yard. Blackberry scooted by her and flew after the red squirrel again. The little rodent scurried up the nearest walnut and sat on a branch chattering at her. Blackberry gave him one last scornful look and trotted off to the springhouse. As he did every morning, Jackson had left the mail and newspaper on the wicker stool. Laney sifted through the mail. There were a couple of bills she would give to Marshall and a few more condolence cards. She picked up the *Lexington Post* and glanced over the front page.

Her heart braked cold. For a moment, the page blurred and she thought she would faint.

"Oh God!" Her words echoed thinly in her buzzing ears. The photo gradually came back into focus and she read again the headline under the picture:

BUSINESSMAN FOUND DEAD IN FREEZER
The body of a Lexington man was found yesterday morning in an unplugged chest freezer in a storage unit at Valu Mini Storage on Dalton Lane. Police identified the man as Tony Richards, 38, part owner of the Owens–Richards RV dealership in Lexington. The owner of the storage facility, Mason Jennings, called police

yesterday when he discovered the body. He used his master key to enter the garage after detecting a strong odor coming from the unit. Police report that Richards had been shot and they believe he had been dead for at least ten days.

Laney's hands were shaking so violently that the newspaper crinkled. A motion out of the corner of her eye made her look up. Jackson's Rover pulled up in the circle drive. Not knowing why she did it, Laney folded the newspaper in half and thrust it under the mail. Forcing a smile, she greeted him. "Good morning, Jackson."

Jackson strode onto the porch. "Red Dust still hasn't foaled, but I'm sure it will be tonight or tomorrow." He smiled and the dimple danced.

Laney stuck her hands into her pockets to keep them from trembling and gazed away for a moment.

"Is there something wrong? You look like you just saw a ghost." Jackson studied her face.

He doesn't know just how close he is, Laney thought. "I just didn't sleep well last night," she mumbled.

"Were you ill?"

"No."

"I saw Prescott's car here."

"He was here."

"Something wrong with Blackberry?"

"No."

Jackson popped a toothpick in his mouth and chewed. "I've got to get down to the barn and check that mare. Don't forget your mail there."

"I won't. Thanks for dropping it off." She picked up the pile and hugged it to her chest and opened the door. Jackson was so considerate, she thought, and slammed the door behind her.

Laney raced into library. The letters were still on the red chair where she had dropped them after Gray had left the night before. She raked through the envelopes like some wild woman, pulling out letters, business cards, and photos. "Where is it?" Then suddenly, the photograph slid from the envelope and fell to the floor. Snatching it from the carpet and grasping the envelope and newspaper, Laney sat down at the desk. With fingers fluttering like butterfly wings, she removed the letter from the envelope and laid it next to the photo. Snatching up the newspaper, she spread it out next to the photograph. Taking a deep breath, she turned on the desk lamp and compared the photos.

"My God, they're the same man! Oh God!" The photograph in the newspaper even looked like it was taken from the same picture although it was only a head and shoulders shot. The photo in the letter showed the man with a mustache leaning casually against a black convertible.

Next, she looked again at the name of the murdered man: *Tony Richards*. Laney held her breath and scanned the signature on the letter: *Tony*.

Laney reread the letter. Her heart gave another lurch where Tony stated that he owned a RV dealership.

"It can't be!" Laney breathed, but knew it was.

"Natine, may I speak to Gray, please. This is Laney."

"I'm sorry, he just left on a call. May I give him a message?" Natine asked.

"No . . . well . . . no, I'll call him later."

"Laney, you sound upset. I can give you his mobile phone number," Natine said.

"Would you?" Laney scribbled down the number and thanked her.

Gray answered on the second ring. His voice sounded distant and hollow.

"Gray, I'm sorry. I know I shouldn't call you."

"Laney, it's okay."

"I need to talk to you. Something's happened."

"Can it wait until I take this call? I'll be there as soon as I can. I promise," Gray said.

"Thank you. Oh, thank you." Laney hung up the phone and stared at the photos and waited for Gray.

Laney heard Gray's Jeep and met him at the door of the Cherokee. "I'm so embarrassed that I called you, but I didn't know where to turn." She clutched his hand and dragged him into the library and shut the door.

"Whoa, Laney. You're in a lather."

Laney answered by thrusting the newspaper into his hands. She had circled the picture and article. Gray sat down at the desk and read. "You know this guy? That why you're so torn up?"

"No." She snatched the newspaper away and picked up the photo and gave it to Gray.

"Same guy. Where'd you get the photo?" Gray looked puzzled.

Laney pointed to the letter on the desk. Gray read slowly, the muscles in his cheeks working in and out.

"Is this one of the letters you showed me last night?" Gray eyes darkened and his brows fused.

"Yes," Laney said.

Gray studied the letter again. "Must be the same guy. Says he owned a RV dealership, and he signed his name, Tony. Looks like the newspaper picture came from the same photo."

Gray suddenly grabbed the photograph and examined it more closely under the desk lamp.

"Uh-oh! I've seen this car before."

Laney drew in her breath. "What?"

Gray faced Laney. "You're not going to like this. Saw it here . . . right here in the circle drive."

"When?" Laney's heart hammered in her throat.

"Let's see . . . must have been a month ago. Was here to check a mare or open a mare . . . can't remember which . . . but I remember that Camaro Z28 all right . . . black convertible with a black top. Don't easily forget a car like that. Even swung through the circle drive to get a better look."

Laney dropped down onto the rug next to Gray's chair and covered her face with her hands. When she lifted her head, her anguished eyes begged Gray to tell her it wasn't true.

"Gray," she pleaded, "What does all this mean to you?"

"Laney, I'm not sure. It could mean a lot . . . or nothing at all. One thing we know for sure, Cara must have been seeing this Tony. I remember the car being here and I remember something else."

"What?" Laney asked despairingly, her heart beating even faster.

"The car had Fayette County plates. That's Lexington." Gray winced as he told her.

Laney leaped to her feet. "He killed her. I know he did."

Gray stood and clasped her arms, trying to calm her. "Laney, cut it out! You don't know that! There are several things that all this could mean. Just settle down and we'll try to discuss it." He led her to the sofa and sat beside her.

"Laney, we know this Tony Richards was murdered. Police think he died at least ten days ago." Gray looked at his watch calendar. Cara died on the thirtieth. Cara's time of death is certain. Tony's is speculative. But let's assume Tony died before Cara. Kind of rules him out as a murderer, doesn't it?"

"What if someone else killed both of them?" Laney ventured.

"What if Cara killed Tony and then died in an accident," Gray smiled cautiously. "Do you see how silly all this is. Remember, Laney, the police have ruled Cara's death an accident."

Laney sat very still. "What you are saying is that I'm jumping to conclusions again. That all we really know for sure is Cara saw this guy at least once." Her breathing returned to normal.

"Right. For all we know, she may have dated other guys who answered her ad, too," Gray said, as an afterthought.

Laney's eyes were bolts of lightning. "What do you mean?"

"I don't mean to be unkind, Laney, but you may not have known your sister as well as you think."

"Cara and I were very close. We shared everything . . . told each other everything," Laney said haughtily.

"Like what really happened between Cara and me," Gray said cautiously. "You left last spring because of something Cara said. We were becoming so close, Laney. What did she tell you? It's only fair that I know."

Laney sighed like it was her last breath. Tell him, she thought. For God's sake, he already knows. Finally, the words bolted from her mouth. "She told me that you two had dated before she met Joe and when she got pregnant, you gave her money to get an abortion, and then dropped her like a stone."

"Is that what she told you?" Gray walked over to the desk and stood quietly. Laney listened to his controlled breathing. Then, with one great sweep of his hand, he cleared the desk. Papers, photos, letters, pens and blotter flew across the room.

"It's a lie, Laney!" He swung about, his face crimson and contorted with anger.

Laney was on her feet. She had never seen his fury.

"Why would my sister lie to me?" she shouted.

"Why? . . . because she didn't want you to know the truth."

"Which was? . . ."

Gray got up in her face to answer. "She was pregnant all right! . . . but not with my child! We never slept together." His spittle sprayed her face.

"Then who–"

"Karl."

"Karl? . . . my stepfather? . . . she wouldn't!" Tears stung her eyes.

"She would, Laney. She asked me for money to get an abortion. Said Karl denied it was his." Gray's eyes narrowed to tight slits with the memory.

"When was this?"

"Seven years ago. Yes, Laney, Karl was married to your mother at the time. It was three months after their wedding. Cara told me she was about two months along. She was desperate. Said she didn't have the money for the abortion. Said if I didn't give her the money, she would have to ask Maddy. As much as I hated the man, I didn't want to see your mother hurt."

"So you gave her the money."

"Yes. Wish now that I hadn't. Maybe if Cara had told your mother about Karl, she would have gotten rid of the worthless bastard."

Laney's legs threatened to buckle, yet her mind spun on. Sagging into the sofa, she managed, "Then why did Cara tell me that it was your child?"

"I guess when you and I started seeing each other last year, she wanted to break us up."

Laney was puzzled. "But why would she, after what you did for her?"

Gray looked down at his hands and pulled at a hangnail. "I can think of several reasons. You see, part of what she told you was true, Laney. I did stop seeing her after the abortion. She dumped me. Said she was going to marry Joe Collins. Apparently, she had been seeing him all along plus Karl and me. Maybe she thought if we got close, I might tell you about the abortion and all her affairs." Gray settled beside her on the sofa. "She didn't want you to see her halo tarnished."

Through all Gray's explanation, Laney watched him warily, looking for some indication that he was inventing this nightmare. But now that the rage had spent itself, she could see only hurt and bitterness left in his face. She reached out and smoothed the lines in his forehead, her hand small and white against his bronzed skin.

He grasped her hand and brought it to his lips. No words were spoken for a long time. Then, Laney tore her hand away and shook her head like she was trying to disengage herself from this new threat to her peace.

Gray spoke first. "All of this is overwhelming to you, Laney. You have so much to sort out. Please don't leave yet or make any final decisions about selling the farm. And please don't jump to any conclusions about Cara's death. Will you give yourself some time?"

Laney, moved deeply by his passionate plea, could only accede softly, "I'll try, Gray."

10

Thursday, May 9

"Jesse, I won't hear of it. I can't have you clean house for me." Laney doodled a tornado on the message tablet while she talked.

"But I want to do it. I don't work 'til tonight. I love cleaning that house. I did it for Cara when she was too busy. See you in a few minutes." Jesse hung up.

I can't imagine anyone that anxious to clean house, Laney thought. In Pittsburgh, she had a girl to clean her little apartment every two weeks. When she was engaged to Fletch, he berated her for not doing it herself, but he was one of those "my mother always" types. She'd finally wised up and had given him the heave-ho along with his Lawrence Welk tapes and his canary, Twit. In retrospect, she often thought that his name and the bird's should have been switched.

Later in the day, while Jesse cleaned, she tried writing her "After Dark" article for *Three Rivers Magazine* but she couldn't seem to concentrate. She was still struggling with it, when Jesse knocked lightly and peeked into the library.

"I've finished, except for this room. Why don't ya take a break while I clean the library. I put some water on for tea and found some of your mother's poppy seed scones in the freezer."

"Sounds good, but would you have some tea with me? I'll take care of this room myself. All my notes are out where I can get to them and I don't want anything disturbed." Jesse seemed a bit disgruntled but followed her to the kitchen. Jesse must think I might question her about the newspaper ad again, Laney thought, but at once, decided that she didn't want to talk about it either.

The teapot was whistling away when they reached the kitchen. Laney nibbled on a scone while she spooned sweetener in her tea. She squeezed two wedges of lemon.

"These are delicious. Damn, Mother can bake. That reminds me. Did you get hold of the rest of the people on the reservation list?"

"Yeah. They were very understanding about your sister's death. I didn't tell them that the bed and breakfast would be closed for good, just in case any new owner might want to start it up again."

"Why, Jesse, that was brilliant. I hadn't thought of that."

Jesse, who usually beamed with praise, only played at her uneaten scone. She stood unexpectedly and looked at her watch. "I have to get home and get ready for work."

Laney wrote out a check and walked her to the front door. Handing it to Jesse, she said, "Thanks for everything you have done. You don't know what a help you've been."

"See ya." Jesse mumbled, avoiding Laney's eyes.

As Laney closed the door, she was startled by a crash in the parlor. When she ran into the room, a flash of red streaked downward and slammed into one of the floor-to-ceiling windows to the right of the fireplace. Laney retreated into the shadows behind the heavy indoor shutters. A few seconds later, she heard the sound again. Cautiously, she peered around the shutter in time to see a cardinal smack against the window pane. A few seconds later, he hit again and then again and again. After each strike against the glass, he would drop to the sill, seem to recover and then fly to a small branch of a walnut tree near the window. Then he'd repeat the act. The crest on his head was beaten down from the blows and little specks of blood from the bird's beak were splattered on the pane. What a brainless ritual, she thought as she closed the shutters and walked across the hall to the library.

After typing a few words, Laney shut down her computer. It was no use trying to work when she was so restless. She opened the front door and saw that a few heavy clouds were moving in slowly from the west. Blackberry bounded around the side of the porch and bounced and shimmied up to her. "Okay girl, but this time I'm riding, not walking." Grabbing a bike from the wrought iron stand, she mounted it, wondering if what they said was true–that once you had learned to ride a bike, you never forgot how.

"We'll find out, won't we, girl?" She started out with some wobbly wheels, but by the time she passed Unreasonable, she was flying down the blacktop toward the front gate.

She circled at the end of the lane, backtracked through the alley of maples, passing the house in the direction of the lower barn. As she coasted by the foaling barn, she could see a dark figure forking fresh straw into a stall. She pedaled past the barn, Applejack's paddock, and glided right, toward the crossing. Blackberry kept pace, her black hair flowing and her white tipped tail and paws flashing with every long stride. A couple of times the dog cut in front of her bike and she had to brake to avoid hitting her. The wind blew through her hair and ballooned her white cotton blouse. For the first time in over a week, she felt energized.

Dusk was settling in early because of the heavy clouds. By the time she reached the slope down to the crossing, the sky was the color of slate. She braked, dropped her bike, and walked the rest of the way. Her legs felt rubbery as she sat upon a rock and listened to the slap of water against the crossing.

Lapping up her fill, Blackberry lay down in the shallows, cooling her hot body. A fishy smell mixed with the sweet aroma of newly cut grass lingered in the evening air. Tiny gnats hovered over Blackberry's head, and near Laney's feet, a water beetle left minute whirlpools as it skipped through the shallows.

Without warning, a dim shape surged heavily out of the water upstream. Flapping his huge wings, the snakebird sailed high above the creek, his crooked neck pushed forward and his giant tail, like an unfolded fan, trailing behind. Higher and higher he sailed until he vanished in the darkening sky. What a bizarre and ghostly bird, Laney thought, and instantly remembered Cutty's words, "Bet he seen it happen. Wish I coulda known what he seen."

All at once, Laney felt the chill and dampness of Stoney Creek. The creaking branches and the songs of the birds became sinister cries in the approaching night. Against the charcoal sky, the limbs of sycamores flashed white.

When Blackberry moved out of the creek and shook away the water, Laney stood and commanded, "Blackberry, come." Laney lingered a moment longer, scanning the starless sky for the snakebird, then the two of them climbed the grade to the bicycle and raced back through the darkness.

Blackberry kept her on the lane by running in front of the bike, her white markings pale beacons in the night. A light twinkled ahead in the foaling barn as she curved around the teaser paddock. Pulling up to the office, she dropped the bike stand and opened the door.

Jackson was standing in front of the observation window. He turned his head as she entered.

"I just tried to call you. Red Dust is getting ready to foal." He nodded toward the window.

Blackberry found a corner and Laney stood next to Jackson. He smelled like fresh hay and his brown chamois shirt matched his eyes. He flashed his dimple at her and turned back to the window. As they observed Red Dust pace around her stall, he rested his hand casually on her shoulder. The mare was sweating profusely, and occasionally she paused to rub her rump against the walls of the stall. She lifted her rear legs in pain, alternately. To keep the site clean, her tail had been wrapped in a hot-pink vet gauze.

"God, Jackson, what's that?" Laney cried out as a stream of fluid burst from the mare's vulva.

"Her water just broke. Do you want to help me?"

"I guess," Laney said uncertainly.

"Just do what I say and don't make any sudden movements or noises." He grabbed a plastic sleeve and iodine from the desk, a shank from a hook by the door and pulled Laney out the door behind him. He unlatched the stall door. While talking gently to the mare, he crossed the stall and hooked the shank to the halter.

Handing the leather shank to Laney, he said, "Hold the shank with your left hand and calm her with your right while I check her. Stay on the same side of the mare that I am."

Jackson put on the long plastic sleeve and with his left hand on her flank, he reached inside of the mare. It seemed like only a second until Jackson removed his sleeved hand and pronounced that the foal was in the correct position. He took the shank from Laney's hand and unsnapped it from the halter.

"Let's go," he said, and led her out of the stall. They stood outside, observing the mare through the slats in the door. Red Dust resumed pacing, and Laney could see a tiny hoof protruding from the vulva with a veiled substance attached. Suddenly, the mare lowered her heavy body to the straw.

"Stay here," Jackson commanded, and entered the stall again.

The mare stretched out on her side and Jackson pulled on her neck and halter to turn her body so that her rump wasn't against the stall wall. Red Dust grunted and strained. With each contraction, Jackson pulled downward on the foal's slippery legs. When the head emerged he broke the tough whitish membrane surrounding it. Quickly, he cleared the foal's mouth of the mucus with his hand and guided the rest of the foal out.

"Laney, bring me the iodine bottle on the window ledge," Jackson ordered and while she did as bidden, he rubbed the foal dry with clean straw. By the time Laney returned with the iodine, Jackson had severed the umbilical cord. He squirted iodine over the end of the cord and stepped away so that the mare could bond with her baby. Red Dust sat up and reached across and nuzzled her foal with a deep-throated nicker.

"Look at that adorable colt," Laney breathed.

"Filly," Jackson corrected. "Let's give them some time together," he said, as he latched the stall door. "She still has to pass the afterbirth." They watched while the mare stood and the elongated bloody white membrane hung down between her rear legs.

"Gravity will release it gradually," Jackson added.

Laney thought her heart would burst with the thrill of it all and she felt her mouth spread into a bright smile. "That's the most miraculous thing I've ever seen," she said as Jackson held the office door for her. She did a little skip as she entered the room.

"Are there any other mares due to foal?" Laney asked. She wanted to see it again and again. She ran to the window and watched as the foal tried to stand.

Jackson laughed, "Sorry Laney, this was the last of nine foalings this spring. You'll have to wait until next year. You're not going to sell the farm, are you?"

Laney's head spun around. "How did you know Cara left me the farm?"

He stared through the glass at the mare and foal. "I didn't know. I just assumed that since you two were so close, that she would leave it to you. I'd better go help that foal get some of that colostrum." He left

Laney standing at the window.

Jackson guided the filly over to the side of the mare and in a few minutes, she was sucking away. When the placenta slipped to the straw, he pitchforked it into an empty feed bag and carried it to the trash can.

How competent he is, Laney observed. If I were to keep the farm, he'd certainly be the only one I'd consider to manage it.

Jackson gave the mare fresh water and hay. Returning to the office, he washed up in the little utility sink.

"Now, a little refreshment for the night watchers." He opened the small refrigerator and removed a cold bottle of Chablis and two chilled wine glasses. With a deft movement or two, the bottle was uncorked and the pale liquid splashed into the goblets.

"If I didn't know better, I'd believe you had this whole evening planned," Laney said nervously.

Jackson only smiled and handed a glass to Laney. "Here's to the last foaling of the season and my last sleepless night for a while." Jackson clinked his goblet against Laney's and he consumed the wine in a couple of long swallows. He refilled his glass while Laney watched the mare and foal through the window.

"You will keep the farm, won't you?" Jackson repeated, and he downed the wine again in a two loud gulps.

"I haven't made up my mind yet, Jackson."

"I thought I saw Prescott's car again yesterday," Jackson said, refilling his glass.

"You did."

"You're seeing a lot of him, aren't you?"

"He's a very good friend." She noticed he was filling his glass again. When he reached over to pour some into her glass, she covered it with her hand and shook her head.

"Do you consider *me* to be a good friend, Laney?"

"Of course I do. I don't know what I would have done without you this past week," she said, with a slight edge to her voice.

Jackson poured the last of the wine into his glass and tossed the empty bottle into the trash can next to the desk. He took a long drink and Laney saw his bright eyes leer at her over the edge of the goblet. He balanced the empty goblet on the window sill and grasped her arm. "Laney, your hair is the same color as Red Dust's." Jackson twined a ringlet that had broken loose from her braid around his finger. His glassy eyes stared fixedly at her face.

"I think maybe you've had a little too much wine, Jackson." She snatched her hair away and placed her glass on the desk. The wine sloshed over the rim and soaked a open notebook lying there. "I'm sorry. It was an accident."

Jackson frowned and blotted at the pages with a towel hastily grabbed from the sink.

"You should be more careful, you know," he said.

"I think I'd better go. It's going to storm." Laney turned the door knob and was instantly thrown backward by the force of the wind blowing the door inwards. She felt Jackson's arms catch her, spin her around and his body press her back against the door. Behind her, she heard the click of the latch. In one quick movement, his powerful hand squeezed her jaw and his cold, wine-wet lips moved roughly against hers.

With a quick twist of her head, Laney wrenched her mouth away. "Jackson . . . no!" she cried, and was surprised when he released her suddenly.

"Laney, I'm sorry. I didn't mean to do that." His face was tragic with remorse. "I did . . . I certainly did have too much to drink. Will you forgive me? It will never happen again, I promise." He backed away from her and smiled sheepishly. "What an ass I am."

Laney looked at him in amazement. It was as though he had instantly sobered–like he had never had a single drink. His dark eyes were clear and steady.

For some odd reason, she was the one who felt guilty. "Jackson, don't be embarrassed. It's not like *I* never had too much to drink before. It's okay . . . really it is . . . don't think another moment about it," she went on contritely. But I must go. Listen to that wind."

"I'll drive you back to the house," Jackson said, as he stepped toward the door.

"No, I think I can make it before the rain begins. Where's Blackberry?" Laney looked toward the corner where she had been sleeping.

"She must have bolted when you opened the door before," he said, as Laney cautiously unlatched the office door.

The gust was furious, slamming the door against her shoulder. Laney fought back and stepped out into the gathering storm. She yelled, "I'll see you," but her words were lost in the roar of the wind.

Blackberry appeared like a black and white vision beside her bike. Jackson, lit up by the lightning, stood in the threshold like an eerie pale apparition, smiling his dimpled smile.

Laney flew along the farm lane buffeted by the forceful tailwind. The lightning rent the rolling black sky and with every echoing crash of thunder, she felt the ground tremble through the pedals of her bike. As she pumped, her hunched back was pelted by the driving rain.

Just as she approached the entrance to the circle drive, Blackberry abruptly cut across her path. Laney braked to avoid her. The bike skidded. The rear wheel locked. Laney flew over the handlebars, her arms outstretched.

Laney scrambled to a sitting position and found that except for a few scratches on her arms, she didn't appear injured. Looking about in the light from the coach light, she found herself in the center of a giant yew, her legs spread wide. Next to her, the bike's front wheel spun on and on and on. Blackberry struggled from the branches of the evergreen and scorched a path to the porch. While the storm roared about her, Laney looked up at the creaking sign that read "Stoney Creek Bed & Breakfast." Her tears and laughter mingled with the storm.

11

Friday, May 10

The rain just wouldn't stop. Throughout the night, she heard it hammering on the roof and beating against the window in her bedroom. Blackberry found a safe haven under the crocheted throw on the chaise longue, but one time during the storm, a flash of lightning illuminated a vibrating lump under the dog's coverlet. When the thunder abated by early morning, both Laney and Blackberry finally slept.

But the rain went on steadily through the morning. Laney had no sooner crawled out of bed when Jackson called.

"Did you have any trouble getting home last night?" he asked.

"No." She didn't tell him about her fall. "Thank you for letting me see the foaling. It was wonderful."

"I'm glad you caught it. I hope I didn't ruin the rest of the evening for you. I can't believe I did that to you, Laney." His voice sounded truly repentant.

"Please, no more about it. Okay?"

"All right, Laney."

"Anyway, while I have you on the phone, I thought you should know that I have decided to sell the farm. I'm sure you will have no trouble finding other employment or perhaps the new owner, whoever he may be, will ask that you stay on."

The silence lasted until Laney wasn't sure that Jackson was still on the phone. "Jackson, are you there?"

The voice was soft and controlled. "I'm here."

"Maybe I . . . I should have told you last night," Laney said, sensing his discomposure.

"You told me last night that you hadn't made up your mind." There was a stony undercurrent to his words.

"I hadn't . . . I mean . . . not for sure," Laney stammered. "What I really mean is that I wasn't ready to tell you."

"You were keeping it from me," Jackson said caustically.

"No, please, I didn't mean–" Laney heard the phone go dead.

The phone rang a few minutes later and Laney let the answering machine pick it up. When she heard Gray's voice, she snatched up the phone.

"Gray?"

"What's going on, Laney?" Laney smiled at his signature greeting.

"Not much," Laney said. "I'm going to try to write that article for *Three Rivers Magazine*."

"Did the storm do any damage?" Gray asked.

"Not that I can see from inside the house."

"Could I come over this evening?" Gray asked tentatively.

Laney debated, "I need to work on this article. How's tomorrow instead?"

"Good," Gray exhaled. "Seven okay?"

"Perfect. I'll fix dinner. I owe you."

"My cup runneth over."

Laney had been at the computer for over an hour when she heard thumps coming from the parlor. She knew it was the cardinal again, but was drawn to the room anyway. The window was still shuttered and when she drew the panels to the sides, she noticed that it had quit raining but the rolling sky was preparing for another onslaught.

She stood very still. She waited. The bird swooped down and into the window. Back he flew to the branch. His beak, a battered battering ram, attacked his reflection over and over. After each pounding of his small head, his eyes stared vacantly for a split second, his tiny body trying to recover from the masochistic hammering. Then, the cardinal repeated his bloody, involuntary dance.

Laney watched transfixed. Something about the bird's pointless performance–the hopelessness of it all–reminded Laney of something, someone. She studied the cardinal's blank stare before he attacked again.

"Good God," she said. "That's me! I'm just like that blasted pea-brained bird with a knee-jerk reflex. I'm letting life just happen to me. When did I decide that I have no control? I've disconnected–tuned out, just like that empty-headed bird."

Laney stepped to the window and beat it with her fist. "Get a life!" she screamed at the redbird, then laughed at herself and whirled about in the middle of the room.

Dizzy, Laney sank to the patterned carpet. She lay back with her arms behind her head. "I've got to start dealing with my problems. Now. Stop ignoring them."

She sat up. "God, look how I dealt with Jackson last night. When he grabbed me, I should have popped him one. Instead, I told him, 'Don't think another moment about it.'" Laney spoke in a childish voice while she wiggled her body to and fro.

"Damn, what's been with me?" she screamed at the bird. "Enough. No more peace at any price."

But Laney knew in her heart what had triggered the slip into her destructive state. Cara's death. She didn't want to face it. There was so much pain there. "But she's gone . . . dead. There, I said it."

"Cara was dead. But was it an accident? Let yourself think about it, Laney. Don't bury your head in the sand this time. Don't think, 'I don't want to be upset.'"

The rain began again and the cardinal flew one last time into the window, then disappeared in the downpour. Laney jumped to her feet and ran through the house to the French doors, grabbing her purse and keys on the breakfast table. She practically stumbled over Blackberry as she rushed off the porch. Over the path to the buggy house she splashed, Blackberry in pursuit. She slid the garage doors wide and when she opened the Whooptie door, Blackberry whipped by her and settled into the passenger seat.

"Why not?" Laney shrugged, and started the engine, the smell of wet dog polluting the car. Laney glanced into the rearview mirror to tidy her damp, tangled hair and saw an extraordinary smile plastered on her freckled face.

Jesse lived above Cohen's Used Furniture Store on Main Street in Hickory. Laney found a tight parking place and gave it three attempts before she managed in.

Laney looked over at the store front and saw that Cohen's sign had been replaced by one that read, "Second Hand Rose." Cracking the window and locking Blackberry inside, she ran through the rain.

"Wipe your feet," a voice with a strange accent commanded. Laney looked about in the gloom. "You deaf or what, already?" Feeling a mat under her feet, Laney did as commanded. "What can I do for y'all?" a massive old woman said from a motley davenport to the right of the open front door.

"I'm looking for Jesse Mills. I believe she still lives upstairs."

"Sure enough. Who are you?" She raised a tufted white eyebrow. Her lips were painted with a wide brush and she blinked a pair of Tammy Faye eyelashes.

"My name is Laney McVey. Jesse is a friend of mine. Excuse me. What happened to Herb Cohen?"

"Herbie aspired about six months ago. I'm his sister, Rose. He left this joint to me. He knew I always wanted to live in the South." Her accent was a cross between Yiddish and a southern drawl. A purple caftan made by Omar the Tent Maker covered her ample form and a pair of fuchsia sandals did heavy duty restraining her swollen feet. Her smile was warm and Laney liked her immediately.

Laney stretched out her hand, "How do you do, Rose." She winced with the strength of her clasp. "May I go on up?"

Rose waved her on.

Laney climbed an elegant staircase–the kind you might find leading to a balcony in an old movie house. It certainly looked out of place in the rough warehouse surroundings. The stairs ended abruptly in front of a small landing. A hollow mahogany door announced one of the entrances to Jesse's apartment. The other access, a metal fire escape in an alley outside of the building, had been added five years before.

Merle Haggard's "The Guitar Man" strummed from inside the apartment. Jesse answered the door in her Finish Line uniform and stocking feet. The turquoise and black jockey outfit and cap set off her large gray eyes.

"Laney, what are ya doing here?" Jesse chewed on her lip and seemed flustered to see her.

"May I come in?" Laney asked, when she didn't welcome her into the apartment.

"Yeah . . . sorry." Jesse opened the door wide.

"I met your new landlady, Rose," Laney laughed. "I love the accent."

"She moved from the Bronx six months ago," Jesse said. "Must've gotten that southern accent from drinking out of a Dixie cup." Jesse sat down on a worn gold ottoman and put on a pair of black leather booties. When she stood up, Laney admired her trim figure. The black satin slacks showed off her long slim legs. "I gotta go." Jesse picked up her purse from the coffee table.

"Jesse, it's four o'clock. I know you don't go to work until five. Now sit down and listen to me." Laney pointed to the ottoman and almost pushed Jesse onto it.

Jesse raised her brows in surprise and sat.

"I asked you the other day if you knew about Cara placing that ad. You said no but you're lying. Now out with it!" Laney bent down and got right in her face.

"Laney . . . you have no right to talk to—"

"Oh yes I do. She was my sister, damn it." Laney reached into her purse and pulled out the letters. "Look, these are the letters she got and I know that she went out with at least one of these guys." Laney removed the photo of Tony Richards from the top envelope and thrust it in front of Jesse. Jesse's face tuned ashen. "She was seeing this man, and he was murdered around the same time Cara died. Now tell me if you know anything about this." The photo quivered in Laney's hand and blood pulsed in her temples.

Laney saw the fear in Jesse's eyes. Jesse shoved Laney's hand away and stood. "Okay, okay. I knew she placed the ad. We were sitting around drinking one night and I dared her. You knew your sister . . . ." Jesse dropped her eyes and turned her head away as she spoke.

"What about this guy . . . or any of the guys for that matter? Did she ever tell you she saw any of them?"

"No, we just sat around and laughed." Jesse fidgeted.

"Laughed?"

"Yeah, we sat around and laughed at the letters. She did it for kicks."

"My God, Jesse. You two sat around and made fun of these guys?"

"I gotta go." Jesse moistened her lips, and started for the door. Laney saw Jesse's hands tremble as she turned the knob.

"Let yourself out," Jesse said and banged the door behind her.

Laney listened to Jesse's footsteps fade down the stairs. She's lying, she thought to herself. She knew this guy.

When Laney reached the bottom of the staircase, Rose was still sprawled across the davenport. She had kicked off her sandals and was drinking something out of a twenties silver flask. "Say, are you the sister of that gal that drowned in the creek a while back?"

Laney flinched but nodded.

"The newspaper said that she was a McVey before she married. You look like her too, except for that rust on your head. She sure was a looker. She had a little flesh on her bones . . . not a rail like you."

"You met my sister?"

She nodded. "Oy . . . and that boychick with her. If I'd been a few years younger . . . ." She fanned her face with an imaginary fan.

"When was this, Rose?" Laney asked, intrigued.

"Hmm . . . maybe three weeks ago. I remember thinking when I saw her picture in the death notices that I had just talked to her a few days before. Oooh . . . he had the most beautiful Valentino mustache . . . and that tush. Oy vey, be still my heart."

"Did they buy anything?" Trying to appear indifferent, she pretended to look at a nice beveled hall mirror leaning against a table.

"No, but she had her eye on that little wicker rocker over there but Valentino said he didn't want to put it in his pretty car."

Laney perked up. "Did you see what kind of car he had?"

"Honey, y'all sure ask a lot of questions, already. Don't know anything about cars. Only know it was a shiny black gangster car without a top. It had white leather seats. I guess that's why he didn't want to put the rocker in it." Rose took another swig from her flask. Her painted mouth smeared onto a front tooth and she belched loudly.

Laney strolled over to the child's rocker and looked at the price tag.

"Rose, I'd like to buy this rocker." Laney couldn't think why in the world she wanted to buy it, but she paid her and hiked the rocker to her hip.

"Hope you don't have to schlepp it too far in this rain. Y'all come back, now."

With a quick, "Thanks," Laney dashed out into the rain. She placed the rocker in the trunk of the Whooptie but couldn't close the lid. She and Blackberry made a quick run by Ben's Market and listened to the trunk lid bounce all the way home.

Laney wiped the rocker down with an old terry cloth towel. Now, why did I buy this? Laney wondered, sitting back on her heels, admiring her purchase. But it would look darling in one of the bedrooms. But I won't be here in a few days, she remembered.

Suddenly hungry, Laney left the chair sitting in the middle of the kitchen floor and scrounged the freezer for something for lunch. She came up with a small casserole with Natine's name taped on it and she shoved it into the microwave. As she made a small salad to go with her lunch, she reflected on how kind everyone in Hickory had been. All that food and the condolences still continued to come in. Her mother had made a list of every person who had sent food or flowers and insisted on personally writing each thank-you note herself.

The aroma of garlic, shrimp, and smoked hot sausage drifted from the microwave, and just as Laney heard the beep, the front door bell rang. Mouth watering, Laney raced Blackberry to the door.

When it swung open, Karl stood on the porch. Laney instinctively stepped backwards.

"Laney," he said, "How have you been?"

Like he really cares how I am, Laney thought. She had a sudden vision of Cara in bed with him. Momentarily queasy, she swallowed loudly. "Karl, I don't have the time right now." She spoke through the screen door.

"This will only take a minute." His tiny steel ball eyes drilled into her face. "I have come to make an offer." An arrogant smile washed over his dark features. In one stomach-turning flash, Laney recalled what Gray had told her about Karl and her mother being married for only a few months. She pictured Cara begging him for money to abort his child.

Laney opened the screen door and she stepped out on the porch and closed the door behind Blackberry, who followed. She stood with her hand on the door knob. "What is it, Karl?" she said venomously.

Karl hesitated for a moment, his eyes questioning if he should go on, but then plunged ahead. "I want to make an offer to buy the farm." He unbuttoned two buttons on his red and black plaid shirt, reached inside and extracted a folded document. Curly gray and black hair sprung from his makeshift pocket. After unfolding the document, he shoved it into her hand.

Laney looked at Karl in disbelief then moved her eyes slowly down the page. When she read the amount of the offer, she realized that her mother had finally told Karl about her inheritance.

Laney folded the document carefully and looked up at Karl. He was grinning at her. She felt her own lips tremble into a smile as she deliberately tore the paper in half, then quarters, then eighths. When she released the confetti slowly from her spread fingers, a swoosh escaped from Karl's lips and his face metamorphosed into some vile creature of rage. As she watched, his skin turned purple and his lips formed a white slash. Veins wormed black in his temples. Opening his mouth, he managed a croaking, "Why?"

Laney narrowed her eyes and spat, "You know why, you bastard."

He raised his fist and took a step toward her. Laney thought he would strike her but Blackberry let out a low throaty sound and he backed away. With a loathsome glare, Karl moved away from her and mumbled an unintelligible threat and stormed to his truck. He burned at least a ply off his tires as he scratched off. Laney knew she would pay for it.

"God, did I really do that?" Laney said, as she leaned against the door after charging into the house. Her legs abruptly turned into quivering gelatin and she slowly slid down the door until she was a puddle on the Persian rug. She could still see the fury in Karl's black eyes and, for the first time, she felt a cold clutch of fear spiral through her insides. When she played her tongue across her wet upper lip, she tasted salt. Laney stood and walked unsteadily to the kitchen. "Get a grip, Laney. He can't hurt you." But when she looked down and saw Blackberry, she bent and patted her head, "Thanks for being there, sweet thing."

Natine's shrimp gumbo was worth the wait. Though a bit overcooked by the second heating in the microwave, the flavor was not lost. Laney indulged in an extra spoonful before she hid the leftovers in the refrigerator.

Laney studied the little rocker in the middle of the kitchen floor. Impulsively, she picked it up and carried it into her sister's bedroom and placed it at an angle next to the fireplace. She ran up the back stairs to her room and lifted the brown box that she had brought from Pittsburgh out of the closet. Cradling it carefully, she hurried back down the stairs and into Cara's room. She took a pair of silver handled scissors from the carton she had packed with all of Cara's personal items. Scoring the tape, she snapped the lid open. Tenderly, she pushed the white tissue aside. There it was–the most exquisite bisque doll in the whole wide world. Laney had bought it because it looked so much like her sister. Her friend, Judy, at *Three Rivers Magazine*, collected German dolls and when Laney had seen the 1885 doll on a visit to Judy's Oakland apartment, she just had to have it. She paid dearly for it, but the almost white bisque doll with apple-red cheeks had stolen her heart. Dressed in pink taffeta, trimmed in antique lace, the miniature Cara stared up at her from the tissue. Like her sister, the doll had a heart-shaped face, golden hair, and bright blue eyes. Tiny pink-tinted fingers and laced up high-topped boots completed the lovely doll. Laney reached beneath the doll and lifted her like she was a fragile new baby and hugged her softly. A single tear fell down upon the silky blond hair. Retrieving a lacy pillow from the bed, she placed it on the seat of the rocker and positioned the Cara doll carefully. Blackberry sniffed at it and turned away indifferently. She lay down on the hearth rug and shut her eyes for a quick nap.

In an impulsive assault that matched the attack that had cleared the room on Sunday, Laney returned all Cara's things to their places–the pictures in silver frames, the silver backed brush and comb. Even the lavender sachets were plopped back into the drawers.

Laney ran back and forth to her room upstairs and hauled her clothes and toiletries down to Cara's bedroom.

When everything was put away, she stood back and looked around the room. Speaking to the porcelain doll, Laney announced, "Sis, I'm moving in with you." With a smile so wide it scrunched her eyes, she hip-hopped out of the room. Blackberry padded behind her.

12

Saturday, May 11

"I really don't want you to come tonight, Puccini," Gray said, as he nudged the sleeping tabby on the dash. "What if Blackberry trees you again or worse, you take a swipe at her like you did once before." Puccini flipped onto his back and his white paws curled into tight little mittens.

"I appreciate your deference to my supreme authority," Gray said, as he shut the door and started the engine. He dropped in a Mirella Freni CD and was instantly soothed by her heartbreaking, "Un bel di."

Later, as Gray drove down the lane to the house, he saw that the swollen waters of Stoney Creek were spilling out from the banks. He caught flashes of its swift and muddy center current between the trees. By the time he reached the circle drive, the rain had settled into a chilly drizzle. He couldn't remember another spring as wet as this one.

Gray dragged Puccini off the dash, lifted the bottle of chardonnay from the passenger seat, and dashed to the porch.

Laney greeted him dressed in a knitted silk tunic and pants–both in soft ivory. Her face was aglow and her eyes sparkled. Blackberry couldn't be seen, so Gray dropped Puccini to the rug and the cat disappeared into the parlor.

"Let's have a drink before dinner," Laney said as she took Gray's arm and followed the cat into the room. She had set a small fire in the grate and its warmth was comforting on the damp evening. Gray automatically went to the small wet bar on the credenza between the windows overlooking the front porch. He set the bottle of wine in the wine chiller and made a Bloody Mary for Laney and a bourbon and water for himself.

"What's going on?" Gray said, as he sat on the red damask sofa next to Laney.

Laney smiled shyly, her eyes crinkling and shining in the firelight. Damn, Gray thought, something is different here. He scanned her face closely. Her eyes were shining buckeyes but they seemed brighter, somehow, like they'd been burnished.

"I've had quite a day, but it can wait," Laney said, a serious look clouding those eyes for a second. She sipped her drink, "Mmm, you make an incredible Bloody. There was an awkward silence that seemed forever to Gray. He noted her deep sigh before she spoke. "I've decided to live here," she whispered almost as though the pronouncement were an afterthought.

Gray wasn't sure he had heard correctly. He gulped and choked on his drink.

"Gray, are you all right?" Laney asked, laughing at him.

"Am I all right?" he croaked. He jumped to his feet, grabbed Laney's drink and set both of them sloshing on the center table. Taking Laney's hands he lifted her to her feet and whirled her around the room. Impulsively, he glided to the polyphon in the corner and wound the handle that started the metal disc turning. The tinny strains of a Strauss waltz danced with them around the snug parlor.

Laney had closed the shutters from the rain, and the glowing firelight cavorted about the room like a firefly unwilling to settle. It flickered on the creamy cocoa walls and winked at the richly polished mahogany furniture and wooden floors.

Gray couldn't pull his eyes away from Laney's. Her gutsy fire had returned and underlying her sparkle was the self-assured inner calmness that had bewitched him so a year ago.

"Do you mean it? You'll live here?" Gray still needed reassurance. "How did you . . . why?"

"To tell you the truth, Gray, a little bird told me," Laney giggled, and explained why she came to realize how complacent she had become and how she had lost control of her life. "I was living in a dreamy half-awareness. I wanted peace at any price and so I tuned out. As a result, I became resigned that my life was unalterable. How's that for self-analysis?"

She bounced away from Gray and lifted their drinks from the center table and handed his to him.

"Here's to the new me," she toasted.

"Here's to the old you," he added, "the one I remember from last spring." Their glasses clinked together and they drank. And he drank in her eyes, her freckled nose, the way her lips moved and trembled when she smiled, making her cheeks shine like apples. Again, he put away the glasses. He couldn't help himself and there was no protest from her when he bent and kissed her lips. "Laney," he murmured.

A low growl came from across the room. When Gray looked over at the fireplace, Blackberry was lying on the hearth rug in front of the brass fender, her brown eyes following Puccini as he approached.

"Blackberry," Laney scolded. Blackberry blinked and lowered her head in compliance.

Puccini never wavered in his advance. In fact, there was a determined regal air in the way he pushed ahead across the room. Blackberry seemed to shrink into the rug. Her eyes appealed to Laney to allow her to shelve her obedience training and go after that tender morsel, but Laney just stood there with Gray, the two of them fascinated with the scene that was unfolding before them.

As Puccini closed the gap between them, Blackberry's eyes grew wide with an overwrought stare, and she began to tremble. The cat seemed to know that he was out of harm's way as long as human beings were there. He approached from the left, his black ringed tail high in the air. Blackberry, frozen in a sphinx position, shifted her eyes to the left as Puccini rubbed his ear against her jaw. A viscous ooze of slobber moved down Blackberry's chin and plopped on the rug. Puccini's body began a long slinking journey under the dog's chin. He sidled and rubbed and undulated a slow tortuous stretch, while Blackberry quivered, the hair on her back bristling with torment and her glassy eyes rolling in agony. When Puccini had accomplished what he had set out to do, he gave Blackberry one final look of disregard and glided out of the room.

Gray and Laney collapsed onto the oriental rug in uncontrollable laughter and hugged Blackberry to them. She didn't know what she had done, but joined in the fun, enjoying all the attention.

"God, that was the funniest thing I've ever seen," Laney said, wiping the tears from her eyes.

"I'm afraid I'm going to have to pay for that. He already gives me no respect," Gray chuckled.

"Speaking of paying for something, come into the kitchen while I tell you what happened yesterday," Laney said. Gray noticed that she didn't smile when she said the words. He threw another log on the fire and they walked to the kitchen with their arms wrapped around each other.

Gray helped cut the fresh vegetables for the salad. Layered in the crystal bowl, they looked like jewels. While they worked, Laney rattled on about her visit with Jesse and how she had lied about Cara's ad. "I guess she wanted to protect Cara's image," Laney said. "You know, I'm beginning to realize that my sister may have had a real problem. It's hard to admit, but look at the affair she had with Karl." She sliced at the carrot furiously.

"Easy there." Gray put his hand down on hers.

"How could she do that, Gray?" Laney stabbed the butcher block with the point of the knife. "He's a creep, but Mother married him. It's almost like . . . like incest." Then in a tiny voice, she said, "He knows I know, Gray."

Gray's head snapped up. "He knows you know about the affair . . . the abortion?"

"Yes." Laney told him about Karl coming to the house and his offer on the farm.

"Where would he get the money?"

"Cara left Mother a huge sum in the will. She didn't want Karl to know about it yet, but I guess she finally told him. He was in such a rage, he almost struck me when I tore the offer up. Blackberry made him change his mind."

"That weenie?" Gray thumbed at Blackberry.

Laney nodded. She set water on to boil and brushed olive oil and garlic between the halves of Italian bread. "If you open the wine, we'll start on our salads."

Laney tossed a light vinaigrette and carried the salad bowl into the dining room.

Gray was startled by the depth of color in the dining room. The crimson walls were set off by a gilded picture rail from which a large portrait of Cara's late father-in-law and several gold framed mirrors were hung. Laney lit the white tapers near the end of the table where two places had been set. The crystal chandelier with dancing prisms and the candlelight were reflected in the silvery, beveled Victorian mirrors.

"Laney, this is beautiful." Gray walked through the pocket doors into the parlor and put another log on the fire. Puccini was curled up on a small footstool by the polyphon and Blackberry was still lying near the fireplace. Intermittently, she glanced over at the cat.

"Have you told John about leaving *Three Rivers Magazine*?" Gray asked, when he returned with the opened bottle of wine. He poured the amber liquid into the crystal glasses and sat down.

"No, I'll finish that article this weekend and send it off Monday. Then I'll call him. It will soften the blow a bit if I at least do that. I'll still have to make a trip to Pittsburgh to close up my apartment. Oh dear . . . ."

"What?"

"I just remembered. I told Jackson that I was selling the farm."

"Why did you do that?" Gray was shocked.

"I told him Thursday when I was still in my dark mood."

"You know, you can't find a better manager than Jackson." Gray finished his salad and sat back in his chair. The candlelight played on Laney's hair. The light leaped about changing the color from chestnut to copper to a dark red cloud framing her face. Her chocolate eyes sparkled.

"How did he take it?" Gray asked, his heart still lurching in his chest.

"He hung up on me."

"Not Jackson!"

"He thinks somehow I haven't been honest with him . . . that I don't tell him everything that I do. He sometimes seems possessive." Laney decided not to tell Gray about the incident in the foaling office. "But maybe I should ask him to stay."

"Think you should. He's the best."

Laney collected the salad plates. "I'll be back in a jiffy. Would you stir the fire a bit?"

Gray groaned and patted his full belly. "How did you make that dinner so quickly?"

"Fettuccini Alfredo only takes about ten minutes. Mother made the brownies. They were in the freezer." She frowned. "I'm worried about her, Gray. I've tried to call her several times this week but the answering machine always picks up. I think I'll stop over tomorrow."

"Laney, be careful around Karl. Don't trust him after what you told me. Never trusted him anyway." Gray threw his napkin on the table.

"Let's change the subject." Laney stood and took Gray by the hand and led him through the kitchen and back to her new bedroom suite. At the door to her room, Gray raised an eyebrow.

Laney laughed. "Don't get any ideas. I wanted to show you what I bought. She led him to the rocking chair and he gasped.

"The doll looks just like Cara," he said in wonder.

"I bought it in Pittsburgh for Cara. Yesterday, I bought the rocking chair at Second Hand Rose's. While I was there, I found out that Cara and Tony Richards were there just before their deaths. Cara was going to buy the rocker, but Tony didn't want to put it in his new car."

"How did you find all that out?" Gray probed.

"Rose told me. Apparently, she knows who's who and who's doing who. Amazing in the short time she's lived in Hickory. When she said she had seen Cara and this Tony at the store, I naturally asked a few questions."

"Naturally," Gray nuzzled her hair. "And what are you going to do with all this information, my dear Watson?"

"I don't know yet," Laney said, with a determined set to her jaw that worried him.

Gray collected Puccini and stood at the front door with the huge cat draped over his arm. Blackberry was taking her turn outside.

Gray shifted the tabby to his other arm. He lingered, not wanting to leave.

"To borrow your expression, what's going on?" Laney asked.

"What do you mean?"

"Why so quiet?"

Gray shuffled his feet. "Don't know exactly. Maybe this information about Cara and Karl and Tony is eating at me. Feel a bit unsettled." He frowned. "Promise me something?"

"Maybe."

"Don't do anything crazy."

Laney kissed him hard on the lips. "Like this?"

"Mmm . . . that kind of crazy's okay."

Gray was halfway home and Puccini was purring away on the dash before he realized Laney hadn't made the promise.

13

Sunday, May 12

Hickory dock was closed because of high water. Backwater lapped at the support posts of the office, and Laney could see Karl pulling the last fishing boat up on higher ground near the house. Her mother was carrying white plastic chairs stacked three-high away from the awning covered pavilion that was used for large picnic groups. Even though the rain had stopped, the decking was covered with about a half inch of brown water. Laney parked by the house and jumped out to help. As she sloshed to the pavilion, she was glad she had worn her rubber ducks.

Laney took the stack of chairs from her mother.

"Thanks," she said. I don't think it's going to come up much more but I'd hate to see these chairs float away. The tables are heavy enough to stay put."

Laney lugged the last of the chairs to the house deck and turned to see Karl glaring at her from the top of the flooded boat ramp. She looked beyond his angry stare to the sweeping torrent of the creek. A surge of brown water in the center percolated like a giant coffee pot and with every thundering eruption, it ejected logs and limbs. She followed their twisting journey until they were out of sight. Dear God . . . poor Cara, she thought.

"Laney, did you hear me? How about some coffee?"

They kicked off their ducks outside the door and Maddy led the way into the warm kitchen where the oven timer was buzzing away. The tantalizing aroma of something sweet and yeasty made Laney's mouth water.

"What *is* that?" Laney asked, turning off the timer and peeking into the oven window.

Maddy grabbed two oven mitts and pulled out a square pan that she turned over onto a large plate on the counter. When she lifted the pan, the most gorgeous caramel rolls lay glistening with a buttery brown sugar glaze drizzling down the sides.

"Look at those. I've just got to have one." Laney grabbed a small plate from the cupboard and slid a gooey roll onto it. Maddy smiled at her daughter while she poured coffee into mugs.

While Laney wolfed down the roll, she watched her mother fuss nervously around the kitchen. "Mother, I hope this won't bother you but I need to ask." Maddy glanced over at her.

"Was the creek this angry the morning Cara died?" Maddy stopped wiping the sink and slowly peered out at the water.

"No, but it had been like this the day before. The creek had started to ease back into its banks."

"Did Cara often canoe when the creek was up like that."

"Knowin your sister, I imagine she did, but just didn't tell me about it. Laney, I've gone over this a million times in my head. The water near the banks in most areas of the creek isn't as turbulent as the center when it floods. Look out and see for yourself."

Laney stood and looked out the window with her mother. The backwater at the banks was moving fairly slowly, compared to the center of the creek.

"I think Cara usually stayed close to the banks when the creek was up but that day she must have gotten too close to the center current and when the canoe capsized, she hit her head on somethin and got swept away." Maddy turned away from the window. The rims of her eyes were red and she rubbed her nose with the back of her hand.

"I'm sorry, Mother. Let's change the subject. I want to tell you some good news. I'm going to move to the farm."

With one swift motion, Maddy took hold of her shoulders and looked squarely in her eyes, then hugged her in a squeeze that hurt. Then she began to bawl. "I didn't dare hope . . . I wanted you so to stay . . . are you goin to open the bed and breakfast? . . . What about your writin job in Pittsburgh?" Maddy blubbered.

"Hold on," Laney interrupted. "I've just fallen heir to a farm, a house, horses, the Whooptie, and a sassy Border collie. Please don't ask me yet what I'm going to do with it all."

Maddy's wet face beamed like the sun after a thunderstorm. She wouldn't let go of Laney's hands.

Her joy suddenly froze in mid-smile when heavy footsteps on the deck announced Karl's approach. "Remember, Laney, nothin about my inheritance," she warned.

Stunned by Maddy's overt admission that she hadn't yet told Karl about the will, Laney stood open-mouthed as Karl entered the kitchen. He stood in his sloppy boots at the door.

"Karl, have you heard? Laney's movin to the farm." Maddy tried to recover the excitement in her voice, but it just wasn't there.

"You don't say," Karl said deprecatingly. He stepped off the door mat and muddy water puddled onto the tile floor. Karl reached around Laney and grabbed three rolls with his filthy hands. With a deliberate brush across her breasts with his elbow, he pushed by her, opened the door and stalked out.

Livid, Laney almost followed him out onto the deck, but at the last moment, only held back because of what Gray had asked her the night before.

"You have to excuse Karl's rudeness," Maddy apologized. "The bad weather has made him so moody lately." She rubbed her right eye.

"Mother, don't make excuses for the man. He's a low life. Why don't you leave him?"

Maddy's eyes opened wide. "Laney, what's gotten into you?"

"I've stopped letting things happen to me. I wish a little bit of it would rub off on you, Mother. You're afraid of him, aren't you?" Even Laney was surprised at her own candidness.

"Laney, that's enough. I think you should go."

Laney opened her mouth to say one last thing, but Maddy raised a forefinger in the air, a gesture from Laney's childhood that meant she'd better not say another word.

Laney kissed her mother and Maddy kissed her back. "I'm happy you're movin back, honey."

"Me, too."

As Laney walked to the Whooptie, she could see all the fishing boats lined up on high ground. A rack of ten canoes and a barrel holding the paddles rested beside the house deck. Karl was nowhere around. As she drove away, she realized that she hadn't seen any paddle boats. She recalled that Karl had told Sheriff Powell that he had checked them out in Florence the morning Cara died. Had Karl's friend actually bought them at the derby day auction?

Laney was about halfway through with her article for *Three Rivers Magazine* when Gray called.

"What are you writing about?"

"Pittsburgh pubs," she answered. "There are some good ones. I had a lot of fun researching this assignment."

"Which ones were your favorites?"

"Mullany's Harp & Fiddle was great. It's in the Strip District and they serve the best Irish lamb stew and corned beef and cabbage you ever ate. There's live Irish entertainment and music, too."

"Meet any other McVeys there?"

"Nope, but I think my very favorite pub is the Seventh Street Grill, downtown.

"Why's that?"

"I think it was the beer. I say 'I think it was,' because they have one hundred different kinds and I believe I tried every one, one night," Laney chuckled. "What are you doing?"

"Resting. I had an emergency foaling about two a.m. Didn't get to bed until four. Turned out all right, though. Mother and filly doing fine. Think I'll hit the sack early, though."

"Did Puccini go with you?"

"No, he seemed exhausted after his cheeky performance with Blackberry. He struts around like he's cool, but if the truth be known, he wouldn't have dared approach Blackberry if we hadn't been there. Right now, he's asleep in his bed."

"Which is where?"

"Okay, at the foot of my bed. Where does Blackberry sleep?"

"In good weather or in thunderstorms?"

"Touché?"

"I saw Karl today at Mother's."

"You didn't–" Gray began.

"No, I behaved myself, but it wasn't easy. Mother told him I was moving here."

"Bet it made his day."

"He jumped for joy," Laney said sarcastically, remembering Karl's reaction. "I told Mother she should leave him. I'm sure the reason she doesn't is because she's afraid of him. One of these days I may tell her about Karl and Cara. By the way, she didn't tell Karl about her inheritance after all."

"Then how could Karl make you an offer on the farm?"

"Beats me. But somehow Karl got hold of the information. Maybe someone in Marshall Knight's office has big ears and a mouth to match. You know this town. I'll call Marshall tomorrow."

Gray yawned, "I'm really beat. Talk at you later. Okay?"

"Okay."

Laney worked furiously on her article for *Three Rivers*. After a quick leftover fettuccini dinner, she settled back at the computer. She was surprised when she heard her stomach growling about eight o'clock. She found herself in the kitchen again, heating a cup of instant coffee in the microwave to go with the last two brownies that were calling to her from a small tray in the pie safe. She was on the way back to the library when she remembered that Blackberry hadn't had her dinner, so she placed the tray on the large console in the hall and opened the front door to bring her in for the night.

Blackberry wasn't lying on her favorite spot on the door mat, so Laney called her and was surprised when she didn't come bounding up on the porch. Laney shrugged and went back to her article.

About nine, she finished the spell check and remembered Blackberry, so she went again to the front porch.

"Blackberry," she called, and listened for the rustling of the collie tearing through the weeds in the woods behind the house. Nothing.

Beginning to get concerned, Laney hurried to the library and looked up Jackson's phone number in the address book. After four rings Jackson's clear voice answered and Laney started to speak when she realized the answering machine had picked up and it was the recording of Jackson's voice. She left a short message about looking for Blackberry and hung up.

Returning to the porch, she called her again. Laney began to get a sinking feeling in her stomach. "Where are you, girl? You never miss your dinner."

Locking the front door, she snatched her car keys from the china bowl on the console, dashed through the kitchen and grabbed the magnetic flashlight off the refrigerator.

As Laney tugged on the heavy doors of the buggy house, she wished she had left the Whooptie parked in the circle drive. Laney drove around the house and between the stone pilasters. She swung left and started down toward the horse barn, stopping every hundred feet or so to call out Blackberry's name through the open window.

The air was cold and Laney felt chilled in only her worn white sweatshirt and jeans. When she reached the foaling barn and office, the building was dark. Laney strained her eyes to pick up any signs of life in the direction of Jackson's house, but his house was tucked away behind a pine tree grove that obscured any glimmer of light. She thought about driving up his lane, but decided to go on.

Laney crept along in the Whooptie, stopping and calling, stopping and calling, but the silence was as absolute and foreboding as the night.

God, where is she, Laney thought with growing fear as she approached the decline to the crossing. She inched the car down the grade as far as she dared. Her headlights picked up the glistening slick and muddy gravel where the flood water had receded after reaching its crest earlier in the day.

Laney called out one more time through the open window where an odor of dank and mold slowly seeped into the Nissan. The beams of the headlights were like beacons from a miniature lighthouse and they focused on the center of the crossing where the swirling water rushed and dashed over the rocks.

Laney yanked the emergency brake and turned off the ignition and lights. The night pitched into total darkness. She could barely see the outline of the trees against the inky sky.

Grabbing the flashlight, Laney opened the door and stepped onto the gravel. Rushing water drowned out all other sounds. She inched her way down the slope until she was even with the water and swept her light over the crossing. She gasped when the beam caught the snakebird perched on a snag on the opposite bank. His black onyx eyes watched her.

Frigid lips of foreboding brushed the back of her neck. She swung the light away and stumbled along the bank.

"What's that?" she choked, her thudding heart skidding to a stop. The shaft of light had caught something black and red in the water grass. She dropped to her knees, her hands groping frenetically into the tall grass.

Blackberry lay on her side in the muddy ooze. A hand-sized black and red pool of coagulated blood matted her white chest. "Blackberry!" Laney cried, but the Border collie lay lifeless, her eyes closed.

"Not my Blackberry!" Laney screamed.

At that moment, lights from another vehicle approached the crossing. Laney lifted Blackberry's lifeless body and staggered up the incline. The vehicle jerked to a screeching halt behind the Whooptie and she was blinded by the headlights. A door slammed and she heard Jackson's voice, "Laney . . . my God . . . Laney, let me help you."

"Thank God, Jackson . . . Blackberry . . . I think she's . . . take us to Gray's."

Jackson reached for the dog to place her in the back of the Range Rover. "No, I want to hold her," Laney sobbed. "Please, Jackson . . . ."

Jackson helped Laney into the front seat of the Rover. "Jackson, I can't feel her breathing! . . . I can't lose her! What happened to her?" Laney cried hysterically, as Jackson backed the truck around and raced along the lane.

"I think she's been shot."

"Shot? What do you mean? . . . Shot?" Laney felt Blackberry's blood seeping into her sweatshirt. "Jackson, hurry! She's bleeding!"

"I heard a shot earlier. That's where I was when you left the message on my machine. I was trying to find out who was trespassing on the farm. When I got back and heard your message, I went looking for you." The toothpick in Jackson's mouth was silhouetted against the dim lights in the dash.

The Rover flew down Hickory Hill Pike and Laney bent over Blackberry, kissing her head. "I'll kill whoever did this." She wept into her cold wet fur.

The Range Rover spun out as it lurched into the small clinic parking lot. The headlights flashed on the sign next to the clinic door: Hickory Veterinary Clinic, Graham W. Prescott, D.V.M. Jackson jumped out of the truck and rang the clinic bell. It seemed forever before Laney saw the light go on upstairs in Gray's apartment. When the clinic door finally opened, Gray stood blinking in his red and white sweat pants and Louisville Cardinals sweatshirt.

"Jackson, what the hell–" Gray began.

"Gray, it's me," Laney called from the Rover. "Blackberry's been shot."

Laney paced up and down the waiting room like she was an expectant father waiting for news of a delivery. "Jackson, it's been over an hour."

"Surgery takes time. Natine told you that it would be quite a while. They had to prep her and give her anesthesia before they began. Why don't you drink your coffee before it gets cold?"

Jackson had called Natine for Gray and had made a pot while they waited for her to arrive. Fortunately, she lived only a block away.

Laney reached for the coffee, but withdrew her muddy, blood-covered hand. "I'd better wash up," she said, and rushed into the lavatory.

The harsh fluorescent light in the restroom made her squint painfully, and she gasped when she saw herself in the mirror while she washed her hands. The entire front of her white sweatshirt was thick with blood, mud, and leaves. Could Blackberry still be alive after losing so much blood, she asked herself? Her own face was gray with shock, dark smudges underlining her overly bright eyes.

After splashing cold water on her face, she dried her shaking hands and returned to the waiting room just as Gray emerged from the surgery. His green surgical gown was dotted with crimson and when he pulled off his cap and mask, his face was grim.

"I've done all I can, Laney. I am amazed she made it through the surgery with that blood loss. She was in severe shock. I removed the bullet and gave her plasma."

"Will she live?" Laney asked.

"The bullet punctured a lung and came very close to her heart. Only time will tell," he answered, his expression not reassuring Laney at all.

"Can I see her?" Laney asked.

"She's still out."

Jackson placed his arm around Laney's shoulders and murmured close to her ear, "I need to get back to the farm. I have the farrier coming first thing in the morning."

Overhearing, Gray said, "You go on, Jackson. I'll take Laney home. Thank God you got her here so fast. A few minutes more and she would have been gone."

Laney squeezed Jackson's arm and walked him to the clinic door. She couldn't find the words to thank him enough, so she kissed him lightly on the cheek. "I'll talk to you tomorrow," she said, with emotion. Jackson looked down at her, smiled, and was gone. Laney spun away and followed Gray into the surgery.

While Natine adjusted the flow on the IV, Laney sat on a tall stool and stroked Blackberry's head.

"Natine, I can't begin to thank you for coming in."

"It's part of the job," Natine said.

"No it's not. Gray told me that you come every time he calls you when there's an after-hours emergency," Laney said. "Thank you."

Blackberry lay as still as death. Laney's eyes fixed on the shallow rise and fall of her chest. A large dressing covered the surgical wound. Gray lifted Blackberry's upper lip and pressed on her gum. "Color's coming back. Good sign," he said.

As though his words were a prediction, Blackberry suddenly stirred and her eyes opened. Gray restrained her so that she wouldn't pull out the IV.

Jumping to her feet, Laney squealed, "Look at her!" and began to wail all kinds of endearments to her dog.

"Think she'll make it if we keep her quiet for a few days while she builds back her strength."

"Gray . . . Natine," Laney looked at them both with red, grateful eyes. "Thank you, thank you, thank you."

Gray and Laney cuddled in Gray's truck in the circle drive. "Would you come in for a toddy or a cup of coffee?" Laney asked. Puccini purred on the dash.

"Have to get back so that Natine can go home. I'll have Natine help me put Blackberry on a pallet in my bedroom, so I can hear her tonight. How's that for special treatment?"

"Do you do that for all your clients?"

"Just the good-looking ones with freckles and hair like red hot pepper," Gray said facetiously, then suddenly turned serious. "Laney, Blackberry's injury could have been caused by a gun-happy hunter or by a random act of a trespasser. Either way, it was almost deadly. Will you be extra careful?"

"Okay, Doc," Laney quipped, but she secretly agonized over one other possibility that Gray hadn't mentioned–that someone may have shot Blackberry to get even.

14

Monday Morning, May 13

The sky was sable. Hypnotized by rhythmic clicking like dry gear teeth, Laney advanced toward the water. As she stepped into the oozing bog, the metallic clack grew louder and louder. Embracing her ankles, slime clutched at her calves like grasping tentacles. Her eyes riveted on a dim and eerie form hovering on a golden perch across the swamp. As she descended deeper and deeper into the mire, the clacking grew into a whine and the strange form changed into a massive black shape–a surrealistic inkblot of a strange black bird. Its neck twisted and its spear-like serrated beak stabbed at the night sky. At once, the whine became a whimper, then a monstrous moan. Blackberry was impaled upon the pointed shaft. As the wail split the night, the feathered creature spread its ebony wings and took flight.

Bolting upright, Laney's scream gradually brought her out of the horror. But for agonizing moments, she was still in the midst of the swamp, watching the snakebird carry Blackberry away. A heavy weight still pulled at her limbs as the cry died in her throat. Her gown was as wet as though she were yet in the bog. Only when she saw the faint gray of daybreak through the curtains in her room, did the oppressiveness began to lift.

Still shaking from the dream, Laney pushed the damp sheet aside and walked unsteadily to the window. The clouds that had hidden the moon the night before were thinning. She now could see the crescent in the leaden sky but the dawn was chasing the stars.

The dream wouldn't leave her. Even after a quick shower, the image of that giant bird on the golden limb obsessed her thoughts. Again and again, she was drawn to the vision of the bird, his wings spread, ready to take flight.

"My God!" she said as realization struck her.

She threw on her jeans and a clean gray sweatshirt. With sneakers untied, she hit the door running. Stopping only to tie her shoes, she mounted her bike and rode out the entrance. Swinging left, she pedaled down the lane toward the lower crossing. Past the foaling barn and office she raced.

When Laney saw the roof of the Whooptie on the gravel ramp to the riffle where she had abandoned it the night before, she braked sharply and dropped the bike on its side next to the car. Racing toward the water, her eyes searched the debris that had piled up on the opposite bank. The sun, rising behind her, struck the snag just as her flashlight had when she had seen the snakebird observing her.

Only it wasn't a snag. It was a canoe paddle. Just like the golden perch in her night terror, it jutted out from a pile of rubble that had washed downstream by the flood waters. As she stepped out into the crossing, she remembered her dream. But unlike the nightmare, no slime clutched at her ankles. Instead, cold rushing water swirled about her legs, threatening to upset her. She held out her arms for balance.

By mid-crossing, the water was up to her thighs and she almost turned back. Each step took her breath. Her limbs were numb with cold. When she thought she could go no further, she felt the water level drop and then, miraculously, she was across.

She climbed a few feet up the grade to where a mound of limbs and twigs had washed into a protective circle of gnarled sycamore roots overhanging the bank. Reaching upward into the rubble, Laney grasped the handle of the blond paddle and tugged. It held fast. Determined, she climbed upon the pile, braced her feet against the roots and pulled. Inch by inch, the paddle emerged until with one final jolt, it slipped free, almost tumbling Laney into the water below.

Clutching the paddle to her chest, Laney waded back into the crossing. Focusing on the bank ahead, she approached the deepest and swiftest area of the riffle. Unexpectedly, her foot slipped on a rock, and she lost her balance. She was pitched backward into the sweeping stream. In a panic, she fought the current, but the water closed over her head. Trying to swim against the flow was useless and she only managed to surface long enough to gulp air intermittently as she was driven downstream.

Her greatest fear was that she would be struck by flood debris that was taking the trip with her. But miraculously, when she reached a bend in the creek, she abruptly popped free and was propelled toward the bank. At last in calmer water, she thrashed her way to the creek side and climbed up the wet embankment. She still clasped the paddle.

She had been swept several hundred feet downstream and by the time she reached the Whooptie, her teeth were rattling like a loose shutter and she thought her legs had turned to stone.

When she grabbed the keys out of the ignition and opened the trunk, the odor of moldy carpeting filled her sinuses and she recalled bringing the rocker home in the rain on Friday. God, was that just a weekend ago?

Laney dropped the paddle in the trunk and decided to leave the heavy bike for Jackson to pick up. Thinking of Jackson, she promised herself she would ask him to stay on as farm manager. Gray was right. She could do no better.

As she drove by the barn, she recognized the farrier's truck parked by the entrance. Reaching the house, she swung around to the buggy house, driving through the open doors. She sat quaking in her wet clothes, trying to think about what finding the paddle really meant.

The police had said that only one paddle had been found so they had assumed that Cara was canoeing alone the morning she died. And she remembered that Gordon had said that there were three paddles in the springhouse with the other canoe. Could someone else have been with Cara? But then how did the third paddle get in the springhouse? Laney frowned with confusion. She decided not to tell anyone yet about finding the paddle. But what to do with it?

She considered hiding it underneath the tobacco cottons hanging from the rafters but she didn't see a ladder in the building. Then she spotted the trapdoors to the icehouse behind the car. Perfect, she thought, opening the trunk and removing the paddle. She laid it down on the wide plank flooring and struggled with the heavy trapdoors until managing to lift one side. A rush of cold musty air snapped her head back.

"Whew," she said, tossing her wet curls. Holding her breath, she peered into the dank hole but could only see steep, rotting steps disappearing into blackness. The sound of dripping water pinged off some surface deep inside. Laney's imagination went into instant overtime—visions of snakes and rats, her worst terrors. She dropped the paddle into the inkiness beside the steps and she heard its clattering echo as it hit the bottom. She couldn't drop the trap door fast enough.

When she got back into the house, she showered, letting the hot steamy water warm her bones. She changed into a pair of beige cotton chinos. A denim vest covered her blue and white plaid shirt. Coaxing her damp, wavy hair into a ponytail, she pulled it through the back opening of a Kentucky Wildcat baseball cap that she had found on a hook behind the bathroom door.

She dashed into the library and faxed her article on Pittsburgh pubs to John Bernard at *Three Rivers Magazine*. There, she thought. I'll give it a day and then call him to let him know I'm quitting. She pictured the little man's chubby face turning puce. He would slam around the office and make life generally miserable for Judy and Shar, her closest friends and fellow editors. I'll miss them, Laney thought, sadly, as she shut her computer down. Maybe I can get them to visit me some time. A fleeting thought of opening the bed and breakfast flitted through her mind.

15

Late Monday Morning, May 13

"Could I see your criss-cross reference directory, please," Laney said, handing the graying reference clerk her new Lexington Public Library card. He took her card and pulled a large volume from the bookshelf behind him. Finding an unoccupied table near a window, she extracted Tony's letter from her purse, and spread it open next to the directory. It took only a moment to match the phone number that was on the letter to the one in the directory. Adjacent to the number was the name, *Richards, Tony and Randi.*

"Shazam!" Laney exclaimed, then covered her mouth with her hand. A lady at the next table frowned at her. "Sorry," Laney mouthed, and looked back at the book. Married, she thought. Figures. But the last name confirms this Tony was the same Tony Richards that was murdered.

She then looked up the name, *Richards, Tony.* Next to his name, she read: *part owner Owens–Richards RV h 426 Chapel Court.* So, he has a business partner.

Laney copied all the information into a notebook, returned the directory and retrieved her library card. As she climbed into the Whooptie, Laney felt the dampness seeping through the terry cloth towel she had placed on her seat to absorb the creek water from her dunking that morning.

Her gut flipped when she recalled her close call that morning. Gray had called her just as she was leaving, but she hadn't had a chance to tell him about her adventure. She smiled. Probably just as well, she thought. *He would have just lambasted me for being so foolhardy.*

Gray had told her that Blackberry spent a pretty good night–considering. He was giving her something for pain, so he expected her to sleep a lot. Then Natine had buzzed him from down in the clinic.

Laney found a Lexington street map in the glove compartment and located Chapel Court near the Lexington Cemetery. The subdivision was a new development and several houses were still under construction. Laney turned right onto Chapel Court and found number 426 written on the sloping curb in white letters. A blue Dodge was parked in the drive in front of a double-car garage.

Laney slithered by the house and when she got to the end of the cul-de-sac she circled around. Up ahead, the yellow door of the two-story brick colonial house opened and a woman in black jeans and a tight fitting short-sleeved red sweater emerged. Her long black hair was brushed into a ponytail and tied with a long white scarf. Laney coasted to the curb and stopped–engine idling. She wondered if that was Randi. The woman got into the Dodge and backed out of the driveway.

When the Dodge turned left at the end of Chapel Court, Laney pulled away from the curb. *What am I doing,* Laney asked herself, but kept on her tail, almost a block behind the car. Laney followed it through a maze of streets until it turned into a trailer park named Pillar Estates. She had no idea where she was, only that at one point, she had passed a green sign marked New Circle Road, a bypass around Lexington.

Laney stopped at the office and watched the Dodge brake in front of the fourth trailer, parked perpendicular to the road. The woman jumped out of the car and ran to the trailer door. When the door opened, a hand grabbed the woman's arm and pulled her inside.

Laney sat in the Whooptie, wondering if she were out of her mind while her eyes scanned the names on the mailboxes in front of the office. One read N. Owens # 4.

Maybe he's Tony's RV partner, she thought. Laney scribbled the name and number on a post-it and stuck it on the dash. A new navy Mercedes was parked in the short car port next to the front door of the trailer. *Wow, the RV business must really be hot.* Her thoughts were interrupted by the appearance of the woman again–this time, in a very agitated state. Tearfully, the woman rubbed her forearm as the door slammed behind her.

She climbed into the car and as she passed Laney sitting in the Whooptie, her tragic eyes were fixed straight ahead. Her shoulders were hunched. The woman's miserable expression tugged at Laney.

Laney contemplated her next move. "Nothing ventured, nothing gained," she said shakily, stepping out of her car. As she approached the trailer she thought she saw mini-blinds move at a window, but when she did a double take, the slats were still.

Just as Laney raised her hand to knock, the door jerked open. A man in an expensive looking dark silk suit, silk shirt, and flashy silk tie leered at her. Hmm. Owns silkworm farm? Mercedes? Trailer? Definitely nouveau riche. she reasoned. No accounting for taste.

"Whatta you want," he said gruffly.

"I . . . I'm looking for Randi," Laney lied.

"No, you ain't. You followed her here. If you wanted to talk to her, why didn't you?" His gray-brown eyes narrowed to slashes and his full, red-lipped mouth curled. He was vintage movie star, Edward G. Robinson, minus the sweetness.

"Okay. I saw your name on the mailbox. Are you Tony Richard's partner?"

"Not anymore, I ain't. He checked out a couple weeks ago."

"Excuse me . . . checked out?" Laney asked.

"Checked out. Got wasted. Murdered." He looked by her to the trailer next door. "Get in here, will you? The neighbors have enough to talk about." He opened the door wide and stood aside.

Laney hesitated, remembering Randi rubbing her arm, then stepped inside, anyway. Her eyes took a moment to adjust to the gloom. Every mini-blind that she could see was shut tight.

"I'm inquiring about Tony's death," Laney ventured.

"You some kind of dick or something?" He placed his hand on the wall behind Laney's head and leaned toward her.

Laney's back hugged the flimsy trailer wall like a strip of wallpaper. "No, but I need to find out how Tony died."

"What was Tony to you?" His breath smelled rotten.

Laney scooted under his arm and took a step toward the door. "He was a friend of my sister's, Mr. Owens." Treat him with respect, he'll respect you back, her father had taught her.

"Name's Nick."

"Nick, my sister asked me to find out what happened to Tony. She really cared for him." Laney was surprised at how easily the lies came after she got started.

"What's wrong with your sister? She break a leg?"

"She's away on a business trip." Laney felt her nose grow by the minute.

"If you want to find out who killed him, ask that wife of his."

"Wife? Tony was married? I thought Randi was his sister."

"Sister? That's a good one." He laughed loudly, throwing his head back so that Laney could see a flash of gold fillings, even in the gloom. "Their divorce would have been final in a few weeks if Tony hadn't been snuffed."

"You think Randi killed him?" Laney could see Nick's eyes going over her body like a metal detector. So much for respect. I've got to get out of here, she thought frantically.

"Randi's a boozer and every time he'd even look at a broad, she would go into one of her pub-crawls. He kicked her out the house at least a dozen times, but he always let her come back. I don't know why I'm telling you this." He took his forefinger and stroked the back of her hand that was grasping the doorknob like she was hanging from a cliff.

Laney's stomach was in a wad. "Do the police think she did it?"

"Who the hell knows? I told them what I thought. They questioned Randi again at the club Saturday night."

"Club? What club is that?" Laney opened the door a crack. Daylight skittered over Nick's pricey snakeskin boots.

"What's the hurry, baby? Maybe we both can go to the A Club tonight to see her." Nick kicked the door shut.

In your dreams, buster, she thought. "I'm busy tonight, Nick. Maybe another night. I've really got to go." This time when she opened the door, she shoved it against Nick with all her might. It slammed him backwards and surprised him long enough for Laney to slip out.

"Hey, you little bitch . . . ," he snarled, recovering. Laney ran from his grasping hand into the street, fully expecting him to be breathing down her neck. But as she scrambled into the front seat, she heard the bang of the trailer door.

Laney ran through McDonald's before leaving Lexington. It was three o'clock and she hadn't eaten since dinner the night before. She was shaky and hungry, at least part of her shaking could be attributed to hunger. *Sure glad I didn't cross my heart when I promised Gray I'd be careful,* she reflected. As penance, Laney crammed some French fries into her mouth, washing them down with a gulp of pop. By the time she reached Hickory, the hamburger, fries, and a chocolate chip cookie were history.

Laney's lunch crunched when she drove through the rock entrance to the circle drive. The sheriff's car was parked in front of the house, and Gordon and Freddie were on the front porch taking turns punching the door bell. They both looked grim. Flashes of the day that Cara's body was found streaked through Laney's mind.

"Gordon, what is it?" Laney said, climbing the steps to the porch. Freddie grinned and tipped his cap.

"Don't be alarmed, Laney. This is just police business," Gordon reassured her. He hooked his fingers around his belt and holster and hiked his khaki pants. She heard the creaking of leather.

"My guess is that Gray told you about Blackberry being shot," Laney said, clearly relieved.

"To be honest, I haven't talked with Gray," Gordon said. "When did this happen? Is she all right?"

"Last night. It was touch and go for a few hours but Gray thinks she'll be okay," Laney said.

"Who shot her?" Freddie asked, plopping down on the wicker stool. His soft belly ate his belt and it was uncomfortable to watch.

"Gray thinks it may have been a trespasser or a hunter," Laney said.

"Nothing's in season in May," Gordon replied. A long silence ensued.

Laney broke it. "What can I help you with?"

"We had a call from the Lexington Police Department this morning. A man named Tony Richards was murdered in Lexington about two weeks ago. The police found a personal ad at Mr. Richards's house that Cara had placed in the *Lexington Post* on February seventh."

Laney's stomach took an elevator plunge.

"Here's a copy of the ad they faxed to the Hickory Police Department." Gordon showed her the fax. Laney saw that her sister's ad had been circled. The fax was of the same clipping that she had in her purse. "The Lexington police have reason to believe that Tony

Richards was seeing Cara at the time of his death."

"Laney, I have to ask you if you know whether or not Cara owned a gun." Gordon looked down at his shoes as though embarrassed to be asking the question.

Laney drew in a deep breath. "Actually, Gordon, Joe Collins owned a thirty-eight Smith and Wesson. He showed it to me about a year before he died. He kept it in the library desk."

"Laney, Tony Richards was shot two times with a thirty-eight caliber revolver."

Laney saw Gordon's face begin to fade and a tiny hammer pounded her brain. She reached out for the railing and Freddie took her arm and led her gently to a chair. It was a moment before Laney could speak. "You don't think—"

"Laney, I have a search warrant. I need to search the house. Does the house have a safe?"

"Not that I know of." Laney handed Gordon her key and he unlocked the door. He and Freddie disappeared into the hall.

It was some time before the two men emerged. They were empty handed. Laney hadn't moved from the chair.

"We didn't find the gun," Gordon said.

"Did you check the desk?" Laney asked.

"I took everything out of the desk. Checked the file cabinet. We did a search of the whole house. I hope we didn't make too much of a mess," Gordon said apologetically.

Laney didn't speak. For some reason, she was glad she had all the letters and photos inside her purse in the car. She wondered if that was obstructing justice or withholding evidence or some other naughty thing that she always read about in the suspense novels she loved.

"The police have to follow all leads in a murder case, Laney. Don't let this gun business get to you," Gordon said soothingly. "We'll be on our way."

Laney watched them drive out the gate and still she couldn't move from the chair. Her familiar paralyzing fear of dealing with problems crept over her. Her whole being cried out to shut down, to wipe out all the pain, to be in peace. She dragged herself into the house, curled up on the library sofa and instantly fell to sleep.

When Laney woke up, it was after five and she still felt a bit slug-gish and weary from the day's happenings. She had a list of things to do but didn't feel like doing one. Piles of files were on the floor from the house search and Laney resentfully gathered up the first pile and placed them back in the drawer. When she got to the last pile, she saw one titled LAST WILL AND TESTAMENT OF CARA COLLINS. After she slipped the files into the cabinet, she extracted the file and opened it. It was empty. Curious, she found Marshall's business card in the top drawer of the desk and dialed his phone number. Marshall himself answered the phone.

"Marshall, this is Laney McVey. Sorry for calling so late but I have a couple of questions."

"It's perfectly all right, Laney. I often work over. What can I do for you?"

Laney heard his deep exhalation of cigarette smoke over the phone. "Did Cara have a copy of her will? I can't seem to find it in her files."

"Yes she did. I sent her a copy as soon as it was typed up by Mrs. Stillwater."

"Strange," Laney said. "One other thing. Please don't be offended by this, but did you tell anyone about my mother's inheritance?"

"Certainly not! Nothing leaves this office! Mrs. Stillwater is com-pletely trustworthy!"

"Please, Marshall, I was only asking because my stepfather Karl made an offer on the farm and I can't imagine where he would get the money, if not from Mother's inheritance."

"You're selling to Karl?" She could hear disapproval in Marshall's voice.

"When Hell freezes over. In fact I think you'll be happy to hear that I have decided to keep the farm."

Marshall went into a coughing fit. "I certainly am," he choked. "That's wonderful news."

"I think it is, too."

"Call on me if you need any legal help, will you?" Marshall asked, clearing his throat one last time.

Laney next dialed the number for USAir. A sense of finality struck her as she canceled her Wednesday flight to Pittsburgh. She knew it would be a while before she could return to Pittsburgh to pack up her things and have them shipped to Hickory. But at least her rent was paid through May.

Laney heard the cardinal as she walked by the parlor. When she approached the window, she looked at his ragged crest and bloody beak. Surely there was something she could do to stop his senseless brain bashing. "I'll fix you up tomorrow," she said to the bird as he swooped down one more time.

16

Monday Evening, May 13

Laney finally got the second wind from her little nap and she bounced down the path to the springhouse. She had one more task before her long day was over. Damn, she missed Blackberry. She kept expecting to see her bounding ahead, then retracting to make sure she was keeping up. At least she knew her newly acquired pet was in Gray's good hands.

When she reached the springhouse, she found the door ajar. She descended the two steps to the rock floor. The beautiful gray stone walls were coated with a delicate green moss. Inside, the unusually large springhouse was cool and damp, and the pungent smell of mold and decay worked over her sense of smell. Because of its size and proximity to the creek, it was ideal for storing the aluminum canoes, although Laney thought the building a bit too damp for the wooden paddles.

The remaining canoe lay against the far wall, and three paddles leaned against the far right corner. Laney wondered what the police had done with the destroyed canoe and other paddle.

Laney examined the paddles carefully. All three were made of a highly polished blond wood about four feet long. The manufacturer's logo was stamped in green ink on each broad flattened blade. All had been made by the River Craft Manufacturing Company in Mississippi, just as the one she found at the crossing that morning. Inside a red oval, a small wave of blue ink underscored the name.

Laney noted one difference. One of the paddles was more worn than the other two. Perhaps Cara randomly grabbed it more often for her daily ride. Then she remembered that during the year, unless a prolonged rain was forecast, Cara left the canoe and paddle on the small dock so that she didn't have to haul the boat from the spring-house every day. When Laney canoed with her, she always had to retrieve another paddle and a life jacket from the building.

Remembering the life jackets, Laney turned to her left where the orange jackets hung from a nylon line strung from corner to corner on two rusty hooks. She counted four adult and three children's jackets. All were in almost new condition Laney noted ironically. "If only Cara—"

A small sound made Laney spin around. Jackson stood in the doorway. He smiled and his toothpick shifted to the corner of his mouth. "I was on the way to your house when I saw you cut out the back door and swing down toward the creek. Are you going to take the canoe out?"

"No, I was just taking a walk," Laney said, admiring his felt outback hat that was pulled jauntily down over one eye. "The door was open when I came by. Shouldn't there be a padlock on it? With trespassers shooting anything that moves, I think we should keep it locked."

"I'll pick one up and give you a key. How is Blackberry?" Jackson's eyes showed deep concern.

"When I spoke to Gray this morning, he said she had a good night."

"I stopped by after the farrier left and you weren't home." Jackson stood aside as Laney stepped out of the springhouse.

"I cycled down to get the Whooptie this morning. After that, I went to Lexington. Jackson, would you mind picking up my bike at the crossing when you get a chance?"

Jackson nodded. "I saw the police car at the house this afternoon. Is something wrong?" Jackson pulled the springhouse door closed.

"No, just some routine police business." Laney decided to keep the gun search to herself.

"Jackson, I've changed my mind about selling the farm. I'm going to move here and run it myself. Would you stay on and manage it for me?"

Laney watched Jackson's face for some sign that he was surprised or pleased, but his expression didn't change.

"I'll stay as long as you want me," he said with just a hint of a smile. "It's getting late, Laney. May I walk you back to the house. On second thought, why don't you come to my house and I'll fix dinner."

"I really appreciate the invite but I've had a long day."

"I promise I won't keep you up past your bedtime. Come." Jackson took her hand and she allowed him to guide her up the hill to the Rover parked in the drive.

Jackson's house was in a secluded area of the farm but was still quite accessible to the horse operation. From her house, they drove the lane toward the office and turned left between the horse barn and foaling barn, continuing along a straight drive that led into the grove of pines.

When they reached the little frame house, Jackson parked the Rover in a small port at the right side of the house. Behind her, a paintbrush was slathering the sky with a breathtaking sunset but as Jackson guided her toward the back of the cottage, evening shadows followed them.

Laney stopped short at steep wooden stairs that led to a small enclosed porch, her eyes instantly drawn to the creek. In a twilight grayness, as though the scene were being filmed in black and white, she watched the water flow over the dam. She had known the house overlooked it, but the power of the water still unnerved her. She shivered and Jackson's arm darted to her waist, maneuvering her to the stairs.

They climbed to the porch. He lit two citronella candles and went into the house, emerging in a couple of minutes with one of his pullover sweaters flung over his arm, an opened bottle of red wine and two glasses. Sensing Laney's uneasiness, he put the bottle and glasses on a large square table made of redwood and patted her hand. "Don't worry," he smiled, "I learned my lesson."

Laney couldn't tear her eyes away from the dam. Even after she pulled the beige sweater over her head, her eyes darted back to it. "I've never seen the dam from this vantage point," she said, "When Blackberry and I took a walk that day, she led me down the steep path to below the dam where I could see the water crash at the bottom.

From up here, you're almost level with the top of the structure . . . but I can still hear it.

"You can see the millstone from the gristmill that used to be over there." Jackson leaned against her and pointed toward the bank. She felt the heat of his hand on her shoulder.

"I'll start dinner," he murmured into her ear. "Help yourself to the wine."

Laney relaxed when she saw that he hadn't poured a glass for himself. She filled her goblet and sat in a canvas chair. While she sampled her wine, she noted the spareness of the porch. It was rustic–almost primitive. Another canvas chair faced the railing, with only enough room for a pair of legs, as though Jackson sat staring directly at the creek for long periods of time. Oddly, in front of the chair, small holes had been jabbed in the screening enclosing the porch. A plate of chewed toothpicks sat on a small twig table beside the chair. About a third of the porch was covered with a frayed, mildewed sisal rug.

Laney stood and drifted into what appeared to be a small sitting room. She could hear Jackson puttering around in a room to her left. Making out a small lamp on a nearby table, Laney turned the switch. The room, like the porch, was austere and unadorned. The lamp cast harsh shadows against the bare walls. Even the end tables were devoid of a single photo or knickknack. She assumed the small wood stove in the corner provided extra heat in the winter.

Jackson entered the room with a tray and handed it to Laney. "Why don't you take it out to the porch and I'll bring the rest."

Laney set the table with two straw place mats, paper napkins and flatware. She smiled while placing the dusty white silk rose in a small vase on the table. She wondered why Jackson was trying so hard to please her.

Jackson carried out two plates and set them on the table, retrieved her chair and grabbed the other for himself. With a grand flourish, Jackson invited her to sit down and as an afterthought, transferred one of the citronellas to their table.

"Look at this salad. It's beautiful, Jackson." She was truly astounded by its almost perfect symmetry. A delicate herb dressing had been drizzled over the sliced citrus and avocado resting on a beautiful lettuce leaf. A sprig of cilantro garnished the salad. "This is wonderful."

"I hope you like the rest of the meal," Jackson said, as he refreshed her drink and poured a small glass of wine for himself.

Noticing the chipped and peeling paint on the porch rails she said, "Jackson, if you wouldn't mind, I'd like to do some remodeling of the cottage. I remember Cara telling me that she planned to redecorate. I don't think anything has been done to it since before your father died. That was about seven years ago, wasn't it?"

Jackson's face darkened like an eclipse. "Laney, I don't want to talk about him . . . if you don't mind." His voice was without warmth and his dimple moved in his cheek.

"I'm sorry–"

"I'll get our dinner." Jackson rose abruptly and left the porch.

"Shazam! Seems a bit touchy about dear old dad." I wonder what that's all about, she mulled while she worked on her salad. But all was forgotten when Jackson returned. The tray held two steaming bowls of corn chowder, a basket of hot hard rolls, and a tub of real butter.

Laney's mouth watered from the aroma. "You couldn't have possibly made this chowder in such a short time."

"No, I made it earlier."

"Mmm . . . did your mother teach you to cook like this?" Laney asked after her first spoonful of the thick soup.

"My mother's a slut," Jackson said, with no emotion. He dipped into his bowl with his spoon.

Laney almost choked on the soup. Suddenly, the croaking frogs in the creek below turned up the volume and her heart did a drum roll. She wondered what in the world could have precipitated Jackson to offer such an offensive description of his mother.

A long silence followed.

"Your not eating, Laney. Don't you like the chowder?"

"Laney coughed, "It's the best I've ever eaten." But in a moment, she had lost her appetite. She forced a mouthful.

"You are very beautiful, Laney."

Startled, Laney looked over at Jackson, but he was intent on eating his dinner. "Thank you," she said.

Jackson quickly placed his hand over hers as though he might lose his nerve if he waited a moment longer. "I really care for you, Laney."

"I care about you too, Jackson," she said, almost afraid not to concur. She squirmed in her seat. She slipped her hand away, pretending to reach for a roll.

"I do a lot for you, don't I?" Jackson said without looking at her.

Laney thought it was a strange thing to say and wondered what he was getting at. "Yes you do, Jackson. You're the best horse farm manager in the county."

"I didn't quite mean that," Jackson said, taking her hand again.

I was afraid you didn't, Laney thought. Damn, why did I come here? "Jackson, dinner was great. I really need to go." Laney snatched her hand away and rose.

"Please sit down, Laney. I'm not finished."

She was completely wrung out over the whole evening. She had developed an instant mouth twitch and her gurgling insides were fast turning her dinner to liquid. Suddenly, it crossed her mind that perhaps Jackson wanted to borrow some money. It always amazed her how accommodating someone could be when they wanted something.

She was just angry enough to let it rip. "How much?" she blurted, sitting back down.

"What?" He raised an eyebrow. "You think I want money?" He looked hurt.

"All right, Jackson, maybe I don't know what you want. Tell me." Laney deferred against her better judgment. She knew she was allowing Jackson to yank her around.

"I want to marry you."

Her eyes blinked and her mouth gaped in amazement. Oh my God, she thought. Press the panic button. What do I do?

"Uh . . . Jackson, that's awfully sweet but we don't know each other that well," Laney managed to say.

"I know all I need to know about you."

She couldn't think. The proposal seemed to have come out of nowhere. She was completely caught off guard. She gulped air, praying something would come to her. Then in a flash she knew what she had to do. Simple. She just had to stop this right now.

"Jackson! . . . enough!" Her voice was harsh. "You are a kind man who will make some woman a fine husband . . . but it won't be me. I just don't feel that way about you." She jumped to her feet, pulled his sweater over her head and tossed it into the seat of her chair. "I'd like to go home please."

"So, it's Prescott," Jackson said, reaching across the table to the candle. He snuffed out the flame with his thumb and forefinger. Staring at Laney with uninhabited eyes, he stood. "I'll take you home."

17

Tuesday, May 14

After the bizarre evening with Jackson, Laney didn't know what to think. The man was an enigma. There wasn't any doubt he was a first-rate manager and everyone seemed to have the greatest respect for him. He was a deacon in the church, and according to what her mother had told her, he was the first to offer to help out in local charity drives. He seemed very giving. God knows, he had been there for her since she had arrived in Hickory. That he wasn't socially disposed or that he didn't follow the courting rules of behavior, shouldn't be held against him, she decided. She only hoped her bluntness hadn't hurt him too deeply.

Earlier, Laney had called her mother to ask her to go to lunch. Upon arriving at the dock, she couldn't help scanning the lot for Karl. He was nowhere in sight.

She parked beside the deck to the house and as she hopped out of the Whooptie, she noticed that because of the recent high water, the rack of canoes had been moved back from the boat ramp and the paddles were under the office supports. Looking timorously around for Karl one more time, she walked quickly over to the rack of canoes. She counted only seven. Three must be out on the creek, Laney figured.

When she counted the paddles in the barrel, there were thirteen. If there were two boaters in each canoe, there should have been fourteen paddles left in the barrel–if there were twenty to begin with, she thought. Lifting each paddle, she studied them individually and checked the logo on the blade. All matched the logo of the three paddles in the springhouse. Could someone have replaced the missing paddle with one from this barrel? She noted that all the paddles seemed equally worn like the third paddle in the springhouse.

Laney strode to the house. When she knocked, she didn't get an answer. Looking out over the parking lot, she saw Maddy's Cavalier, but Karl's green pickup was gone. When she got no response after knocking a second time, Laney assumed Karl and Maddy had gone somewhere together. She sat on the top step to wait for her mother, her anxiety beginning to rise over the possibility of seeing Karl again.

She thought she heard a muffled sound coming from inside the house–like a mewing kitten. She scrambled to her feet, turned the doorknob, and pushed the door open a crack.

"Mother?" she called. The cry intensified as she entered the kitchen. When Laney passed through the kitchen, she saw that two places were set at the table and two slices of cold toast were in the toaster. Starchy oatmeal coagulated in a pot on the unlit burner of the stove.

The sound again.

Alarmed, she ran down the hall, stopping at her mother's bedroom door. Not stopping to knock, Laney shoved the door open.

Maddy lay curled on her side on the quilt-covered four poster. Laney stood next to the shaking form of her mother and whispered, "Mother, what is it?"

When Laney touched her arm, Maddy groaned and drew away. "Mother, you're hurt." She took her mother's hand and pulled her to a sitting position on the side of the bed. Maddy was still in her worn gray velour robe and her thin bare feet dangled over the edge of the bed. She covered her face with her hands and continued to cry deep heaving sobs.

Laney crossed to the window and opened the shade. The sunlight poured through the crisp white Priscilla curtains onto Maddy's tangled, lusterless hair. Laney knelt in front of her mother and pried her fingers away from her face. "Mother, tell me what happened."

Slowly, Maddy opened her swollen eyes as though leaden weights were attached to the upper lids. Her umber eyes were glassy with tears and her pupils instantly shrank into black pinheads in the bright light.

Red blotches mingled with the freckles on her cheeks. Maddy hiccuped a gulp but couldn't speak. She shook her head in frustration.

But Laney knew. She reached over and lifted the loose sleeve on her robe and gasped at the blue and red fingerprint bruises forming on her upper arm. Laney slid the other sleeve up and saw the matching discoloration on her right arm. "Mother, Karl did this to you, didn't he?" Laney thought she was going to burst into tears herself.

"I provoked him," Maddy blubbered.

"There's nothing in the world that you could do to deserve this," Laney said through clinched teeth. "Did he injure you anywhere else?"

Maddy shook her head.

"The stinking coward. He made damn sure the bruises were in a place that you could cover with clothing. Has he ever hurt you before?"

Maddy looked away, her silence the answer.

Maddy blew into the tissue that Laney retrieved from the bedside table. Laney waited until Maddy was down to shaky breaths before she asked, "What happened?"

"Marshall called this mornin to say that you had called him about Karl knowin about the inheritance. He wanted to assure me that he hadn't been the one to tell Karl. While I was talkin with Marshall, Karl must have picked up the extension here in the bedroom and overheard the call. When Marshall hung up, Karl went crazy . . . said I had kept it from him. He shook me 'til I thought my head would snap off. I've never seen him so mad."

"Mother, Karl came to me on Friday and made an offer on the farm so he must have already known about the money," Laney said.

Maddy's eyes grew large. "He did what?"

"He offered a fair amount for the farm. I turned him down."

"So when you were here on Sunday and I told Karl you were movin here, he already knew?" Maddy said, her eyes blinking in surprise.

"Actually, I didn't tell Karl that I was moving here, but he definitely understood I wasn't going to sell to him." Laney remembered how angry Karl was when she had torn up the contract.

"How did he find out about the money?" Maddy asked.

"There's one possibility. Cara's copy of the will is missing."

"Missin?" Her mouth opened to protest, then closed. A moment later she said softly, "You think Karl took it, don't you?"

"Mother, I wouldn't put anything past that son of–"

"Laney!" Maddy jumped up from the bed. "Please, don't . . . ."

"He must have known about the will," Laney said, her anger igniting. "How else could he come up with that kind of money?"

"He really seemed surprised about hearin about the inheritance this morning."

Laney couldn't believe her mother's gullibility. "He ought to get an Oscar. He's a good enough actor . . . no, liar is a better word for him. Overhearing your call just gave him a good excuse to knock you around again." Laney's crossness dissolved into concern. "Mother, I'm afraid for you. I want you to leave him. Next time he . . . he may kill you. Come stay with me."

"I won't leave the dock, Laney. This is my home." Maddy stood in front of the window and looked out on the creek. She began to cry again. "I have to get dressed. The boats are back and Karl isn't here," she sobbed.

Laney watched as three canoes pulled up to the ramp. "I'll take care of them. You get some rest." She embraced her mother and felt her thin shoulders tremble in her arms. "Mother, how many paddles are there?"

Her mother sank onto the bed and mumbled, "Twenty."

Laney covered her mother with a blanket, stooped and kissed her. "Please think about what I said. And for God's sake, call me if you need me."

Laney helped the six canoeists drag in the canoes and place them on the rack. As they drove away in a small van, Laney dropped the paddles into the barrel. She counted them again.

Nineteen.

18

Late Tuesday Morning, May 14

Natine and Gray were in his office going over the morning calls.

"What is this?" Natine pointed to chicken scratches on the bottom of a client appointment sheet.

Gray grinned, knowing how tough he made it for her. "Anyone can tell that's 'calfhood vac.'"

"And the moon is made of green cheese," she said scanning the sheet again. "Do all docs take "Scrawl 101" before receiving their licenses?" She stretched and rolled her shoulders. A wide yawn followed.

"Wish you'd quit that," Gray said, as he followed suit with a yawn of his own. "It's contagious." But when he noticed his secretary's droopy brown eyes, he said, "Why don't you knock it off after lunch. I don't think you've caught up from Sunday night's surgery on Blackberry."

"I've half a mind to. Warren is off today and tomorrow. It would be nice to have a little time with him." Natine's husband was a member of the St. Clair County Fire Department and worked twenty-four hours on and forty-eight off.

"What's the schedule for the rest of the day?" Gray asked.

Natine reached for the appointment book. "You only have one call at three, but it's a doozy–working a hundred head at Deaver's Angus."

"Blast, forgot about that."

The bell in the clinic waiting room rang and Natine peeked around the door.

"Laney, we're in here," Natine called.

"I came to see Blackberry," Laney said, as she entered Gray's office.

Gray stood and shooed Puccini off the remaining chair. Suddenly he felt fuzzy inside.

"How is she?" Laney asked, sitting down. Standing behind her, Gray's eyes focused on her brilliant hair. The sunlight from the window behind his desk frolicked with the color, turning her curls from cinnamon to burnished copper. The light seemed to caper through it with a vitality all its own. How he wanted to feel its energy in his fingers! He cleared his throat and moved back to his chair.

Never taking his eyes from her, he sighed. Damn striking woman, he thought. Her jeans pressed her thighs just enough to tantalize. A snow-white blouse peeked from a lightweight fitted jacket in a golden beige that matched the freckles peppered across her nose and the flecks in her brown eyes.

"Gray," Laney repeated, "how's Blackberry?"

"Sorry," Gray said, glancing over at Natine and catching her tongue-in-cheek smirk. "She's coming along . . . slowly."

Natine stood, collected her appointment book, client sheets, and waved. "See you tomorrow, Gray. Don't forget that three o'clock." She winked and hurried out the door.

"How about some lunch? Have some tuna upstairs." Gray really wasn't hungry. He just wanted to keep Laney around as long as possible.

"Sure, if I can see Blackberry first."

Gray pulled Laney to her feet and led her down a long hall past a closed door with a sign that read "Pharmacy & Supply," a couple of examining rooms, and the surgery. Laney heard a dog yipping through a metal door at the end of the hall. Gray opened the door next to the surgery and with his foot, held Puccini back until he could shut the door. They were inside a small room with a short wall lined with cages stacked three high. A stainless steel table anchored the center of the room.

"This is the post-op," he said.

He strode over to a large unit in the middle tier of cages and unlatched the door. Laney swooped past him and practically climbed into the cage with Blackberry.

"You poor baby," she crooned, while smothering her forehead with kisses.

Blackberry managed to thump her tail weakly and lick Laney's hand. An IV was hooked up to her front leg and a drain tube was protruding from the wound.

"Gray, when will she be able to come home?"

"Not for several days. She still isn't eating well. Gave her electrolytes in her fluids this morning. But think seeing you was her best medicine." Mine too, Gray mused.

After a series of kisses and pets, Gray closed up the cage and they left the room and retraced their steps to the waiting room. Gray locked the clinic door, and he and Laney, along with the tabby, climbed the inside stairs off the waiting room to his apartment over the clinic.

Not expecting company, Gray was embarrassed by the apartment's untidiness. He managed to kick a sock under a chair as they entered the living room, and he snatched a dirty glass and dinner plate from the coffee table on the way to the kitchen. Gray recalled that Laney had been in his apartment only one other time. The occasion had been his derby party the previous spring. Though both Laney and he had gone through school together, they'd never dated, and after graduation, Laney had moved to Pittsburgh. But last May, while Laney was visiting her sister, they'd been reacquainted. For almost a week, the two of them had been inseparable and when Laney appeared at the door for his party, he realized for the first time that he was falling in love with her. Later that night, Cara told Laney about her abortion years before and that the child had been his. The following morning, Laney was gone. Cara's lie had driven her back to Pittsburgh.

Laney helped him prepare lunch. While he mixed the tuna with the mayonnaise, Laney chopped a limp stock of celery and half an onion she had found in the crisper. She minced a sweet gherkin and dumped it all into the tuna mixture. After toasting a couple of frozen hamburger buns, he spread the tuna salad while Laney plopped a slice of cheddar onto each half. The tuna melts went back into the oven until they were hot and bubbly. Bottom-of-the-bag potato chips had to do for something crunchy.

While they ate, Laney's scintillating eyes darted about his face and she squirmed in her seat.

"Out with it, Laney. You're about to bust a gut."

"Cara's will is missing . . . and I know who stole it."

He sighed. "Let me guess. Poor, dead Tony."

"Wrong. It was Karl. That would explain how Karl thought he could make an offer on the farm; he already knew Maddy was getting the inheritance because he read it in the will."

"How would he get a copy of the will?"

"Marshall told me Cara had a copy, but the file was empty. Karl and Mother are at the house a lot. He could have lifted it any time." Laney went on to tell Gray about Karl injuring her mother this morning.

"Damn him!" Gray slammed his fist on the table. He took a calming breath and continued, "But it's still pure speculation about Karl stealing the will," he said, but he couldn't help thinking that if Karl could abuse Maddy, he could do just about anything.

Laney wasn't finished. With trepidation, she told him about her visit to Nick Owens's trailer.

"My God Laney, are you away with the fairies? This is dangerous stuff! And though you may find it hard to believe, you're not a cop." His insides twisted into kinks.

"Come on, Gray. I won't tell you anything if all you're going to do is yell at me," Laney said, her eyes firing sparks.

"You said you won't do anything crazy. What's nuttier than going onto some hood's turf."

"If you go with me next time, it won't be crazy, will it?" Laney asked timidly. She caressed his hand coyly.

"Oh no you don't. I'm not–go with you? Where?"

"To the A Club. Randi sings there. I want to talk to her."

"What the hell for? She may be the one that killed Tony, for God's sake. That Nick creep thought she did it." Gray tipped his chair back onto its rear legs and rested his left ankle on his right thigh.

"That sweet thing couldn't have done it."

"Spoken by a true believer of scientific reasoning."

"Oh Gray," she giggled. "That partner of Tony's is more the killer type. Anyway, I want to find out more about this Nick Owens. I bet Randi could tell me plenty."

"Why are you so interested in who killed Tony anyway?"

"Okay . . . there's something I didn't tell you."

Gray lunged forward and the front chair legs banged against the tile floor. "Uh–oh . . . don't think I'm going to like this something."

"Gordon and Freddie were out at the farm yesterday." Laney wriggled in her chair, folding and unfolding a paper napkin several times.

He saw that Laney was struggling to get it out. "What did they want?" Gray asked quietly.

"They searched the house."

"What the hell for?" Gray's stomach knotted another kink.

"They were searching for Cara's gun."

"Gun? Cara had a gun?"

"Well . . . it was Joe's. He said he kept it for protection because they were so isolated in the country. He showed it to me once."

"Why in the world did Gordon want to know if Cara owned a gun?" But Gray thought he knew what was coming.

"The Lexington police found the ad that Cara placed in the *Lexington Post* at Tony's house. The post office number she was assigned at the newspaper was circled on the ad page. The police faxed a copy of the ad to Gordon." Laney started tearing the napkin into little strips. "Since Tony was shot, they naturally wanted to know if Cara owned a gun."

Gray reached over and took Laney's hands. "Did they find it?"

"No, and they searched the house thoroughly."

"Do you know what kind of gun she had?"

"A thirty-eight Smith and Wesson."

"What kind of gun was Tony shot with?"

"A thirty-eight."

Gray began to clear the table. This raised all kinds of possibilities. The obvious struck him first. Could Cara have murdered Tony? Cara and Tony's deaths were so close together that it was possible that Tony had been killed first. But what motive would she have had?

As though Laney had read his thoughts, she said, "Don't even think it, Gray. My sister did not kill Tony . . . but I'm going to find out who did."

Gray dropped the dishes into the sink, squirted liquid detergent, and turned on the hot water. He watched the level of the water creep up over the plates until, with a last bubbly bobble, they sank beneath the surface.

"I worry about you doing this alone," he said. "I'll go with you to the A Club."

Gray walked around the table and leaned over Laney's back and wrapped his arms around her. He plunged his face into her glorious hair. It smelled of clean herbal soap. "Laney, I think I love you," he murmured into her ear.

"Gray." Laney covered his hands with her own and turned her head and kissed his warm lips with an intensity she hadn't shown before. Gray placed his hands on her shoulders, urged her to her feet and pulled her into his arms. He felt her arms stretch around his waist and draw him tight against her. Her soft breasts flattened against his chest and he ached to press his lips into their fullness. He heard himself groan, an alien sound. Their kiss was hard and strong and deep. When Gray separated his lips from Laney's, he could see tears in her eyes.

"God, I want you," she moaned, but stepped back and opened her gold-speckled brown eyes. She took his hands and placed them on her breasts. Gray caught his breath and felt their softness. Laney touched his mouth with her fingertip. It was like a whisper on his lips that told him all he needed to know. He crushed her to him in one final embrace, then led her into his little room under the eaves.

Pavarotti was singing "E lucevan le stelle" from *Tosca* on the stereo.

"I have to go, Laney. Have that herd to work." Gray looked down at her. She was curled on her side watching him dress. Even with her deep chestnut hair askew and her face rubbed red with their love-making, she glowed with a natural loveliness. He bent and kissed a freckled shoulder peeking from the wrinkled sheet. "I love you, you know."

"I know," she said.

"Can you let yourself out? Or better yet, you can stay here until I get back and we can do a encore." He slipped on a green scrub shirt and tucked it into his old jeans. When he sat on the side of the bed to pull his boots on, Laney rubbed her hand across his thigh.

"Love to, but I'd better go home. I've got to call John Bernard to tell him I am resigning. You'll go with me tomorrow night?"

"Yes, Nancy Drew, but only to keep you out of trouble. The A Club isn't exactly 'uptown.' I'll check Blackberry and feed the animals before I go. When you leave, please lock the clinic door." Gray scooped up

Puccini from the bottom of the bed and reluctantly left the apartment.

Gray dialed the number for the St. Clair County Sheriff's Department. "Nancy? Gray Prescott here. Would Gordon be around?" Gray stroked Puccini who was getting forty winks on his desk blotter.

"Yeah, Doc. What can I do for you?" Gordon asked.

"Did you get a chance to look at that slug I dropped off yesterday?"

"What slug?"

"You were out, so I put it on your desk. It's in a white envelope with my name on it."

Gray heard Gordon shuffling papers in the background.

"My desk is the black hole of the department. Drop something there, it's never seen . . . wait a minute. Here it is." Gray heard him ripping the envelope open. "Hmm. Beat up little thirty-eight."

"It's a thirty-eight?"

"Yeah. Where did it come from?"

"From Blackberry's lung."

"Oh yeah. Laney said she'd been shot. She thought a hunter did it."

"I'm not so sure about that, especially since you told Laney that Tony character was shot with a thirty-eight."

"Think there's a connection?"

"Don't know. Any way you can find out if the bullets that killed Tony and this slug came from the same gun?"

"Possibly. I'll have to send it up to Lex and let them check it out. Unfortunately, they don't have the murder weapon for a ballistics check. Say Doc . . . something gnawing at you?"

"Nope, just curious about the bullet. Probably just a hunter. Thanks." Gray hung up and collected Puccini.

"Like hell it is," Gray said, as he strode out the door.

19

Tuesday Evening, May 14

The phone was ringing as Laney let herself into the house. "John, I was about to call you," she huffed into the phone, out of breath by her dash to the library. "Did you get the article I faxed Monday?"

"Yes, it was great. When did you find time to go to all those pubs? I hope you didn't charge all that beer drinking to our expense account."

"Heaven forbid if I have a little fun on assignment," Laney snorted.

"When are you coming back to work? You were due back yesterday. You've been gone two weeks."

Laney braced herself. "That's the reason I was going to call you. I'm not coming back, John." She held the phone away from her ear in anticipation of John's explosion. She wasn't disappointed.

"What do you mean you're not coming back?" John bellowed.

"John, you had no way of knowing, but my sister drowned the day before I left Pittsburgh. The story is too long but the short of it is that she left the bed and breakfast and the farm to me. I'm moving to Kentucky to write."

There was a moment of silence, then in a subdued voice, he replied, "Awe Laney, you're right. I didn't know. I'm sorry." His voice was thick with empathy.

"I know this isn't the professional way to resign, but I think I can make it up to you by promising to write articles for your next four issues. That will cover two months. I have enough Pittsburgh notes and information on my computer to write them from down here. My first article will be on Pittsburgh musical theater."

"I'll accept that, but it won't be easy to lose you. It will be rough around here for a while."

That's the understatement of the year, Laney thought. Poor Shar and Judy.

Laney opened the shutters wide. Her eyes flew up to the cardinal's perch in the walnut tree. Instead of a flutter of scarlet, a brown and black owl bobbed about on the limb. It didn't look very life-like to Laney, but the plastic, inflatable bird had convinced the cardinal. He was nowhere in sight.

"Gotcha!" Laney said as she looked out into the trees that were aglow with the evening sun. Below, the ripples in the creek sparkled gold and white on their way to the dam. A little brown muskrat broke the surface on her way to the bank with a mouthful of green. Laney's gaze followed her V trail until, with a silent blurp, she dived below to her nest.

Laney wound the polyphon and with open arms, waltzed about the parlor imagining Gray's arms around her. Into the dining room she danced, through the kitchen, and into her room behind the back stairs. And as the music box ran down, she spun slower and slower until, with its distant fading notes, she floated over to the little wicker rocker, intending to take one last spin with the Cara doll. Her outstretched arms reached down for the doll—and recoiled in horror. She stumbled backwards, her flailing hands flying to cover her face. Her terrified scream muffled the final notes of the Strauss waltz.

Laney paced the porch, afraid to go back into the house. She had grabbed the portable phone on the desk in the kitchen and had called Gray's cell phone number from the front porch. When he didn't answer, she left a message to call her before he drove home from the stockyards.

Dusk settled in and the yellow coach lights cast bleak shadows on the porch. Finally, she saw headlights along the lane, but it seemed an eternity before Gray's Jeep screeched into the circle. She met him at the drive and practically toppled him as he jumped out of the Cherokee.

"What's going on?" He grabbed her around the waist and pulled her to him. "Your message only said to hurry. You sounded so frantic I almost called Gordon."

"Maybe you should have. Wait until you see." Laney trailed after Gray as they went into the house, nudging him from behind as they made their way down the hall. When they entered the back hall, she was reluctant to precede Gray into the bedroom. Standing at the door, she chewed on a fingernail while Gray passed into the room.

"Good God," he said, when he saw the doll. Laney crept up behind Gray and clung to his green scrubs.

"I can see why you didn't explain this over the phone," Gray told her, revulsion warping his mouth.

Peeking from under his arm, Laney forced herself to study the doll with him. The doll's head was twisted into an unnatural contortion and its blond hair had been pulled out wildly. It lay in fuzzy clumps on the hearth rug. The Cara doll's blue eyes gawked crazily at them like some lunatic in an asylum and from the center of the bloody chest, a black-handled butcher knife protruded. The red stain radiated from the knife to the hem of the doll's pink taffeta dress. Laney buried her face into Gray's chest, and his arm enclosed her shoulders protectively.

"Laney, I think we should call the police. This is a clear threat."

Laney looked up into his blue eyes that were bright with concern. "We can't, Gray. Not yet, anyway."

"Why not, for God's sake?" Gray pushed Laney to arm's length, his fingers pressing painfully into her shoulders.

Laney pried away his fingers and turned her back to him.

"Laney, answer me."

Laney twirled to face Gray. "Whoever did this is either trying to get back at me for something or is trying to scare me into selling this place. If we tell the police, we may never know who did this."

"You think it's Karl, don't you?"

"Yes, and I still think he stole Cara's will. That's how he planned to buy the farm." Laney was about to tell him about finding the second paddle, but suddenly decided that Gray would overreact and certainly tell Gordon. Instead, she said, "Before we scare Karl off by involving the police, I want a couple more questions answered."

"Like?"

"Was Karl really in Cincinnati the morning Cara was killed?"

Gray blinked and his mouth opened in surprise. "I . . . I thought Gordon checked out his alibi."

"He did . . . rather he had a buddy of his on the Cincy police force check it out. When Gordon called me the night before the funeral, he told me Ben Smith talked to Jake Rudnik, the guy who was supposed to bid on those paddle boats for Karl on Derby Day. Ben owed Gordon a favor and since both he and Rudnik live in Cincinnati, Ben gave Rudnik a visit."

"What did he find out?" Gray persisted.

"Jake Rudnik told Ben that Karl was at Bailey's Warehouse about nine o'clock on April thirtieth, checking out the boats. Sounds just too convenient to me."

"What do you mean?" Gray asked.

"What if this Rudnik guy was lying for Karl or something?"

"Come on, Laney. Why would he do that?"

Laney shrugged."I don't know. It's just a hunch. Anyway, I don't think this Jake Rudnik bought the paddle boats on Derby Day for Karl because they're not at Hickory Dock."

"Maybe he just hasn't picked them up," Gray offered.

"Too many maybes to suit me."

Gray was thoughtful. "Tell you what, Laney. I have to go to Cincinnati on Thursday for a herd health management seminar. I'll run by the warehouse and try to find out something."

Laney's face lit up like Christmas morning and she gave Gray a sloppy lip bruiser.

"Thank you," she said, truly grateful.

"Now, about this doll." Gray stepped over to the rocker and stooped. Laney followed like a puppy dog.

"My God, I think that's my butcher knife," she gasped. She dashed into the kitchen and glanced at the wooden block that held her knives. One of the slots was empty. When she returned to the bedroom, Gray was holding a small dark bottle with a tissue.

"Here's the 'blood.' Red food coloring . . . probably from your kitchen, too. Found it in the waste basket there. Seems almost like a kid's Halloween prank . . . except for one thing–" Gray said.

"The hair and the twisted neck," Laney finished.

"The way the hair was yanked out. Look at these haphazard tufts on the floor and the force that had to have been used to pull it away from the head. Looks like it was done by someone who was in a wild, uncontrollable rage."

"Gray, you're scaring me," Laney said, taking his hand in both of hers.

"Damn it, Laney, I want you to be scared. I don't think it's just a prank. It's a warning. And I think Blackberry's close call could be one too."

"You think Karl shot her?"

"Another maybe, Laney. But you need to be on your guard. I'll be quiet about this for a couple more days, but if there are anymore threats, I'm calling Gordon."

"Fair enough," Laney said.

"How do you think they got in?" Gray asked.

"You got me. I locked up when I left this morning and the house was locked when I got in this afternoon. Uh-oh . . . Mother has a key."

"You better get it from her tomorrow. Better yet, get the locks changed."

"I'll see to it tomorrow. You still on for the A Club?"

"Said I'd go–against my better judgment."

Laney rummaged around in the linen closet in the bathroom and came out with a large, worn terry cloth towel. Spreading the towel on the floor, she carefully laid the doll in the center. When she reached for the knife, she hesitated, "Think there are any prints on the knife?"

"Probably wore gloves, but let's be on the safe side." He dashed to his truck and returned with a pair of disposable surgical gloves and a large plastic sleeve that he used for palpating and pregnancy-checking large animals.

"Just like a regular forensic expert," Gray quipped and dramatically donned the gloves and carefully removed the knife from the doll's stuffed chest. He was about to place it into the sleeve when Laney held up her hand.

"Hold it. I read that plastic sweats and destroys prints. Patricia Cornwell's protagonist, Kay Scarpetta, uses paper bags," Laney explained.

"Damn, I was really getting into this," Gray said.

Laney retrieved a brown grocery bag from the kitchen and Gray lowered the knife along with the empty bottle of food coloring into it. Laney secured it with a rubber band. After gathering up the tufts of blond hair, Laney laid them on top of the doll. Folding the towel over, she placed the bundle in the top of her closet.

"I really loved that doll," she said with watery eyes. "How about a cup of tea?" she said with a heavy sigh and walked into the kitchen and put the pot on to boil.

Gray came into the kitchen with Puccini leaping behind. "He was lonesome out there by himself."

"I bet he was sound asleep on the dash."

Gray grinned. "Well, I was lonesome for him."

"I miss Blackberry, too."

"When I checked her before I left for the yards, she was a lot more chipper. She ate a little soft food. I'll probably remove the IV when I get home or in the morning. Think your visit helped."

Laney was reaching in and out of the refrigerator and darting back and forth to the stove while they talked. Before long, she produced the most fragrant smelling fresh herb omelet, hot sausage, and toasted bagels to go with their hot tea.

"What is that smell?" Gray asked, placing his nose so close to the omelet, the steam moistened his face."

"Fresh parsley and thyme. Don't you just love it?"

"I love *you*," Gray said.

20

Wednesday, May 15

Laney left the light on all night. With every creak and squeak in the old house, Laney's heart would give a lurch. When some time near dawn she finally fell asleep reading, she slept like a cat on hot bricks. Rather out of sorts and grumpy, she crawled out of bed. *Maybe I should have allowed Gray to stay all night like he offered,* she thought, but had to giggle knowing that the two of them together definitely wouldn't have slept at all.

As soon as she was dressed and drinking her first cup of coffee, she called Frank Hobble, the local locksmith, and was told that the earliest he could change her locks was first thing Friday morning. *Damn,* she brooded, *two more sleepless nights.*

No sooner had she hung up when Gray called.

"What's going on? Nothing I hope. Had trouble sleeping, worrying about you."

"I slept with the light on myself, what sleep I got."

"Blackberry's doing great. She's up and eating much better. See you tonight about nine, okay?"

"Right."

"Get those locks changed. Bye."

"Gray–" Laney said, but before she could tell him it would be Friday before she got the locks changed, she heard the phone click.

Freddie Rudd was having a hard time eating his third giant taco and balancing a large soft drink while he read the local news page of the *Lexington Post*. With every crunch, shredded lettuce, cheese, and chopped tomato mixed with hot taco sauce plopped onto the printed page. It didn't help that Gordon seemed to jerk the wheel of the sheriff's vehicle or braked every time he tried to take a bite. The two of them were on their way back to Hickory after dropping off the thirty-eight caliber bullet that Gray had given Gordon. The Lexington Police Department had promised to compare the bullet to the two that had killed Tony Richards.

Freddie took a long pull from his soft drink. "Say, what was the name of the guy Karl Webster gave us the day Cara Collins was pulled out of the creek?"

"The guy in Cincy who told Lieutenant Smith that he saw Karl at the warehouse the morning she drowned?"

"Yeah. Was it Jake Rudnik?"

"That's him. Why?"

"Listen to this. Freddie scooped up a piece of cheese from the newspaper, stuck it in his mouth and began to read:

> *Jake Rudnik, 48, was arrested Tuesday morning by Franklin County police when his truck that was hauling a large boat trailer, overturned on Route 421 just outside of Frankfort, Kentucky. When a patrol car stopped to render aid, they discovered plastic bags full of a powdery substance spilling from a rent in the boat's hull. Rudnik was taken to the county jail and was to be arraigned this morning in the Franklin County courthouse on trafficking of cocaine. Police would only say that the cocaine had a street value of almost a half a million dollars.*

"Well, what do ya know," Gordon said. "I wonder if birds of a feather—"

"Wouldn't surprise me," Freddie said, as he took another slurp of his soft drink.

The A Club was on the northeast side of Lexington, not far from the trailer park where Nick Owens lived. Gray had driven the Whooptie because he was afraid his beloved Buick might get stolen or vandalized while they were in the sleazy bar.

Gray parked the car near the only light in the small lot and locked the doors. Under a grimy A Club sign, a poster tacked to a billboard portrayed a girl holding a guitar. Laney recognized the woman before she even read the bill: "Featuring Randi Richards."

Laney's quick sweep of the lot, didn't turn up Randi's blue Dodge. A couple making out by a pickup glanced up briefly as they passed and were back at it as Laney and Gray entered the club.

Gray groaned as he paid the five-dollar cover charge, and they found an unoccupied table two tables back from the tiny stage. A waitress in a low-cut blouse and black mini-skirt took their drink orders. It was karaoke night and two gals were singing off key to Reba McIntire and Linda Davis's duet, "Does He Love You." Laney smiled at Gray's pained expression.

"How long do we have to endure this before the star appears?" Gray whispered in her ear.

"I have no idea," Laney said, as their drinks came and the duet ended with scattered applause. From right stage, a pumped-up man dressed in an orange, green, and purple Hawaiian shirt appeared and took up one of the microphones.

"Wasn't that wonderful. Thank you, gals. Now . . . Gary Hawkins, ladies and gentlemen."

Stepping onto the stage, a handsome black man took the microphone from the announcer. Laney instantly recognized the opening strains of "Can You Stop the Rain."

When the man began to sing, he had a voice very much like Peabo Bryson, the artist that had made the song a hit. This guy obviously hadn't had any voice training, but he was pleasant to hear and on key. Laney and Gray gave him a big hand.

Laney noticed that the small club was suddenly filling up. "Must be time for the big show," Laney said, placing her hand on Gray's arm. He smiled at her through the cigarette haze and covered her hand with his own.

Laney thought he had the sweetest smile in the whole world. It was open, yet at the same time, vulnerable and shy like a little boy's. Every time he smiled at her it was like plunging her face into a fluffy towel just out of the dryer. It warmed her heart.

The lights dimmed and the announcer in the gaudy shirt pulled a tall stool to the center of the stage and leaned a guitar against it. After adjusting the mike, he bent over and said, "Ladies and Gentlemen . . . Randi Richards."

The small club vibrated with applause as Randi, under a single spotlight, strolled to the stool. She was dressed in a soft turquoise and white silk tunic that reached below her hips and covered black tights that hugged her slim form. Her only adornment was a pair of turquoise drop earrings that matched her eyes. Resting on her left shoulder, a long single braid of raven black hair glistened. She reminded Laney of an exotic Indian maiden.

Randi smiled and her pretty face lit up with the applause. Laney couldn't help recalling how she had looked the last time she'd seen her–crying and rubbing her arm from Nick's roughness.

When Randi reached down and lifted her guitar, the club instantly hushed. Laney could tell this crowd knew Randi and they were loyal followers of her music.

Her first notes on the guitar set the mood for the song. The simple arpeggio of chords introduced a ballad that Laney hadn't heard before. She wondered if it was an original composition. When Randi began to sing, Laney heard the voice of an angel. At times it reached down into deep throaty notes, only to soar into a piercing falsetto that left chills along Laney's spine. My God, Laney thought. She shouldn't be singing in this hole.

The lyrics seemed to ascend from Randi's soul:

> *Seems no matter how I've tried,*
> *An emptiness has crept inside.*
> *When did everything go wrong? . . .*
> *I start to feel I don't belong?*

> *Where do I go from here?*
> *I'm sad apart or when we're near.*
> *Even when you're close to me,*
> *We are not together.*

> *There's no room left for hurting,*
> *No more tears left to cry. Should I . . .*

Stay another day . . . or go away?
Where do I go from here?

The beautiful lyrical song ended with a single tear rolling down Randi's cheek. There was a moment before applause fractured the pin-drop quiet in the club. Unaware that she had been holding her breath throughout the last verse, Laney exhaled. She glanced at Gray who locked eyes with her at the same moment, speechless.

Randi sang several more songs. Most were ballads and were unfamiliar to Laney. But one was a rip-roaring bawdy number that got the crowd clapping along with her and laughing boisterously.

When Randi finally left the stage and disappeared through the exit at right stage, Laney leaped to her feet and followed her, almost upsetting the Hawaiian shirt guy in her rush through the door.

"Hey, Lady, you're not allowed back–" He bellowed as Gray also exploded through the door, spinning the man around.

Laney had already caught up with Randi in the dark hallway and was asking Randi if she could talk with her when Gray caught up. Randi appeared frightened by the intrusion.

"I'll only take a little of your time, Randi. It's about Tony's death," Laney pleaded.

"Hawaiian shirt" had recovered and was stomping down the hall like some nettled bodyguard of Randi's.

"I'll take care of this, Randi," he growled, managing to take hold of Gray's right arm and twisting it behind his back. Gray kicked backward with his left heel and caught "Hawaiian shirt" on his kneecap. The big guy hit the filthy floor with a yowl and Laney's mouth parted in surprise.

Randi hardly gave the guy a second look. "What do you know about Tony?" she asked Laney, in a hushed voice.

Recovering from Gray's unexpected response, Laney took Randi's arm and asked, "Is there somewhere we can talk?"

"My house. Do you have a car?"

Laney nodded. She was astounded by Randi's receptiveness, with only the mention of Tony's name.

"I live at–"

"I think I remember where you live," Laney said.

"How–"

"It's a long story," Laney interrupted.

Randi looked over to her right. "Hawaiian shirt" had struggled to his feet and was scowling at Gray, his fists opening and closing, raring to have a go at him. Gray looked like he was ready.

"Bruce, it's okay. This is personal business," Randi said.

"Randi, I'm Laney McVey and this is Gray Prescott, a friend of mine." Gray shook Randi's hand, all the while keeping an eye on Bruce.

"I'll see you at the house in about a half hour," Randi said. She seemed reluctant to talk in front of Bruce. Pivoting, she disappeared through a door marked "Dressing Room."

"Hawaiian shirt" bored one last hole through Gray with his eyes and limped back to the stage door.

Laney and Gray made it to the house on Chapel Court before Randi arrived. They parked next to the drive and Gray turned off the ignition. They didn't have long to wait. When Randi's blue Dodge pulled into the driveway, her remote opened the two-car garage door and she swung into the garage. The door dropped down behind the car.

"Did you see what I saw?" Gray asked.

"Sure did. The black Camaro Z28. Did you get a chance to see the plates?"

"Nope. The door closed too fast."

"Let's go." Laney was out of the Whooptie and waiting for him at the yellow front door before Gray could remove the keys and lock the doors.

Randi led them to a large, tastefully decorated living room. She turned on a couple of lamps and invited them to sit down. Laney sat on the edge of a blue and red plaid sofa. Gray found a navy wing-back chair, piped in scarlet.

"Can I offer you something to drink?" Randi asked. "A soft drink? Coffee? Sorry, I don't have anything stronger."

Laney recalled what Nick said about Randi being a heavy drinker. "No thank you," Laney said, and Gray shook his head.

Randi sat on the matching wing-back chair. She had changed into a pair of black jeans and a pale yellow short-sleeved sweater at the A Club. She looked even more exotic and beautiful than on stage.

"Please tell me," she said, "what do you know about Tony's death?" Her turquoise eyes immediately began to pool.

"Randi, my sister was Cara Collins. She was seeing Tony before he died." Laney was blunt, assuming that Randi knew about the ad that was found in their house by the police.

"Cara Collins? That can't be," Randi said, surprise showing in her face.

"I'm afraid so. Please . . . I don't want to hurt you."

"Laney . . . it is Laney, isn't it?"

"Yes."

"I have no illusions about my husband. I knew he was seeing someone. We were getting a divorce. But her name wasn't Cara."

"What?"

"I overheard him on the phone one day, but the name he called her wasn't Cara," Randi said.

"May I ask what her name was?" Gray asked.

"Jesse."

Laney glanced over at Gray and their eyes bonded for just a second.

"Jesse? Are you sure?" Laney asked.

"Positive. I didn't hear the whole conversation, but I definitely heard him call her Jesse."

"Did you hear a last name?" Laney was on the edge of her seat.

"No. Like I said, I only heard him say, 'Jesse, tomorrow? Good.' Then he hung up."

"Can you remember what day that was?" Gray pressed.

"It was on Thursday, April twenty-fifth. I remember because it was my first night at the A Club and thinking about Tony seeing her the next day almost ruined my performance."

"Randi, we noticed Tony's car in the garage when you pulled in. How long has it been there?" Gray asked.

"Ever since Tony disappeared. On the Sunday after I overheard Tony talking to Jesse, I left for rehearsal at the A Club. When I returned, the car was here and Tony was gone."

"Didn't you call the police?" Laney asked, drinking in every word Randi said.

"No, Tony had told me earlier that he was thinking of going to Atlanta that week on one of Nick's boat buying trips so I figured he and his partner had gone in Nick's truck. Nick usually was gone for a week or so." Tracks of anxiety formed between Randi's eyes and she took a couple of deep breaths.

Gray came right to the point. "Who do you think killed Tony, Randi?"

"Nick Owens. He and Tony didn't get along. In fact, I think Tony was going to end the partnership. I wouldn't be surprised if he told Nick that and in a fit of anger, Nick shot him. I later found out Nick didn't go on that trip south after all and was here in Lexington all that week."

"Did Nick have a gun?" Laney asked.

"I don't know, but he had a key to the rental garage. They rented it together." Randi stood and rubbed the back of her neck. She excused herself and left the room. When she returned she carried a tall glass filled with what looked like ice water.

"Sure I can't get you something to drink?" she asked.

"No, thank you," Laney replied.

"Randi, I followed you the other day from here to Nick's trailer," Laney said.

"Why did you do that?" Randi seemed surprised.

"I wanted to find out more about Tony. He had been seen with my sister before she died."

"Died? Your sister died?" Randi became alarmed and she placed her drink on a small chest used as an end table and stepped over to Laney as though to touch her. "What happened?"

"She drowned in what the police think was an accident. I . . . I don't think it was."

"But what does this have to do with Tony? You don't think he—" Randi exclaimed.

"I don't know what to think anymore," Laney interrupted, then covered her face with her hands and rested her elbows on her knees.

"Laney, I can tell you this. Tony did not kill your sister. He may have been unfaithful to me, but he wouldn't kill. He was a gentle man. I drove him away with my drinking. He would throw me out but would always let me come back here when I had nowhere else to go." She began to cry softly. "I loved him."

Laney stood and held her until she calmed. Randi finally pulled away and sank back down on the blue chair.

Gray interrupted the long silence. "Why did you go to Nick's trailer on Monday?"

Randi's eyes moved to Laney as she answered. "I wanted to ask

Nick where the boat was."

"What boat?" Laney inquired.

"Tony and Nick bought and sold boats as well as recreational vehicles. Tony took a liking to one of these boats and he parked it in the storage unit they rented together." Laney remembered that in the letter Tony had sent Cara, he had mentioned owning a boat.

"Nick kept after Tony to sell the boat, but Tony held out. When the police mentioned to me that the garage was empty . . . ex . . . except for the freezer, I went to Nick's to see if he had sold the boat. As Tony's widow, Nick owed me half of the money, if he had."

"Who held the title?" Gray prodded.

"Nick's name was on it, so I was surprised when Nick gave me the money at the trailer. I thought he would give me a hard time. He told me he had sold the boat and threw the cash at me, saying he didn't want to hear anything more about it."

"What kind of a boat was it?" Gray urged.

"A twenty-foot runabout. A real beauty. I wouldn't have bothered to see that creep if I hadn't needed the money. After the police went over Tony's car with a fine tooth comb, I thought I could sell the Camaro but Tony's estate isn't settled. I have house payments and the A Club doesn't pay much." Randi collapsed into her chair and seemed completely drained.

Gray stood and took Laney's hand. "We need to go, Randi. This information may be a big help after we sort it all out."

"One moment, Gray," Laney said, stooping to look into Randi's face. "Randi, we were out front listening to you sing this evening. You were absolutely sensational. What an incredible voice!"

Randi managed a tired smile. "Thank you."

"You shouldn't be singing in a dive like that. I have some connections in Pittsburgh. May I see what I can do?" Laney asked.

"I'd really be grateful. It's tough getting started in this business."

Randi took Laney's hands in her own and struggled to her feet. Walking them to the door, she said, "I hope you discover how your sister died. I wouldn't be surprised if somehow there is a connection to Nick. I'm hoping the police will arrest him for Tony's death very soon. I don't know why they are dragging their feet."

"Without the murder weapon, they may not have enough evidence," Gray said.

Laney dug a scrap of paper out of her purse, wrote down her name and phone number and handed it to Randi. "Please keep in touch," Laney said, "and, thank you."

"Laney, you can't stay here alone one more night. I won't get any sleep." Laney had just told Gray that the locks hadn't been changed and the locksmith wouldn't get to them until Friday.

"It's so sweet you're so concerned about me," Laney said.

"Seriously, I'm going to sleep here tonight," Gray announced.

"You'd do anything to canoodle me," Laney laughed.

"For your information, I'm camping right here on the sofa." Gray patted the tan leather on the library sofa.

"Don't you have to leave early in the morning for your seminar in Cincy?" Laney protested. "And feed Blackberry?"

"Listen, my little sleuth, I fed your hound dog before our great adventure and I'll set my watch alarm to wake me at six a.m."

"You're ready, aren't you? Speaking of being ready, where did you learn that slick little foot move you performed on 'Hawaiian shirt' tonight?" Laney asked.

"Liked that, did you? Thought you knew about the karate course I took while I was in vet school." Gray's eyes sparkled with mischief.

"Refresh my memory."

"There was this cute assistant professor at Auburn that was my anatomy instructor. Fell head over heels, so when I found out she taught a karate class, I signed up. Pictured myself rolling around on the mat with her. The first night of class, she paired me up with 'Attila the Hun.' Found out after three weeks of bruising that he was her husband. I stuck it out for three more weeks and learned just enough to get me into trouble."

"Serves you right," Laney laughed, "but I have to admit I was impressed tonight."

"Makes all the pain and suffering worth while," Gray grinned.

"Changing the subject, Randi seems awfully sure Nick did Tony in."

"Sounds as though there may be a motive there . . . generally not getting along and wanting out of the partnership. Opportunity, too. Randi said Nick was in town that week. Didn't go on that boat buying trip south after all. Had a key to the garage."

"I wonder if that is enough evidence for an arrest?"

"Sounds pretty circumstantial to me. I'm more interested in what connection Jesse–if it's the same Jesse–has to do with this."

"I'll try to talk to her tomorrow," Laney said with a yawn. "Now it's your bedtime. Let me get your blankey."

"Will you tuck me in?" Gray asked in a little boy voice.

"You betcha."

21

Thursday, May 16

Gray usually dreaded the continuing education seminars, but this one hadn't been so bad. The professor from Purdue who had lectured on herd health management in the afternoon session, was knowledgeable and had cracked the class up by peppering his talk with humorous anecdotes from his wide experience in the field. Also, two of his classmates from Auburn had attended and they'd made plans to meet for dinner later that night. It would make for a late night, but Gray needed the diversion after the stress of the past week.

His class ended at four and Gray jumped into his Buick, dropped in his Jussi Bjoerling CD of favorite arias and took I-75 south out of Cincinnati to the Florence, Kentucky exit. After a few wrong turns, Gray saw the large Bailey's Warehouse sign perched above a building. There wasn't much activity at that late hour, only a couple of guys unloading a used Case tractor from a huge trailer. The tractor was just one of at least fifty parked in the lot waiting for the next auction.

Gray parked by the gaping entrance and strolled inside. He was astounded by the size of the concrete block building. There're three acres in here, he thought, scanning the equipment arranged in row after row as far as he could see. As he walked down the nearest aisle, he could tell that the majority of the equipment was farm related, but here and there were small groupings of appliances, building materials, furniture, and recreational equipment. Gray spotted a rack of canoes and two pink paddle boats in aisle seven.

"What can I do for you, buddy?" a friendly voice asked.

Gray turned around to see a barrel-chested man approaching him. A smile stretched across the man's round face and crowded his eyes into two twinkling crescents.

The man held out his hand, "Pat Bailey here. Did you want to consign for the sale?"

Gray shook his hand and introduced himself. "No, but I have some questions about those paddle boats over there." Gray pointed to the two boats.

"Hope to get rid of them this sale," Bailey said. "I bought them back the last auction when I only got one low bid on them. If you're interested, I might sell them to you privately."

"So they're your boats?" Gray asked.

"Yes sir. I have a small lake on my farm and the grandkids used to paddle around in them before they discovered computers. They're all growed up now and going to college."

"Did a guy named Jake Rudnik bid on them in the last sale?"

The sparkle dimmed a bit in Pat's eyes. "You a cop?"

Gray was surprised at Bailey's question and assured him he was a veterinarian and just wanted to talk to him.

"I guess you haven't read the paper lately. Come into my office." Gray followed the burly man through a door near the front of the building into a spacious room lined with metal file cabinets. Pat sorted through some newspapers on his desk and came up with Wednesday's *Lexington Post*. He pointed to a small headline on the front page of the local news section and handed the paper to Gray, motioning to him to take a seat.

As Gray read the short article, he felt the newspaper grow damp in his hands. My God, he thought. Could Karl have a connection to this drug trafficker?

"Mr. Bailey, you didn't answer my question earlier. Was Rudnik the bidder on the paddle boats in the last sale?"

"Hell, no." Bailey's jovial face had turned grim. "He's banned from the warehouse."

"Banned? Why?" Gray asked.

"About a month ago, I caught him pocketing some small tools. Told him I wouldn't have him arrested as long as he never stepped foot in the warehouse again. After that article, I guess I should've had him busted." Pat pulled out a pack of generic cigarettes and offered one to Gray.

"No thanks. Do you know a man named Karl Webster?"

"Sure do. He consigned some leaky canoes here about two months ago. Bitched and didn't want to pay the commission when he got what they were worth. Him and Rudnik are buddies."

"Have you seen him in the last month?" Gray asked.

"I haven't seen him since he sold those canoes. Say, you sure seem awfully interested in this Rudnik guy," Pat said, lighting up. "Did he try to do it to you, too?"

Gray stood up to go. "Actually, Mr. Bailey, by getting arrested, he may have done me a favor."

22

Thursday Night, May 16

As Laney microwaved her low-fat dinner, lightning lit up the sky. "Another spring thunderstorm," she grumbled, as she listened to the dismal pattering of rain against the breakfast room window. She poured a cup of hot tea from the blue and white teapot and squeezed a slice of lemon. While she stirred sweetener into her tea, her finger ran down the index of the *World's Life List of Birds* until she found snakebird. "See Anhinga," she read. Turning to the correct page, Laney immediately recognized the unusual bird in a full page photograph. The bird appeared almost primeval, his outstretched wings displaying the silver patches that Laney's flashlight had captured the night Blackberry was shot. Reading quickly through the text, she discovered that the bird was really tropical and rarely seen this far north. The photo called to mind her frightening dream the morning she found the paddle. She shuddered and closed the book.

Shaking the image away, Laney went over her day. I sure didn't accomplish much, she reflected ruefully. After visiting Blackberry and lunching with Natine, she had gone to Jesse's only to be informed by the all-knowing Rose that Jesse had left the apartment earlier. She had called her several times up to five o'clock when she knew Jesse started work at the Finish Line. When she ran by the dock late in the day, she had found her mother also gone. Thankfully, Karl had been nowhere around.

The microwave dinged and she retrieved the chicken stir-fry dinner. She picked around the meal, then having enough of its cardboard taste, fed the disposal the rest. Losing the battle with her conscience, she made her way to the pie safe and seized the apple turnover she had snitched from the top of her mother's stove when, as usual, she'd found Maddy's door unlocked. She had left a brief note to her mother that she would be by tomorrow.

"Now this is more like it," she said and devoured the whole pastry. As she washed the last morsel down with her tea, a crash of thunder set her heart racing. "Poor Blackberry," she groaned. "She'll be terrified." Laney dialed Gray's number but only got his voice mail. She left a short message that she hoped Gray would allow Blackberry into his apartment when he got home from Florence. Laney checked her watch. Nine-fifteen. Maybe Gray had stayed over because of the storm.

Laney put her dishes into the dishwasher and went through the house checking all the doors and windows. One last night, she thought. The locksmith would be there in the morning. As she picked up her purse from the hall table, the telephone startled her. She answered it in the library.

"Gray?" she said, delighted to hear his voice.

"I just checked my voice mail. Got your message. Only worrying about Blackberry, I noticed. I don't like storms either," he said with a slighted whine.

"Where are you?"

"I'm still in Cincy. Met some old buddies of mine and we're having dinner. Are you okay?"

"I'm fine. I was just worried about Blackberry. She hates storms so."

"So does Puccini."

"But he isn't in a cold cage all by himself. I bet he's draped over your arm, as we speak."

"Nope. Left him at home."

"Blackberry seemed great when I saw her today," Laney said. "She's standing some and Natine says she's eating better. I know she was glad to get rid of the IV."

"Laney," Gray's voice had turned serious. "I won't be home until late. I have lots to tell you, but I need to get back to my dinner. Please lock up carefully. I'll call you first thing in the morning." He hung up.

Laney felt unnerved by Gray's obvious concern for her safety. Did he really think someone would try to harm her?

The storm crashed around the house and she knew she wouldn't be able to sleep until it passed over. Restless, she sat at the desk to ponder Tony's murder and if somehow it could have been connected to her sister's death. She reached into her purse and pulled out the manila envelope containing the letters to her sister. As they slid out of the envelope, the newspaper clipping Cara had placed tumbled out with them. Laney's eyes were drawn to the red circle around the ad.

She read it again. The address that the newspaper had assigned to Cara and that each of the respondents had copied onto their envelopes was at the end of Cara's ad: L-P Box 12H, Lexington, Kentucky 40510. The L-P stands for *Lexington Post*, Laney thought. The 12H must be the identifying code for Cara Collins. She remembered that almost all the letters began with "Dear 12H."

Laney scanned over the rest of the personal announcements on the clipping. Three were advertisements for singles' clubs, one was an ad from a Miss Crystal, a psychic who promised to tell your fortune over the phone, and two others were personals from men who were lonely. One other ad next to the torn edge of the clipping read:

> *Tall, slender, attractive, independent female, 32, interested in meeting mature, professional, sincere male who likes traveling, dancing and dining out.*

The woman's identifying code was 11G. Laney suddenly perked up. Sounds just like Jesse, she thought. Could this second ad be Jesse's? She was thirty-two–just like Cara. Tall. Slim. And the wording was similar to Cara's ad–interested in meeting mature, professional, sincere male for . . . dancing . . . dining out. And her identifying code was 11G. Cara's was 12H. Could they have placed the ads at the same time?

Intrigued, Laney began to read the letters one at a time. When she got to Tony Richard's letter, she paused, recalling meeting his wife the night before. Tony definitely had lied about already being divorced, Laney thought wryly, as she scrutinized the photo of Tony next to his Camaro Z28.

One of the other two letters that contained photos was next. She spread the letter and the photo out on the desk. The man's face wasn't very clear but she definitely could discern that he was dressed in an expensive suit and his boots must have cost a great deal.

Those boots! Laney snatched up the photo and held it under the lamp. Still not clear enough, Laney scrounged around in the desk drawer and came up with a miniature magnifying glass–the kind that was used to repair eye glasses. She held the glass over the photo.

"Shazam!" Laney exclaimed. "They sure look like Nick's boots." She'd never forget those shiny snakeskin boots that were between her and escape from Nick's trailer. She moved the glass over the photo. "Looks like Nick. Has his same snarly mouth." She began to read the letter that he had sent with the picture:

Dear you:

(Nicely put, Laney thought.)

> *I like them tall and slender so let's see what else we have in common. Me? I'm over forty, six foot, and a smart dresser. I own my own business so I can show you a good time. That's my two bits. You can "can" this or send me your bits back plus a picture. Could be the "thrill of victory" or the "agony of defeat." Who knows?*
> *N. O.*

"N. O.! Nick Owens? Double shazam! Could it be?" He has an attitude problem like him too, Laney concluded, as she turned the envelope over. "Wait a minute . . . ," Laney said, as she studied the address on the envelope:

> *Lexington Post*
> *Box 11G*
> *Lexington, Ky. 40510*

"This letter wasn't addressed to Cara. It was for 'tall and slender,' Box 11G. Jesse? Well, well, well . . . this hasn't been a lost day after all. But how did Cara get hold of this letter?" Immediately, she recalled Jesse telling her that she and Cara had sat around laughing at the letters. Maybe Jesse had also placed an ad and gotten one of her letters mixed with Cara's when they'd read them together? God, I can't wait to talk to Jesse tomorrow, Laney thought to herself.

She gathered up the letters and photos and stuffed them into the top drawer of the desk. Turning off the lamp, she moved down the hall to her bedroom. The last thought she had, as she pulled the covers up, was that the storm had ended.

Her eyes clicked open. No reason. Just suddenly awake. Laney lay as though cemented to the bed, holding her breath. Nothing. She relaxed. Exhaled.

"What was that?" She held her breath again. The wind? She turned her head and listened.

There it was again. A small, faint rustle. A shadowy whisper of sound. Far away. Near the front of the house.

She pushed the covers aside and sat on the edge of her bed. She listened again.

Nothing.

Like a shadow, she tiptoed to the bathroom in the dark and felt for her robe on its hook behind the door. Its flannel warmth took the chill from her arms but her trembling hands were stiff with cold. She slipped them into her deep pockets and curled her fingertips into fists.

She wondered if she had locked the front door. Like some obsessive-compulsive, she knew that she had, but had doubts just the same. She passed silently to the door of her room and peeked out into the short hall behind the back stairs. The small night light in the hall reassured her and faintly led the way to the kitchen where once again she was in darkness. She lifted the portable phone from its cradle on the desk. She was about to dial the police when she thought she'd better be sure that she had secured the front door and that it hadn't blown open during the night. Explain that to the police.

But what if someone was in the house? She looked around in the blackness. Besides the green light in the phone cradle and the illuminated digital clock on the coffee maker, she could see nothing. She felt her way to the countertop where she knew the knife holder sat. She ran her hands over the block, feeling the empty slot where the butcher knife had been. Sure could use it now, she thought, and settled for the knife in the adjacent slot. Running her finger gingerly along the edge, she knew she had grabbed the serrated bread knife. It'll have to do, she rationalized.

Grasping the knife in her right hand and holding the portable phone in her left, she inched her way through the kitchen and turned into the hallway leading to the front of the house. Instantly, she felt the cool rush of air. Straining her eyes to the end of the hall, she could see a narrow pale rectangle of the night sky through the partially open door. I did leave the front door unlocked, Laney thought, and discharged a deep breath of relief. How could I have been so stupid, she reprehended herself, and padded down the hall toward the front door.

As she rushed past the library, she halted dead in her tracks, then lurched backwards toward the door of the library. A sliver of light beneath the door! She gasped.

Oh God, I know I turned that light out. A hot current of pure terror ran through her body. Again, she heard the rustling sound but this time it was less muffled and it came directly from the library. Her bare feet suddenly sprung roots and her knees threatened to buckle. Opening her mouth to scream, she was abruptly struck mute. Rapid breaths threatened hyperventilation. Mind reeling, she laid the phone on the rug next to the door and dropped to one knee. With fingers like fluttering moths at a light, she groped for the door knob. But when her hand made contact, it suddenly had purpose. Slowly and firmly, she rotated the knob and eased the door forward until she could peek through the tiny crack.

By the light of the desk lamp, Jesse Mills was on her knees, digging deep into the bottom drawer of the file cabinet. For a startled moment, Laney did nothing. Then, as total rage consumed her, she burst into the room, the door slamming into the paneled wall.

"What are you doing here?" Laney screamed.

For an instant, Jesse froze, her brown eyes wide and ghastly in fear, her face bloodless like her arteries had been sucked dry. She scrambled backwards and struggled to her feet. Her arm flew upwards to shield her face. "No! . . . Please!" she begged.

"Answer me!" Laney lifted her knife hand.

"Don't hurt me! . . . I'll tell you! . . . I'm sorry!" Jesse cried, backing away from the file cabinet, still holding her hand out to shield her body.

Laney moved toward Jesse, gesturing with the knife for Jesse to move to the sofa and sit. Jesse sat, her head strangely tilting to the right.

"Put the knife down," a voice demanded from behind Laney.

She spun, the knife raised to plunge.

Gray stood in the doorway, his hand outstretched. Gently, he pried the knife from her fingers and placed it on the desk–all the while staring at Laney in consternation. A grateful, shuddering sob burst from Jesse.

When Gray spoke next, his voice was marked with tightness. "Decided to check on you before I drove home. Jesse's car was parked in the middle of the lane and so when I couldn't get by, I walked back here to find the door open and you holding a knife on Jesse. What in the hell's going on?"

"Ask cat burglar here," Laney said hostilely. "I woke up and found her here."

"Jesse, how did you get in?" Gray asked.

The color was returning to Jesse's face but she trembled with fear. "I . . . I have my own key. Cara gave it to me so I could come and clean when she wasn't at home."

"Give it to me," Laney demanded, holding out her hand. Jesse reached into the pocket of her Finish Line slacks, pulled out the key, and handed it to Laney.

"Why are you here?" Gray asked.

When Jesse didn't answer, Laney stepped to the desk, grabbed the phone and put it to her ear.

"Who are you calling?" Jesse's face again turned pale.

"The police," Laney spat. "I'm going to press charges." Laney couldn't remember ever being so incensed.

"Laney, no! I . . . I was looking for the letters and the ad," Jesse sobbed.

"Why?" Laney said, replacing the receiver.

"I was afraid if the police found them, they would try to pin Tony's murder on me."

"How could they do that? It's Cara's ad," Gray said.

"I placed an ad, too," Jesse replied. Gray looked confused.

Stepping to the desk, Laney removed the letters and ad from the center drawer. "Cara and Jesse both placed ads in the newspaper. I just discovered that this evening." Laney pointed out the two different ads on the same clipping to Gray.

"I'll be damned," he said.

"Jesse, where are your letters?" Laney demanded.

"When I saw the article in the newspaper that Tony had been murdered, I burned them."

"Jesse, Sheriff Powell showed me Tony's copy of the ad. Only Cara's ad was circled. Evidently, the police don't know that you placed an ad too . . . unless I fill them in," Laney said snidely, her forefinger tapping the phone. "How did you meet Nick?" she asked quickly while she had Jesse's attention.

Jesse shrugged. "He answered my ad. We just started seeing each other."

Laney picked up a letter and waved it in Jesse's face. "Here's Nick's letter. It was mixed in with Cara's."

Jesse jumped up and tried to snatch the letter away.

"Oh, no you don't," Laney said, flipping her hand with the letter behind her back.

"Did you know Cara was seeing Tony?" asked Gray.

"Yeah, Cara told me and later I met him," Jesse said.

"When was that?" Gray prodded.

"One day about three weeks ago, me and Nick stopped at Valu Mini Storage. That's the garage Nick and Tony rented together. I waited in the car. When Nick didn't show after about twenty minutes, I went looking for him. When I got to the unit, I heard Nick arguing with some guy he called Tony."

"What were they arguing about?" Gray asked, encouraging her to open up.

"Some boat they owned together. Tony wanted to keep it. Nick was trying to get him to sell it. Finally, Tony said he would sell it when Nick told him he had seen a nicer runabout in Atlanta."

Gray's voice was gentle, "So, that's the day you met Tony?"

"Yeah. When I heard them arguing, I ran back to the car so Nick wouldn't get mad that I overheard them."

Laney sat down on the desk chair. "And . . ."

"When Nick got to the car, Tony was with him. Tony introduced himself, then Nick and me drove off."

"Did you ever go out with Tony?" Laney asked.

"Oh, no. He was Cara's boyfriend."

Honor among thieves, Laney mused. She suddenly remembered Tony's phone call that Randi had overheard. "Did Tony ever phone you?"

"Yeah, he did . . . a couple days later. He wanted to know when Cara was getting home from her workshop in Frankfort."

"What did you tell him?" Laney asked.

"That she would be home the next day."

"Jesse, tomorrow? Good." It fits, Laney thought.

Jesse stood up like she was ready to bolt.

"Sit down!" Laney shouted at her. Jesse flew back onto the sofa. Gray gaped at Laney in wonder.

"Were you the one who broke into the house Tuesday and stabbed my doll with a butcher knife?" Laney asked.

Jesse's hand flew to her mouth, and her eyes once more grew into huge circles of fear. "What doll? I didn't know you even had a doll. I wouldn't . . . I couldn't . . . believe me, Laney," she cried, total shock on her face.

"Do you still see Nick?" Laney asked her, a mite softer.

"Are you kidding? He told me to get lost when Tony died . . . just like that." She snapped her fingers. "I can really pick em, can't I?"

"Jesse, he's a toad," Laney said.

"Laney, I think we should let Jesse go home now. I parked in the grass, so she should be able to get out of the lane." Turning to Jesse, he added, "We'd appreciate it if you would keep all this to yourself."

Jesse charged off the sofa. "You won't have me arrested?" Her eyes pleaded through tears.

"As long as you promise," Gray pursued.

"I promise . . . and Laney . . . I'm sorry. I was so scared."

"Go home, Jesse," Laney said, waving her away, suddenly feeling like all her steam had evaporated.

Without another word, Jesse dashed out the door.

As soon as he heard Jesse close the front door, Gray asked, "Do you believe she was telling the truth about the doll?"

"I do. She couldn't have done that."

Sitting side by side on the sofa, Gray told Laney about his trip to Bailey's Warehouse and the drug trafficking charge against Karl's friend, Jake Rudnik.

"You don't mean it!" Laney exclaimed. "Jake Rudnik? Do you think there might be a drug connection there with Karl?"

"Don't know, but I'm sure as hell going to find out more about Karl's sorry friend. Rudnik didn't bid on those paddle boats for Karl on Derby Day either, because he was banned from the warehouse after Bailey caught him stealing."

"But what about the day Cara died? Did this Bailey fellow see Karl at the warehouse looking at the paddle boats?"

"Nope. Hasn't seen Karl at the warehouse for two months."

Laney jumped from the sofa, her brown eyes shiny aggies above her freckled nose. "If Karl wasn't at the warehouse that morning, Rudnik must have lied to that cop friend of Gordon's." She pounded Gray on his knee for emphasis. "Gray! There goes Karl's alibi for the morning Cara died!"

"Exactly," Gray said, settling back into the soft leather cushions. "I think it's time to talk to Gordon." His expression shifted into serious gear.

"Hey, you. You promised you'd wait before getting the police involved. Please, just a little longer." She bent and kissed his cute nose and nibbled on an ear. He pulled her into his arms, and it wasn't long before his serious gear disengaged. Laney stretched out on the leather sofa with her head resting in Gray's lap. His fingers massaged her temples until she felt like a pot of buttery noodles. "No more intrigue tonight . . . please," she murmured.

"No more. I promise."

23

Friday, May 17

"Hold your horses," Laney shouted, yanking a comb through her wet curls as she ran down the hall. Glancing into the hall tree mirror, she saw the hated frizzles already drying at her temples.

She had overslept. By the time Gray had left, it had been after two and the confrontation with Jesse had played over and over in her mind, keeping her awake. She knew there was a connection between Tony, Nick, and Karl, but she still didn't know what it was. If she could find the link, perhaps it would shed some light on Cara's death.

The bell rang for the fourth time as she opened the door. "All right. What's the hurry?"

Gray and a little bald man with a pockmarked face and handlebar mustache were standing on the porch. "Oh-my-gosh. I forgot you were coming. I'm sorry, Mr. Hobble. Come on in."

Gray followed the locksmith into the hall and while Laney gave him instructions, Gray disappeared into the kitchen. It was fifteen minutes before she joined Gray.

"I had to go out to his truck and look at some of his locks. Looks like he won't have to go to town for any of the replacement locks. I told him I wanted dead bolts on all the doors. Oh good, you fixed coffee," Laney said.

"Stopped by to tell you that Unreasonable is back in heat," Gray said, pouring two cups of coffee.

"That's bad, right?"

"That means she didn't get in foal on her first cover so she'll have to go back to the breeding shed," Gray explained.

"Did you tell Jackson?"

"He's not here. Went to Maryland for the Preakness."

"He what? He didn't tell me," Laney said, recollecting the last time she had seen him at the awkward dinner at his cottage. He probably was too embarrassed to see me so soon, she thought.

"Who is taking care of the horses?" Laney asked, suddenly anxious about their care.

"Aaron Sloan. Apparently Jackson had this trip planned for some time. Aaron says he goes every year and he'd lined him up over a month ago."

"How long has he been gone?"

"Left some time early yesterday. Aaron said he was gone when he got here. He called me first thing this morning after he teased Unreasonable. She was showing interest in Applejack yesterday morning. Today, she has almost a three-centimeter follicle on the right. Just took a culture." Gray finished his coffee and poured a second cup. "Aaron's competent enough, although he's terribly shy. Wouldn't hurt if you called the breeding shed and booked Unreasonable for him," Gray suggested.

"What do I do?" Laney asked.

"Aaron will help you, but I suggest you do it right away if you want to get her booked for tomorrow afternoon."

"This makes me nervous, Gray. I really don't know anything about horses, except a little about foaling . . . thanks to Jackson."

Gray scrounged around in the refrigerator and pulled out a sack of sesame seed bagels and a tub of margarine. "Be good experience for you."

"They look kind of stale, Gray. Let me." Laney sliced two bagels, spread them with a little margarine, and toasted them in the toaster oven. While they were hot, she spread them with crunchy peanut butter and topped them with fresh peach slices. Another minute in the oven, and they melted into a wonderful nutty-smelling, gooey treat.

Gray noshed both of his and one of Laney's. "I have a call at Jason's farm. Hate to eat and run. Talk at you later." He gave Laney a sticky peanut butter kiss and let himself out.

Laney threw a pink scarf around her still damp hair and pulled out her horsy jacket from the hall closet. Cara had given it to her last spring when she'd complained she didn't have anything appropriate to wear on the farm. It had seen better days but the rough woolen tweed didn't show the soil and it had a comforting British warmth. That it had belonged to her sister made it dear to her.

The morning was cool and windy with specks of azure peeking out from behind the fast disappearing gray clouds. Maybe the spring storms are finally over, Laney hoped. In the yard, catkins hung from the wild cherry trees and wagged to and fro like little kitten tails in the breeze. When she saw that Jackson had returned her bike to the wrought iron stand before he had left for Maryland, she opted for the bike instead of the Whooptie.

Aaron met her in front of the office. He was a muscular young man with short blond hair and bright green eyes that crinkled his upper cheeks into tiny fans when he smiled. Laney introduced herself. He blushed furiously and avoided her eyes when she shook his hand.

"Now Aaron, you're going to have to help me book this mare. I've never done this before."

"Miss McVey, I'll tell you what I know," he said.

"Please call me Laney."

Laney followed Aaron into the office. He handed her a notebook with "Teasing Records" printed across the cover. "This is Jackson's book for the mares on the farm. He keeps track of the daily teasing results." He opened to the page with "Unreasonable" printed at the top. "You can see that today is the seventeenth day since she was bred to Captain Jim at Wilmere Stud."

The entry read: bred, April thirtieth, eight-thirty a.m. Good cover.

That it was only seventeen days since her sister's death flashed through Laney's mind.

Aaron's voice interrupted her thoughts, "When Dr. Prescott palpated her this morning, he said to book her for tomorrow afternoon, if you can get it."

"Where do I call?" Laney asked, and Aaron pointed to the phone number next to the name of the farm.

Laney sat down at the desk. She noticed a large stain that went through the whole notebook and recalled spilling her wine the night that Red Dust foaled.

Laney lifted the phone and dialed. "This is Stoney Creek Farm. I'd like to book a mare," she said. She gave the secretary at Wilmere Stud the name of the mare and the stud she would be bred to and told her it would be her second cover.

"Uh-oh." Laney put her hand over the phone. "She said Captain Jim is booked tomorrow afternoon. The earliest she can give us is Sunday morning."

"Take it," Aaron said.

"That was easy enough," Laney said when she hung up the phone. "She's booked for Sunday morning at eight-thirty. Will that be too late?"

"You can only take what they have. If we miss her, we can try again next heat."

Laney sighed. "There's a lot to this horse business, but you know, I kind of like it. I may go with you Sunday morning. Okay with you?"

Aaron's cheeks suddenly blotched with irregular circles of color, reaching an alarming shade of rose. "S . . . sure, Miss Laney. Be ready no later than seven-thirty. I . . . I'll pick you up as I swing by the house."

Laney wondered why Aaron was so ill at ease when she said she would accompany him to breeding shed. She found out soon enough.

24

Late Friday Morning, May 17

Maddy was sliding a canoe into the water as Laney swung into the Hickory Dock parking lot. Laney parked the Whooptie and hurried to help her mother. Her mother grinned at her and turned to help an older couple fasten their life jackets. The creek was a bit muddy from the storm the night before but it wasn't out of its banks. A soft breeze rippled the surface.

"Stay fairly close to the banks and you'll be just fine," Maddy said, as she and Laney steadied the canoe while the couple climbed in. When they were settled with their paddles, Maddy gave the boat a small shove and the gray-haired woman smiled at them as they glided off downstream. "Have fun," Maddy called.

Laney put her arm around her mother as they walked to the house. "You love doing this, don't you?"

Her mother tucked a wisp of her graying red hair under her floppy-brimmed knit hat and grinned at her daughter. "I really do. I can't imagine doin anything else."

"Can we go inside? I need to talk to you about something," Laney said, remembering why she had come.

A worried expression crossed Maddy's face. "Sure."

Laney looked warily around the dock as they climbed the steps to the deck.

"He's not here, Laney," Maddy said.

"Where is he?"

"I don't know. He barely speaks to me."

"That's no way to live, Mother."

"I know," Maddy said, as they entered the kitchen.

"What are you going to do?"

Her mother sat down at the table while Laney poured two mugs of coffee. "I don't know."

Laney sat across from Maddy and took her hands. "I'm worried to death about you. I'm going to be up front with you about what's been going on, because it involves Karl."

Maddy's eyes flared with ready anger as she prepared to jump on Karl's band wagon once more. She snatched her hands from Laney's.

"Mother, please don't say anything before I'm through," Laney demanded, her jaw tightening with impatience.

Maddy cast down her eyes and began turning her mug around and around.

"Mother, this will hurt, but it should have been said a long time ago."

Laney began with the affair that Karl had had with Cara one month after he and Maddy had married. She told her how Gray had paid for the abortion in order to spare Maddy from hearing the truth.

Maddy continued to rotate the coffee mug. When Laney reached across the table to remove her mother's hat so she could see her eyes better, Maddy didn't move.

Laney continued, "I learned about Cara's abortion last year when I was here. But at that time, Cara told me it had been Gray's child."

That got her mother's attention. "Why would Cara lie to you?" Maddy asked.

"Gray said Cara probably wanted to scare me away from him before he told me the truth. It worked for a while. I ran back to Pittsburgh."

"Why did he tell you now?" Maddy still looked unconvinced.

Laney let out a sigh, hesitated, then continued, "Because I just wouldn't believe some things I've found out about my sister."

The mug stopped. "What things?"

Laney reached into her jacket pocket and pulled out the manila envelope. She shook out the letters and the ad.

"What are these?" Maddy asked guardedly.

Laney separated the ad from the letters and handed it to her mother. Maddy read quickly and tossed it back at Laney. "Cara placed this ad, didn't she?" Maddy asked impassively.

"Yes."

"And those are the letters she got from men." It wasn't a question, but a straightforward statement.

Laney paused. "You don't seem surprised by this."

Maddy looked away. Laney swept the mugs away with the back of her hand and took hold of her mother's trembling fingers. Maddy was quiet for a long moment. When she spoke again, Laney couldn't believe what she was hearing.

"Everyone thought Cara was charmin and perfect. But, if the truth be told, Cara only cared about herself. It was an act . . . a role she was playin." Maddy sighed, like it was coming from the deepest part of her. "She was always lookin for applause . . . like she was actin out her life on a stage. But I knew her behind the scenes." A veil seemed to drop over her eyes like the final curtain. She blinked it away and glanced at Laney. "She even had you fooled."

"Mother, this was your daughter," Laney protested.

Maddy's voice was thick with suffering as she spoke, "She was so beautiful and she knew how to use it. She would flirt . . . you know . . . seductive like. Sometimes she flaunted her body. She wanted everyone to love her. Especially men."

Laney was incredulous.

"She would go with a man until she got what she wanted, then strike him off the list if someone else came along. Think about it, Laney–all the men she had in her short life."

"But she was married to Joe for seven years." But as soon as she said the words, Laney recalled Gray telling her that after Cara had gotten pregnant by Karl and had had the abortion, she'd dropped Gray and married Joe Collins.

"Laney, I know of two, maybe three men that she saw while she was married to Joe. There were probably more."

"My God."

"Gray was probably right, honey. She didn't want you to know that she wasn't perfect. It was easy with you livin away all those years."

Laney was beginning to believe her mother. "Did you ever say anything to her?"

"Everyone has the right to live their life the way they want." Maddy got that far-away look again. "And I guess I blamed myself a little for the way she was."

"You?"

"After your father died–and to be honest, even before–Cara was my whole life. I've often wondered if my dotin on her . . . all that attention . . . made her expect that from everyone when she was grown. It was like she didn't feel limited in any way . . . almost like she didn't have a conscience."

Laney was astonished at her mother's insight. Recalling her mother's obsessive focus on her sister, Laney realized with surprise that she had never resented the extra attention Maddy had showered on Cara. In fact, perhaps her own unconditional love for Cara, had contributed to her sister's limitless lifestyle.

Laney could tell her mother had nothing further to add. "Mother, there is more I have to tell you. A man named Tony Richards was murdered about the same time that Cara died. Cara was dating him. He was one of the men that answered her ad." Laney passed Tony's letter over to her mother along with the photo of him in front of the Camaro Z28.

Maddy's voice was barely a whisper. "Murdered? I never met him. You don't think that Cara–"

"I don't want to think there's a connection, but look at this." Laney opened Nick's letter to Jesse and gave her Nick's photograph.

After a brief glance, Maddy thrust the photo back at Laney. "Nick Owens." Her mouth twisted his name. "Tell me Cara didn't date this nasty man."

"You know him? How? Where?"

Maddy scrambled to her feet and stood at the sink, her back to Laney.

"Please, tell me," Laney cried, breathing in tiny sips of air.

"He's a friend of Karl's."

"How do you know this?"

"He was here Derby Day. He brought a boat here for Karl to take to Jake."

Laney sprung to her feet and crossed over to Maddy. "Jake? Jake who?" Laney asked, spinning her mother around to face her.

"I don't know his last name."

"Where was Karl supposed to take the boat?" Laney placed her hands on her mother's shoulders and looked directly into her eyes. "This is important."

"When I asked that Nick character the same question, he told me to mind my own damn business, but I did hear him tell Karl to call him when he got back from Frankfort."

"Frankfort?" Laney's head was spinning. "Are you sure this is a picture of Nick Owens?" Laney asked.

"His face isn't very clear in the picture, but he looks just as mean as I remember him," Maddy said, studying the photo again. "But those boots. I'd remember them anywhere."

"Mother, do you remember what kind of boat it was?" Laney held her breath.

"I sure do. It was a white runabout with a green stripe down the hull. Pretty thing."

Laney pushed the air out with a swoosh. "Mother, Jake Rudnik was arrested this week on drug trafficking. The police found a huge amount of cocaine in another boat he was hauling."

"Good Lord, Laney. Karl has delivered several boats to Jake. Do you think Karl is involved in drugs?" Maddy sat down hard as though her legs wouldn't hold her another second.

"He could be involved in more than drugs," Laney said, and told her mother about the doll-slashing, Blackberry, and Karl's alibi not holding up at Bailey's Warehouse.

It was all too much for Maddy. Her face paled and she crumpled into tears. "If he wasn't at the warehouse that mornin, where could he have been?" Something in Laney's face told her. "Laney . . . no . . . it was an accident," Maddy sobbed.

"There's more but I won't go into it now. Enough said. You must not confront Karl with any of this. It could be dangerous for both of us. Do you promise?"

"Yes," Maddy murmured and rushed into the bathroom. Laney heard her retching.

When Natine led Laney into the infirmary, Blackberry struggled to her feet to greet her.

"Gray thinks she'll be ready to go home some time this weekend," Natine said, as she unlatched the cage so that Laney could give Blackberry another dose of adoration.

"Golly, but I've missed you, girl," Laney said between hugs and kisses and slurps. "I wish I could take you home right this minute."

Turning to Natine, she asked, "Why can't I?"

Gray said there's some infection in the wound. Another day and you can continue the antibiotics at home," Natine explained.

"Nothing wrong with her tongue," Laney laughed, wiping her cheek.

"She's a sweetheart."

"Where's Gray? On a call?" Laney asked, shutting and latching the door reluctantly.

"He'd better be. Billy James has called twice about a cow prolapse. I told him Gray was on the way."

"I'm going home. I'm beat. If you talk to him, tell him I booked Unreasonable for Sunday morning. I couldn't get anything earlier. I'm going to the breeding shed with Aaron."

"Sounds as though you and the boss have been keeping some late hours lately," Natine said with a twinkle in her eyes.

"It's not what you're thinking. Wish it were," Laney said with a troubled sigh.

25

Friday Afternoon, May 17

"What's going on?" Gray stood in the doorway of the sheriff's office in the St. Clair County courthouse.

It was a high-ceilinged room with narrow dark oak wainscoting traveling a third of the way up the walls. The crazed plaster above was painted a putty gray that matched the metal desk, the file cabinets, the tubular chairs, the worn carpeting and the dusty venetian blinds. The only spot of color was sagging red tulips in a gray mustard jar on the window sill behind Gordon's desk.

"Shut the door, will you, Doc?" Gordon asked from a creaky chair behind the desk.

Gordon waited while Gray closed the heavy door to a larger room where Nancy West, a sheriff's department deputy, sat behind another gray desk doing her nails.

Gordon motioned for Gray to take a seat. "I asked you to come in because there are several developments in the Tony Richard's murder case that may involve persons in this county," Gordon said.

Gray raised his eyebrows.

"I don't usually discuss police business with anyone outside the department, but in this case, I think maybe you can help me."

"How's that?" Gray asked, sitting back in his chair and crossing his ankle over his thigh.

"Did you read the article in the *Lexington Post* on Wednesday about a Jake Rudnik getting busted for drug trafficking?"

"Sure did."

"Seems this Rudnik fellow is a buddy of our upright citizen, Karl Webster." Gordon spoke the words like he had a bad taste in his mouth. He paused and looked at Gray. "You seem surprised at my open dislike of the man."

"I have no fondness for vermin," Gray said.

"I can't imagine how Maddy stomachs him. That brings me to why I asked you here."

"Shoot."

"This Rudnik guy spilled his guts to the Franklin County police. He implicated Karl in almost every aspect of the drug scheme."

"No," Gray exclaimed.

"He thinks he'll save his ass by cooperating with the police," Gordon said sarcastically.

"What did he tell them?"

"I can't give you details, but I can say this much. Some guy named Nick Owens was a partner of Tony Richards, the man who was murdered in Lexington."

"Yeah?" Gray perked up.

"Nick Owens and Tony Richards owned a RV dealership together and sold boats as a side line."

"How does this tie in with Rudnik?" Gray said, anxious for a connection.

"I'm getting to that. Nick bought pleasure boats in Atlanta and hauled them to Lexington." Gordon smiled. "Nothing irregular about that, huh?"

"Then why do I smell a rat?" Gray said, playing along.

" 'Cause occasionally, one had a bilge stuffed to the yin-yang with coke."

"Thought most cocaine was smuggled in planes that landed on small air strips," Gray said.

"We think that's how the cocaine got as far as Georgia. Nick would pick a boat up after it was outfitted to take the coke. Feds think Nick was one of the mules to get the dope as far as Central Kentucky."

"So, Nick hauled a boat to Lexington. Then what?" Gray asked.

"Nick would deliver the boat to his RV lot. The occasional one that was hiding coke in its hull was taken to our friend Karl Webster at Hickory Dock."

"And our good citizen, Karl? . . . "

"Would haul the boat to Frankfort where his buddy, Rudnik, would take it north to some town or city on the Ohio River. Actually, Karl and Rudnik were just small-time spokes in a bigger wheel."

Gray scratched his head and sat forward in his seat. "A regular relay team. Seems like a lot of runners with their fingers in the pie."

"Evidently. And that relay system may have been Tony Richard's undoing."

"How's that?"

"According to Rudnik, Tony took a liking to one of the boats that Nick brought up from Georgia and decided to keep it for himself."

Remembering Jesse's conversation the night before, Gray thought he could put his money on what was coming next.

"Tony put the boat in a storage unit in Lexington that he shared with Nick, unaware that it was loaded with cocaine. At least we think he was unaware."

Gordon stood and walked around the desk and sat on the corner facing Gray. "Tony didn't want to let the boat go and Lexington police think Tony and Nick may have gotten into an argument and Nick shot him and stuffed his body in the freezer."

"Either that or Tony found out about the drugs and Nick killed him to shut him up."

"Yeah."

"What happened to the loaded boat?" Gray asked.

"Police don't know. It wasn't in the storage unit when they found Tony's body."

Gray recalled Randi telling them that Nick had sold the boat. That seemed unlikely now.

"Maybe Nick took the boat to Karl after he shot Tony," Gordon said. "The Feds are still questioning Rudnik. After a few more odds and ends are cleared up, there should be a couple more arrests."

"I just may have some of the ends you're looking for, Gordon." Gray said.

"If you have anything that can help put these guys away, I'm all ears."

A quick double knock and Freddie peeked in the door. "Nancy said Doc was in here. I have some news for both of you."

"C'mon in and shut the door," Gordon said, and when Freddie settled his girth into the other chair, Gordon asked, "Whatta ya got?"

"That bullet Doc took out of Blackberry . . ."

"Yeah? Gordon said.

"It came from the same gun that killed Tony Richards."

The hair on Gray's arms and neck stood at attention. "Then the person that killed Tony, shot Blackberry!" he shouted.

"Don't jump to conclusions," Gordon said. "Two different people could have used the same gun."

"Either way, Laney could be in danger. She's already been threatened." Gray winced as he remembered his promise to Laney.

"What kind of threat?" Gordon was on his feet.

"Someone with a key entered the house on Tuesday and violently stabbed Laney's doll with a butcher knife."

Freddie looked over at Gray. "The doll that looked like Cara?"

"How did you know about the doll?" Gray asked suspiciously.

"We searched the house on Monday. Didn't Laney tell you?" Freddie said.

"Forgot. Anyway, the doll had red food coloring, like blood, smeared all around the knife and its hair had been pulled out by the roots. Looked like the person who did it must have blown his cork."

"Why didn't Laney report it?" Gordon asked angrily.

"Told her to, but she's been doing this little investigation on her own–" Gray began.

"Damn it! She could get herself killed," Gordon spouted, then settled and chewed a cheek. "What did she find out?" he mumbled from a hand covering his mouth.

Gray suppressed a smile. "Quite a lot, actually. And when I went to Florence, I–"

"Not you, too! Who do you guys think you are? Nick and Nora Charles?"

"Don't get in a lather, Gordon. Listen to what we've got."

Gray settled back in his chair and let it all out–Laney and Maddy's inheritance, the missing will, the ads and letters, Cara and Jesse dating Tony and Nick, Karl's offer to buy the farm, and Randi and Jesse's conversations about the boat in the rental unit in Lexington.

He didn't tell Gordon about Jesse breaking in or Laney's suspicions that Cara's death wasn't an accident. He just wasn't ready to accept Laney's theory that Cara was murdered. Not yet, anyway.

When Gray was finished, Freddie lifted himself out of his chair and loosened his belt a notch. "Hey Gordon, why don't you deputize those two?"

Gordon ignored him. "Doc, this drug operation would explain how Karl had the funds to make an offer on the farm."

"That's what I'm thinking. And when Laney turned him down, maybe he thought shooting Blackberry would scare her into selling," Gray said.

"Then the doll-stabbing . . . one more threat to get her to sell," Gordon added.

"Maddy had a key to the house. He could have used hers or had a copy made for himself," Gray said. "But if he stole Cara's gun, that makes him a suspect in Tony's death, doesn't it?"

"It could, but now with Nick, Rudnik and Karl connected in this drug operation, anyone could have gotten hold of the gun. If we could find the gun, it might answer some questions."

"I hope she had the locks changed after the incident with the doll," Freddie ventured.

"Hobble's changing them as we speak," Gray said.

"Now, Sherlock, what did you find out in Florence?" Gordon asked.

"What?"

"You were about to divulge the results of your snooping," Gordon snapped.

"Discovered Rudnik lied to your detective friend, Ben Smith. Karl wasn't at the warehouse the morning Cara died."

"Son of a . . . ," Gordon began.

"And Rudnik didn't bid on those paddle boats Derby Day either. He's banned from the warehouse."

"Why's that?"

"Bailey caught him lifting some tools a while back," Gray said.

Gordon slammed his fist on the desk. "Dammit!" A couple of reports slid off the desk and fluttered to the floor.

"Think we can arrest Karl on what we've got?" Freddie asked.

"We're close. I'm worried about Maddy if Karl gets cornered. Laney too. I don't want him to know we're on to him."

"He's probably already read the article about Rudnik getting arrested–if the guy can read," Gray said.

"Yeah, but we're keeping Rudnik's confession under wraps. You understand?" Gordon said.

"Can I tell Laney? Think she should be forewarned, don't you?"

"Okay, but hold off telling Maddy. I don't think she would warn Karl, but he's her husband and she's never reported any of his abuse in the past."

"Laney said he roughed her up again this week."

Gordon's face darkened. "He won't get a chance to do it again, if I have anything to do with it," Gordon said. He was quiet for a moment, trying to get his rage under control. "Doc, you didn't think to handle that knife so that we might lift some prints, did you?"

Gray was aware that his smile was cocky. "Just might have worn surgical gloves and dropped it into a paper bag."

Gordon's pale brows leaped. "Now, I'm impressed. Mind dropping it off? I'd love to add breaking and entering and vandalism to that growing list of charges against Karl."

26

Saturday Morning, May 18

As Gray open the door to his vet truck, he waved at Jeff Irwin who was loading his cattle into the gooseneck trailer parked adjacent to him. Climbing into the Jeep, his eyes swept the dash. Empty.

"Meow."

Gray's gaze shifted to the floor of the truck. Puccini, curled around the brake pedal, looked like a gray floor mat.

"What's gotten into you?" Glancing out the passenger window, Gray spotted the problem. Jeff's boxer, Morgana, was guarding Jeff's trailer from the vantage point of a built-in toolbox in the bed of the pickup.

Morgana was sixty-five pounds of pure muscle with a massive head and undershot jaw. Her graying muzzle looked like it had been flattened by a two-by-four and her neck rippled power. Her menacing head barely turned and she gave Gray the bad-eye. Scooping Puccini from the floor, Gray felt him stiffen. He dropped him onto the dash and started the engine.

"Terrorized by that hateful old bat, are you?" Gray laughed to the cat, remembering how Puccini had bullied Blackberry earlier in the week. "Serves you right."

Gray had just ear-tagged and vaccinated a small herd of cattle for his friend, Jeff, at the stockyards. It hadn't taken as long as he thought it might and he was looking forward to the rest of Saturday off.

Maybe Laney would have dinner and go to a movie with him later. He couldn't wait to tell her about the latest on Karl and Nick.

He circled the wide gravel lot and stopped at the end of the long driveway to wait for a dump truck to pass before turning left onto Hamilton Road.

What happened next was a blur in slow motion. A flash of white light. An earsplitting explosion. The sound of glass shattering. A rush of hot air as the window let go, followed by the tinkling of glass shards as they spewed over the interior of the Jeep. Gray's shout mingled with the howl from a gray body hurtling through the air. Something tore at his face and when he reached upward, his hands came away wet. The slippery, furry body of Puccini clung in a death grip. "Oh, God, I can't see," Gray cried.

The phone was ringing as Laney stepped out of the tub. She snatched a towel on the way into her bedroom and picked up the phone.

"Mother, what's wrong?" Laney said, when she heard sobs over the line.

"Laney, please come over. The police were just here," Maddy's voice cracked.

"Police? What did they want?"

"I can't talk anymore. I'm afraid Karl's coming back." She hung up.

Laney pulled on a pair of jeans and jerked a fuchsia sweatshirt over her head. She wondered what the police had been doing at the dock. Had they finally accumulated enough evidence to arrest Karl?

Laney snatched her new key off the kitchen counter and raced barefoot out the French door to the screened porch, stopping only to check that it was secure. She raced to the buggy house where she had parked the Whooptie after visiting Natine the day before. With her adrenaline flowing, the doors slid open effortlessly. Throwing her sneakers onto the passenger seat she jumped into the Whooptie.

Only when her hands clutched the steering wheel, did Laney deflate. She lowered her head until her forehead was resting on the back of her hands. A familiar heavy fog moved into her head, threatening to block out the reality of the moment.

She turned the key and the engine hummed. Through the entrance she drove, passing the paddock where Unreasonable had cribbed the fence. Ahead of her, a bluebird flew down the lane as though caught in a wind tunnel of green trees. Laney's foot hit the accelerator like it was weighted. For a second she thought she would overtake the bird before he could escape from the channel. She was almost upon him before he grabbed his opportunity and darted upward through an opening in the trees.

Somehow, Laney mustered the courage to drive to Hickory Dock. Karl's green pickup was parked by the deck to the house. She saw the kitchen door slam behind the screen door as she nudged the truck's bumper. Still barefoot, she leaped from the car. "God, please let Mother be all right," she choked aloud. She heard her mother's desperate cry from inside the house. Bounding up the stairs to the deck, she burst through the door.

Two figures stood at the kitchen sink, and for a second, Laney's eyes couldn't adjust to the dimness of the room. But in a blink, the image of Karl's upraised hand ready to strike her mother registered, and she reacted instinctively. Laney lunged at her stepfather like a striking rattlesnake. Her nails were deadly fangs that raked across his face. Vivid tracks of blood followed her fingers. Karl's little eyes shrank to black gashes of contempt when he saw who had assaulted him.

"You little bitch!" he yelled, and thrust his fist brutally into Laney's stomach.

A heaving rush of air flew out of Laney's mouth and she crumpled to the floor. At the same moment, she heard her mother scream and a commotion at the door. Laney's arms flailed about her body as she fought to get her breath. Just as she thought she would fall unconscious for lack of air, she caught her breath with a loud whooping gulp. By taking hold of the kitchen chair, she dragged herself to her knees. As her eyes refocused, Gordon and Freddie were handcuffing Karl, and another officer was holding a gun on him. Maddy reached Laney's side and helped her to her feet.

"Laney, are you all right?" Gordon called.

Laney managed a nod and Maddy sat her down in a chair.

"Gordon, how did you know that he was here?" Maddy sobbed.

"We weren't gone, Maddy. We were staked out up the street. We saw him drive through the gate and Laney go in almost right behind him." Karl struggled against the cuffs, his face fiery with fury and blood. Freddie and the other officer led him out the door. "Read him his rights," Gordon called to his deputies.

Maddy, on her knees, held on to her daughter with both arms. Gordon crossed over to them and placed his hand on Maddy's shoulder. "Maddy, I have to go. Explain to Laney what I told you earlier, and Laney, I may need a statement from you about this incident." He paused, then added, "Karl Webster won't hurt either of you again."

Laney looked up into Gordon's severe face–his crooked nose and deep parenthesis enclosing his stern mouth. His gray-green eyes caressed her mother with a surprising tenderness. He's in love with her, she thought. Somehow, the realization gave her comfort.

Gordon and the other officers were gone. Through the screen door, Laney saw a couple of fishermen loading their johnboat onto a small trailer at the boat ramp.

"Are you sure you're not hurt, honey?" Maddy asked.

"Mother, this has to be the fourth time you've asked. I'm sore, but I'll be fine. Now what did Gordon want you to tell me?" Laney asked, as she filled the teakettle from the tap.

"It's what you said. Karl was mixed up in that drug thing."

"Mixed up how?"

"Gordon came here earlier lookin for Karl. They were goin to arrest him for drug traffickin or somethin."

"How did they learn that?"

"I asked the same thing. He said he couldn't say right now."

The police must have gotten enough evidence for an arrest somewhere, Laney thought, as she spooned loose tea into her mother's ironstone teapot. When the kettle began to sing, she poured the boiling water into the teapot to steep. "Mother, why did Karl try to hit you?"

"Someone must have told him they saw the police car here earlier. I guess he thought I had called them."

"Why would he think that?" Laney asked.

Before Maddy averted her gaze, Laney caught her look of guilt.

"This mornin, I happened to mention to Karl about readin about some guy bein arrested for haulin cocaine in a boat."

"Mother, you didn't read that. I told you that and you promised you wouldn't tell Karl," Laney scolded.

"I just wanted to see what he would say."

Laney poured the tea into pink flowered teacups and passed the sugar to her mother.

"So when he heard the police were here earlier, Karl thought you had made a connection and had called them?"

"Just before you came abustin in here, he accused me of callin them. Laney, what if Gordon hadn't got here in time?" Maddy dropped her spoon onto the saucer with a clink.

"Mother, it's over. He's gone. Try to relax." Laney retrieved a plate of sliced lemon from the refrigerator and removed the cellophane. Before she could sit down, the phone rang.

Putting the wall phone to her ear, Laney heard a breathless voice say her name. "Natine?" Laney asked.

"Finally. I had hoped you were at your mother's. I've already tried the farm."

"You're in a wad. What's wrong?" Laney's heart sank. "Blackberry, she's not–"

"It's not Blackberry. Gray–"

"My God, what's happened? Gray's not–"

"Laney, stop, for heaven's sake. Let me finish," Natine said crossly.

Laney took a quivery breath and let Natine continue.

"There's been an accident–"

"Oh God!"

"There you go again. He's all right, Laney. I swear he is, so don't get yourself all torn up."

"Thank God. Where is he?"

"He's in the emergency room getting a couple of stitches."

"Stitches? I thought you said he's okay." Laney couldn't stop her mouth.

"Laney, what's going on? What's wrong with Gray?" Maddy interrupted.

Laney put her hand over the phone. "Gray was in an accident. He's okay. Just stitches."

"Which hospital? Hickory Memorial?" Laney asked into the phone.

"Yes, he asked if you could pick him and Puccini up."

"Is Puccini okay?"

"Yes, Laney. I guess he had his seat belt on." Natine quipped condescendingly.

"Funny. Would you call the hospital and tell Gray I'll be right over?"

Laney hung up and took a big swig of tea. "I have to pick up Gray. Will you be all right?"

"Yes, honey. Call me when you get home," Maddy said, walking Laney to the door. "Excitin week, huh?" she added.

Laney bent over and kissed her mother on the cheek. "You don't know the half of it," she said, as she dashed out the screen door in her bare feet.

When Laney arrived at the emergency entrance of the hospital, she could see Gray sitting in a chair in the hallway just inside the double doors. She pushed through the doors and stood in front of him. His eyes were closed. The back of his head rested against the wall. A lock of brown hair partially covered a white bandage on his forehead and a couple of deep scratches, painted orange along one cheek, made him look like he was wearing war paint. His arms were crossed over his favorite beige and blue windbreaker, now stained with blood. A suspicious swelling in the chest area satisfied Laney's curiosity about Puccini's whereabouts. As though reading her thoughts, a black nose and one copper eye peeked out from above the zipper.

Suddenly aware of her presence, Gray's eyes opened. "There you are," he said, straightening in his chair and tucking Puccini's nose back down in his jacket and zipping it higher.

"You look like a size forty-four D," Laney said, as she bent over to kiss Gray on the lips, moaning as the aftereffects from Karl's punch grabbed her diaphragm.

"What's all that about?" Gray asked, a frown clouding his features.

"Long story . . . another time . . . you first."

"My windshield exploded."

Laney sank down in the chair next to Gray. "Windshields don't just explode, Gray."

"This one did. Fortunately, the safety glass kept me from getting cut. The glass just seemed to melt into all these rounded pieces and showered me, the truck and Puccini."

"How did you keep control of the Jeep?"

"I wasn't moving. Must have been a rock or something that flew out of a passing truck. Puccini was so scared, he turned into a damn flying squirrel and ripped into my face." He pointed to the bandage and the deep scratches.

The image of Puccini slamming onto Gray's face was so vivid, Laney's eyes began to water and she could feel her mouth beginning to draw into a smile. Please don't let me burst into laughter, she said to herself and turned her head away.

"This is just tearing you up, isn't it?" Gray said, his feelings hurt.

"I can't help it," Laney said, exploding into a giggle.

Stepping out of the emergency room office, a severe looking nurse with legs like fence posts gave them a dour glare. Pivoting, she marched back into the office.

Gray leaped out of his chair. "Let's get out of here before she calls the humane society and they confiscate Puccini. After I got stitched up, I smuggled Puccini into the men's room and washed the blood off him. 'Nurse Ratched,' there, followed me in–can you believe that?–and read me the riot act."

Once inside the Whooptie, Gray unzipped his jacket and his cat sprung out and landed on the dash. He sniffed around–Blackberry territory here. Satisfied that nothing had ever claimed the dash, he settled down to wash his damp matted fur.

Laney put her arms around Gray and gave him a tender kiss. "I'm sorry I laughed at you. You could have been killed. Where's the Jeep?"

"At Jay's Station, waiting to get a new windshield. I had it towed. Jeff Irwin drove me here in his truck, and if we weren't a sight–fifteen head of cattle, that mean momma boxer, one wounded vet and a bloody cat."

"Want to go home?"

"I do. I need to talk to you but it can wait."

She pulled into the clinic parking lot. Gray looked so exhausted. She decided that her story about Karl's arrest could wait until tomorrow, too.

Gray gathered up his sleeping tabby and with the cat between them, he kissed her on the mouth. "I love you," he said. Nodding at Laney's bare feet, he added, "Nice touch."

When Gray turned into Jay's Station, he saw Gordon already parked in front of a cyclone fenced area where Jay parked vehicles waiting to be repaired. Gordon hopped out of his car and waited for the pink Buick to come to a stop behind his patrol car.

As Gordon walked back to the Buick, Gray was surprised to see that he was dressed in civvies–a navy polo shirt and a pair of jeans. The shirt was pulled taut across his wiry but well-built chest. He wore a Cincinnati Red's baseball cap over his graying dishwater blond hair.

"Sorry you had to come out on a Saturday afternoon, but Jeff Irwin said I should report it."

"It's okay. I'm on call on the weekend anyway. The station has been crazy. Say, Puccini really did a number on you, or did you have a fight with Laney?" Gordon cracked.

"I could have been killed," Gray said without a hint of a grin. Puccini slept on the dash.

Jay called to Gray from the station door, "I unlocked the gate. Gordon has the key to your Jeep."

They found his Cherokee parked between a Plymouth Voyager with a busted headlight and a Chevrolet pickup with a front bumper dangling by a thread. Jay had thrown a small tarp over the windshield to keep out the weather.

When Gray flung the tarp aside, Gordon gasped, "You're right about that. If you had been on the road, you probably would have lost control."

Gray had been so upset after the accident, he had forgotten how frightening the damage appeared. The center of the windshield was completely gone. Framing the gaping hole was a nine-inch mosaic of glass. Broadcast throughout the front of the Jeep and over the dash were hundreds of tiny rounded pieces of glass.

Gordon unlocked the driver's side door and bent down to look over the interior of the vehicle. Except for the glass and a blood-soaked paper towel on the passenger seat, the seats were empty. The floor-board on the driver's side was covered with dried mud, manure, and a sprinkling of glass particles. Gordon suddenly straightened and walked around the front of the Jeep to the passenger door and unlocked it. Like a puppy, Gray followed.

Gray watched while Gordon reached into his pant's pocket and removed a penknife. He pulled out a worn blade and moved his head and shoulders into the cab. A minute later, he emerged.

"Well, lookie here," he said, holding an object between his fingers.

Gray held out his hand and Gordon dropped it into his palm.

"A slug," Gray cried.

"I dug it out of the back cushion of the seat."

Leaning over, Gray could see the small hole in the upholstery, only inches from where he had been sitting.

"Looks like another thirty-eight," Gordon said.

Gray felt queasy. "Think it was meant for me?"

"Unless it was a random drive-by shooting."

"Who would do something like this in broad daylight?"

"Someone who just didn't give a damn if he got caught. What time did this happen?"

Gray's hand shook as he gave the bullet back to Gordon. "About nine this morning."

"Tell me exactly how it happened," Gordon said, as he threw the tarp back over the opening.

Gray explained as they walked slowly back to their cars. "I was out at the yards about eight o'clock to work a small herd for Jeff Irwin. Took about forty-five minutes. When I finished, I got into the truck and was waiting at the end of the drive for traffic to pass before turning left onto the highway. I remember seeing a dump truck pass and there may have been another vehicle right behind it. I can't be sure 'cause BAM, it blew. I thought maybe it was a rock or piece of gravel that flew out of the dump truck."

"Did you see the color or make of the second vehicle?" Gordon asked.

"Couldn't tell you. Too much flying around in there."

"What about before you worked the cattle? Did you notice anyone else in the lot?"

"There were several trucks and trailers. Always are a few, even if it isn't a sale day. I didn't notice anything unusual."

"Think it could be Karl? Maybe he heard you were snooping around in Florence. I didn't arrest him until about ten o'clock this morning."

"My God! Do Laney and Maddy know?"

"They were there."

Gray couldn't believe it. "I saw Laney this morning. She didn't tell me."

"I love couples that tell each other everything."

"Damn! After being attacked by this wildcat, I just wanted to go home." Gray reached into the window of his Buick and lifted Puccini from the dash.

"Laney got to the dock just before we did. We got there just as Karl gave Laney a stiff right to the gut."

Gray's stomach convulsed and his face turned hot like someone had turned the heat on. "I remember her hurting. Thoughtful son of a bitch, aren't I?"

"You're not the son of a bitch. Karl is."

"Why did he hit her?" Gray asked.

"She ran into the kitchen just as Karl was about to hit Maddy. Talk about wildcats. Laney raked his face open with her nails."

"Damn," Gray said, in wonder.

"I don't think he'll hit another woman for a long time."

"A long time isn't long enough. Listen, I'm going home and get some shuteye."

Gordon shook his head as Gray started up the Buick. "How in hell do you have the guts to drive that rosy reject?"

In answer, Gray smirked and drove away accompanied by a flourish of horns from Verdi's *Aida*.

27

Sunday Morning, May 19

Laney was hooking the last of the new house keys onto her key ring, when Aaron honked the horn on the horse van at exactly seven-thirty. Looking up, she peered at herself in the hall tree mirror. The dark circles were gone from under her eyes, but frown lines plowed her brow like furrows in a field of freckles. She smoothed the wrinkles with her fingers as she grabbed her horsy jacket off the hall tree and slipped it on over her white tee. After pausing to tie her sneakers, she twisted, lifted her jacket, and scanned her butt in the mirror. Her skintight jeans left nothing to the imagination. "Will have to scrunch the munch this week," she moaned. After locking the door behind her, she loped across the yard to where Aaron was waiting in the van.

"Beautiful day," Laney said. Aaron colored and nodded his head.

After stopping at Gray's clinic in Hickory to pick up the clean-culture certificate Gray had left in his mailbox, they were on their way.

The ride to Wilmere Stud took almost an hour. They passed through some of the most beautiful horse farm country in the world. Plank fencing undulated along the roadside like endless black and white roller coasters. Interspersed with the fencing were rugged gray limestone walls that were the original dividers of the land. Beyond these partitions, the incredibly lush bluegrass rolled over the paddocks, swept across the lawns of antebellum mansions, and spilled into ponds and streams.

Laney was captivated by it all. When she had left Kentucky to attend the University of Pittsburgh after graduating from high school, she'd never really thought of what she'd left behind. As a budding, callow teenager, all she wanted was the buzz and titillation of the city. Could she recapture the calm of the bucolic life that she'd known when her father had been alive?

During the trip, it was obvious that Aaron wasn't comfortable talking to her, but Laney managed to learn by the time they reached Wilmere Stud that Aaron was married and had a son, Eric, who was nine years old. His wife, Sally, worked as a sales associate for a real estate company in Hickory. Aaron had been night watching and working with horses ever since high school.

Aaron drove through the brick entrance to Wilmere Stud and followed the arrow signs to the breeding barn. After backing up next to another van, he shut off the engine.

Laney followed Aaron to the back of the van. After unlatching the rear door, he lowered it to make a ramp and snapped the wooden side rails in place. Unreasonable nickered softly and stomped the bed of the van, as though anxious to leave the truck. Aaron flipped the fiber mat over the ramp and said to Laney, "Better move to the side."

The gray mare pranced about as Aaron led her down the ramp, her chain shank jingling as she tossed her head. Her ears were perked and she looked from side to side. A young man with "Logan" embroidered in script across his shirt pocket, approached them with a clipboard and compared a name on the sheet of paper with the name on Unreasonable's halter. Aaron handed him the envelope embossed with Gray's letterhead.

"You back, old girl? Made it on time this time, did you now?" he remarked in a thick Irish brogue.

Another attendant took the shank from Aaron and led the mare to a padded area. The teaser was led over. Unreasonable immediately backed up to the teaser, squatted and urinated.

"She's ready," Aaron said to Laney and abruptly cleared his throat, nervously. He led Laney to an elevated partition near the entrance of the shed where they could view the breeding.

A couple of attendants wrapped the mare's tail with white gauze, and her genitalia was gently but thoroughly washed with a mild solution of soap and warm water.

Unreasonable was led to the mating area and a twitch was twisted about her upper lip. The mare handler controlled the tension on the loop of rope around her lip, by turning the attached wooden pole. One of the breeding crew bent her front leg and tightened a leather strap around it to prevent her from kicking. A leather apron was swung over her neck and strapped in place to keep the stallion from biting her. Without once looking at Laney, Aaron explained each step in the procedure.

As Captain Jim was led into the breeding shed by the stallion foreman, Laney watched mesmerized. The beautiful bay stallion approached Unreasonable from behind on the left side. He rubbed his nose over her rump and flank, and he sniffed at her genitalia. As he nuzzled her, he danced around the mare. By this time, the stallion was fully erect and as the stallion mounted Unreasonable, the tail handler moved her tail out of the way and guided his one and a half foot penis into the vulva. The stallion arched his neck and with his head down, grabbed hold of the leather-looped apron with his teeth. Laney glanced to her side, but Aaron was gone. She saw him standing in the entranceway to the barn, his complexion as rosy as sunburn. She felt her own face flushing and was glad he couldn't observe her own embarrassment. Turning back to the mating, she saw Captain Jim's tail flag up and down and he rested his head on the side of Unreasonable's neck, almost affectionately. In about ten seconds, the stallion dismounted and was led away to be washed for the afternoon breeding.

"Whew!" Laney said aloud, then looked around quickly, sure that Aaron had heard her exclamation. His neck and shoulders writhed and she caught his constrained smile.

The mare handler untied the leather strap around the mare's front leg and removed the apron from her neck. After the handler ripped off the tail wrap and gave several counter twists to the twitch to release the mare's lip, Aaron strode over and led her back to the horse van.

Aaron wasn't inclined to speak as he loaded the mare, and Laney, respecting his feelings, climbed into the cab of the truck without commenting. She sat thinking about the breeding while she watched Logan, who was standing in the shed entrance observing the final mare get bred to a roan stallion. Aaron hopped into the van and started the engine.

"Stop!" Laney yelled, as they eased away from the dock. Aaron slammed on the brakes and the van jerked to a halt with a clank. Unreasonable protested from the rear of the van with a whinny.

Laney shoved the heavy cab door open and jumped to the ground. She covered the short area to the entrance of the barn in a split second. "Logan!" she called as the Irishman began to walk into the barn.

"Logan!" she repeated. She was out of breath with excitement. "Could I talk to you a moment?"

His blue eyes held a puzzled look, but he stopped and waited for her.

"Your comment when you saw our mare . . . you said, 'made it on time this time.' What did you mean?" She gasped the question.

Logan hugged the clipboard to his chest and tucked a short red pencil behind his ear. "Your mare," he said, "was late for her first breeding."

"How late?" Laney asked, her heart thumping against her ribs like she had run a marathon.

"An hour late," he said, frowning. "She was booked for the eight-thirty breeding but your fellow didn't get her here until nine-thirty."

"How could that be?" Laney asked.

"I got a call about eight-thirty from your fellow . . . what's his name? . . . not this fellow," he said, nodding in the van's direction.

"Jackson . . . Jackson Burns," Laney spurted.

"Yes, he's the one. He said he had had a breakdown. Would be a little late. Came sailing in here at nine-thirty, he did. I was getting ready to cancel the breeding."

Laney's mind was racing, trying to remember what Gordon had said about Jackson's alibi.

"But I understand the record shows that she was bred at eight-thirty," Laney protested.

"You'll have to check about that in the office. The stallion foreman was hot, he was. I saw that man of yours slip him a little green. But don't let on I told you so, would you now?"

Laney thanked Logan and ran back to the van.

"I'll be a few more minutes, Aaron," she said through the open window, whirled and thundered through a door with "Office" printed on the outside.

A pretty girl in beige slacks and a kelly green blouse sat at a computer and was on the phone. From the conversation, Laney deduced someone was booking a mare for the following morning. As she talked, she entered the information into the computer. After a few more entries, she hung up the phone and finally pivoted her chair and smiled at Laney. "May I help you?"

"I'm Laney McVey, the owner of Stoney Creek Farm. My mare, Unreasonable, was just bred for the second time to Captain Jim. Could you tell me when her first breeding was?"

The girl typed in the farm name and waited for the screen to pop up. "Excuse me. I have a Cara Collins listed as the owner of Stoney Creek Farm." She frowned at Laney.

"That was my sister. She died a few weeks ago. I'm the new owner."

"I'm sorry," the girl said and corrected the entry. "Let's see."

Laney held her breath.

"She was bred April thirtieth."

"The time . . . what time of day?" Laney said, impatiently.

"She was booked for the eight-thirty breeding," the girl said.

"Could I see the breeding shed form?" Laney asked.

The girl stood and dug into a vertical file and pulled out Captain Jim's record. "Here it is." she said, and handed a sheet of paper to Laney.

The form showed the name of Unreasonable's dam, sire, owner, the address of the farm, the name of the stud, and the date and time of the breeding: Bred eight-thirty a.m., April thirtieth, Laney read. Attached was a certificate signed by Gray Prescott certifying that the mare had a clean culture.

"If she were bred late, say nine or nine-thirty, would the time of breeding be noted in your record?" Laney asked.

"Yes. The stallion manager is supposed to inform the office if the breeding is unusually late," she said.

Logan's words, *"I saw that man of yours slip him a little green"* echoed in Laney's mind.

"Miss McVey, is there a problem? You're the second person asking to see this breeding record. A police officer was here a couple weeks ago and wanted to see it."

Clearly, Gordon didn't talk with Logan, Laney concluded. "No, I think everything is taken care of," she replied, her voice reverberating in her ears as she backed out of the office.

"Is everything all right, Miss Laney?" Aaron asked, as Laney climbed into the cab. "You look like you are upset about something."

"I'm fine," Laney said, not really feeling fine at all.

"She got a real good cover," Aaron said, flushing with his words.

"I know," Laney said, briefly, not wanting to chit-chat.

The excitement of discovery had been displaced by fear. It was working on her like a gnawing rodent that was feeding, feasting.

"My God–Jackson!"

Laney watched from the front porch as Aaron traveled down the lane to the horse barn where he would park the van. He had dropped her off at Unreasonable's paddock and she had run back to the house while Aaron unloaded the mare in her paddock. She could hear Unreasonable neighing as she kicked up her heels. Sitting in the swing, she looked down at her freckled hands. Trembling and icy, she tucked her fingers into fists. Logan's alarming words played over and over in her head: *"Made it on time this time, did you now? Your fellow didn't get her here until nine-thirty. I saw that man of yours slip him a little green."* My God, that would give Jackson enough time, she realized as her nails cut into her palms.

Laney stood, not knowing what to do first. She looked at the Whooptie waiting in the drive. She raced to the car and pulled away with a screech of tires.

Being Sunday morning, Hickory was almost deserted except for the cars that were parked up and down the streets near the many churches. Organ music poured out of the First Baptist Church on Fourth Street as Laney swung around the corner and parked in front of Second Hand Rose's. A sign that read "Closed. Y'all come back" hung inside Rose's huge storefront window. Laney flew down the alley on the side of the building and took the steps three at a time to Jesse's apartment.

After a second ring of the doorbell didn't produce Jesse, Laney rapped on the door window with a key from her ring.

"Oy vey, lady. Want to raise the dead, already?"

Standing at the foot of the steps was Rose, hands on her well-padded hips. She was dressed in another caftan. Purple pansies smiled from black and yellow faces, and were scattered over yards of apple green material.

"Oy, it's 'rusty hair.'"

There was a click behind Laney and Jesse stuck her head out the door.

"It's all right, Rose," she called, and opened the door a couple of feet. Laney gave Rose a wave and slipped inside.

Laney entered the kitchen, a spacious room with white painted metal cabinets and an old fashioned enameled sink with a bright calico curtain gathered around it to hide the plumbing. A dinosaur stove with a cooking well and an assortment of chrome knobs stood menacingly next to a baking rack with a flour bin. In the center of the room, a blue and white enameled metal table supported by four light oak legs was surrounded by four matching chairs.

Jesse shifted her bare feet on the green and white block linoleum floor. She had flung on a pink negligee with unrolled hems and snags that pulled at the chiffon.

"Jesse, I'm sorry if I wakened you."

Jesse tried to smooth her disheveled hair with her hands and she wiped her mouth with the back of her hand.

"I worked late last night. It's okay, Laney. I should be up by now, anyway," she said, as she glanced at the clock on the wall over the stove. "How about some coffee?"

"None for me, Jesse, but make some for yourself."

Jesse filled a chrome percolator with water and scooped coffee from the refrigerator into the basket. When she plugged it into a wall socket, she swiveled and faced Laney. "I'm so sorry about the other night." Her gray eyes brimmed with guilt.

Laney, from a chair at the table, said, "I know you are, Jesse. Let's forget about it. Okay?"

"Can you?" A tear crested and slipped over.

"Yes. I just think you did something stupid. But I've been there, too."

"I can't imagine you doing anything like breaking into a house," Jesse said, as she reached for a mug hanging on hooks under the cabinet next to the sink.

"May I ask you a couple questions?" Laney asked.

"Anything," Jesse said sincerely. Laney thought maybe she might tell her anything to make amends for breaking in the other night.

"Did Jackson know that Cara was seeing Tony?"

Jesse stared at Laney for a long time. She finally answered, "He knew."

Laney was surprised. "You seem so sure."

"I was the one that told him."

Red hot with excitement, Laney asked, "Why did you do that?"

"He asked me."

"Jackson asked you? When?"

Jesse stood staring at the coffee pot.

"A watched pot never boils," Laney said.

Jesse smiled at Laney, then remembering the question, answered, "It was while Cara was at the seminar in Frankfort."

"Can you remember the day?"

"Sure. It was the Thursday before Cara died. "I was at the house cleaning. I cleaned for Cara every Thursday," she continued in a subdued voice, her eyes downcast.

Sitting forward in her seat, Laney asked, "Jesse, tell me exactly what was said . . . if you can."

The coffee finished perking and Jesse grasped the handle and poured into her mug. She gestured with the pot to see if Laney had changed her mind. Laney shook her head.

Jesse set the pot on the counter and carried her cup to the table and sat across from Laney. "Jeez, Laney, what's all this about?"

"I don't have time right now. Just tell me."

Jesse seemed rattled by Laney's intensity. "I was cleaning the kitchen when Jackson just appeared on the screened porch. I let him in and he sat himself down at the kitchen table and asked me if Cara was dating anyone. He said he had seen a strange car in the drive and part of his duties as farm manager was security on the farm."

"What did you tell him?"

"When he said it was a black Camaro convertible, I told him it was Tony Richards's car and he was seeing Cara."

"What did he say when you told him that?"

Jesse took a gulp of her coffee before answering. "You know, that was the strangest thing. He got all excited like. Like he wanted to know all about him."

"What did you tell him about Tony?"

"Just stuff . . . what he did . . . where he lived . . . junk like that."

"Did you tell him Tony sold RVs?"

"Yeah . . . and boats . . . he seemed real interested in boats."

"Did you tell him anything else, Jesse?"

"I might have told him he had a boat to sell. Yeah, I think I told him Tony and Nick owned a runabout and Tony's partner, Nick, wanted to sell it."

Laney felt a trickle of sweat slide down between her breasts, and her underarms were wet.

"One more question, Jesse. Does Jackson have a key to the house?" She held her breath.

Jesse jumped up to get a second cup of coffee. She flung the answer over her shoulder. "Yeah, Cara had given him a key so he could feed Blackberry anytime she was away."

Laney exhaled.

28

Late Sunday Afternoon, May 19

Gray rang the doorbell for the second time. Gazing out to the pink Buick, he watched Puccini do a long stretch, jump to the seat, and then to the blacktop. The tabby checked out the tires of the Whooptie that was parked in front of the Buick, then wandered off toward the woods that led down to the creek.

Gray loped along the flagstone walk behind the house and when he turned the corner of the screened porch, he practically ran into Laney, who had just stepped out the door. He hugged her from behind and nuzzled the vulnerable spot below her ear that usually produced a squealing response. Instead, Laney wiggled out of his embrace and stepped away.

"Something I ate?" Gray said, holding his hand over his mouth.

"Gray, please, don't be cute," Laney said.

Then Gray saw the tightened lines crowding her eyes and the vague unfocused stare that had been there immediately after Cara's death. But there was something else—an underlying hopelessness.

"C'mere you," Gray said, as he led her back to the porch and sat her down into one of the iron chairs. He snatched the ring of keys from her hand and unlocked the door to the kitchen. "Don't move," he commanded.

When he returned to the porch, he carried a tray with him. Laney hadn't budged. She sat staring through the trees at the creek's surface dancing in the sun. Laney turned her head toward Gray as he poured the tea from the blue and white teapot into the matching cups.

"Gray, I have to tell you," she said, like an automaton. Exhaustion seemed to have overtaken her body. Her hands lay upturned and limp in her lap.

Gray squeezed a slice of lemon into Laney's cup and spooned some sugar on top. He stirred the tea and placed it in front of her like she was an invalid. "Laney, tell me."

She began in a voice so tired and soft, Gray had to bend forward to hear the words. Then, as though Tinkerbell herself were clapping, her voice gradually became stronger, more animated. Her brown eyes began to crackle with renewed energy.

"Jackson was an hour late for the breeding?" Gray roared. "But he told Gordon that he left the farm at seven-thirty that morning."

"He told me the same thing the night I arrived."

"What else did you find out?"

Laney told Gray about Jackson's bribe of the stallion manager. "Gray, this means Jackson's alibi isn't any good for the morning Cara died."

"Karl's alibi doesn't hold up either. Remember, he wasn't at the warehouse the morning Cara died."

"Gray–" Laney began.

"Maybe Jackson did have a breakdown that morning," Gray interrupted.

"Then why lie to the police and me? And there's something else."

"I thought maybe there was," Gray smiled.

"I found the other paddle."

"Paddle?"

"The paddle that a second person used on that canoe ride with Cara." Laney told Gray about her snakebird dream and how she had retrieved the paddle the morning after Blackberry was shot.

"Laney, the police found three paddles in the springhouse. Three plus the one found with the canoe makes four." Gray knew he was patronizing, but he couldn't help himself.

"One of those paddles in the springhouse was replaced by one from the dock. Mother said the dock had twenty paddles. I only counted nineteen."

Gray thought for a long time. "What if that paddle you found belonged to someone else along the creek?"

"The paddles all came from the same manufacturer in Mississippi. When Cara and Joe got married, they bought their two canoes and the four paddles at the same time Mother and Karl replaced their old rigs. I remember Cara telling me they got a cheaper rate by ordering in quantity. It doesn't seem likely someone else had the same kind. Most people around here have the plastic paddles, anyway."

"Where is it?"

"I dropped it in the icehouse."

Gray finished his tea in a big gulp and refreshed Laney's from the pot. "Is that it?"

"No," Laney said. Gray settled back in his chair and fingered the bandage on his forehead.

"Go on," he said.

"I talked to Jesse after I got back from the breeding shed."

"And . . ."

"Jackson had a key to the house. Cara gave it to him."

"What the hell for?"

"To feed Blackberry whenever she was away. I think he stabbed the doll."

"Why would he do that?" Gray said sarcastically.

"I haven't figured that one out yet."

"Guess you think he stole the gun and the will too."

"You said it–not me," Laney said meanly.

"You thought Karl did it."

"I've changed my mind." The frown deepened between Laney's eyes. "Jesse told me that Jackson knew Cara was seeing Tony."

"So what?" Gray retorted.

"Jesse told Jackson where Tony lived and that he had a boat for sale. She said he really seemed interested in that boat."

"Are you implying that Jackson shot Tony? Come on, Laney. Gordon thinks Nick shot Tony over that boat."

"But Jesse told us that Tony had agreed to sell the boat," Laney persisted. "What reason would Nick have?"

Gray told Laney about his meeting with Gordon at the courthouse on Friday. After talking with her mother, Laney wasn't surprised that Jake had implicated Nick and Karl in the drug trafficking.

"Maybe Tony found out the boat was loaded with drugs and Nick had to shut him up. Jackson had no motive to kill Tony," Gray said.

"Damn it, why won't you believe me?"

Gray could see she was at her limit. "Changing the subject, Freddie reported that the bullet that I took out of Blackberry, came from the same gun that killed Tony."

Laney swatted Gray's sleeve on the way to her feet. "Why didn't you tell me sooner? Do you know what that means?"

"I know what you think it means." He smiled, happy to see that her old fire had returned.

"Jackson must have shot Blackberry."

"Why in the hell would he do that? He was the one who helped you that night. Without Jackson, Blackberry would have died."

"Jackson is so good, isn't he?" Laney's voice was icy. Gray looked up and for the first time saw revulsion in her face.

"Laney, he is. I admire him tremendously. Everyone does. As a farm manager, he's a gold mine."

"He's so good, you wouldn't dare think he could do anything bad. He's almost like a self-sacrificing saint. But what you don't know is, Jackson does so much for you that he feels he has rights to you."

"What are you driving at?" Gray asked, amazed.

"He's become possessive with me and his acts of kindness are laden with ulterior motives. I think there is something wrong with the man . . . something a little twisted . . . not quite right."

Gray shifted in his seat with her words. Laney was the only one he'd ever heard who had spoken about Jackson so. "You're mistaken, Laney."

"He tried to jump my bones."

That got his attention. "Jackson? When?"

"It was when I was helping with the foaling. Jackson had had too much wine–"

"Whoa. I don't recall wine drinking being part of the foaling process."

"Jackson said it was to celebrate the last foaling of the season. He had the glasses and the bottle all chilled–almost like it was planned."

Gray didn't comment.

"Anyway, he frightened me. Later, he apologized and said it would never happen again. But not before I saw a side of him I'd never seen before."

Gray was ticked. "Did he hurt you?"

"Let's just say he was rough . . . forceful. Another thing. I thought about this on the way home from Wilmere Stud. He asked me a couple times if I were going to sell the farm."

"When did you tell him that you had inherited it?"

"That's the point. I didn't. When I asked him how he knew, he said he just thought that because Cara and I were so close, she would leave it to me. Funny, the reading of the will blew me away."

"So you think maybe he stole the will and read about the inheritance?"

"Yes. Then, Monday, when I had dinner at his cottage–"

"You had dinner with Jackson after what he did to you?"

"That's what I mean, Gray. He was so remorseful. He keeps me off guard with his sweetness and kind deeds. He had just saved Blackberry. How could I refuse? It was payback time."

"How did the evening go?"

"You won't believe it."

"He didn't? . . . " Gray sat forward in his seat while Laney settled back in hers.

"Just listen. We ate on the porch. He served the most wonderful meal. When I asked him if his mother had taught him to cook, guess what he said?"

Gray shrugged.

"He said, 'My mother's a slut.'"

"No way." Gray felt his mouth drop open.

"Sure put a damper on the evening, I tell you."

"I bet." Gray said, recovering.

"Then he reminded me that he did a lot for me. When I agreed he was the best horse farm manager in the county, he came out with the evening's coup de grace."

"Which was? . . . "

"I want to marry you."

"God, Laney, maybe he misunderstood."

"Are you suggesting that I led him on?" Laney almost tipped over her chair getting to her feet.

"Course not. Did you set him straight?"

Laney's brown eyes never wavered. "That very moment."

"What did he say?"

"He said, 'So it's Prescott.' Then he snuffed out the candle with his fingers and took me home. His eyes were absolutely spooky."

Neither of them spoke for a long time. Laney walked to the screen and focused on the creek again. Gray finally broke the silence.

"Speaking of snuffing, Gordon dug a thirty-eight bullet out of my truck upholstery."

Laney twirled, her face blanching to a deathlike gray. She swallowed and tried to speak but her mouth opened and closed without a sound. Her body swayed. Finally, one word escaped her lips, "Jackson."

"Karl."

"Karl's in jail."

"Jackson's in Maryland."

"Gray, if anything happened to you, I couldn't bear it." She collapsed into the chair and her hands covered her face. Gray pried one finger away at a time until he held her face in his hands. He kissed her trembling mouth. "Laney, sweetheart . . . Karl had time to shoot at my truck before Gordon arrested him."

"But why would Karl shoot at you?" Laney persisted.

"Maybe he heard I was snooping around at the warehouse in Florence, or thinks I said something to Maddy. Who knows what slime will think."

Gray leaned over the table and kissed Laney again. This time it was long and hard. He kicked away his chair as he stood, pulling Laney into his arms. Her cool trembling mouth, his hot open lips, melded into a sensual deep kiss. Gray felt her body lean into his, moving, molding. "Laney," he whispered, as he drew his mouth away.

"Gray, I love you," Laney murmured.

"You don't know how I've wanted to hear that." Gray buried his face in her chestnut hair. "But Cara is still between us, Laney."

"I have to know."

"I know." Gray held her at arm's length. "Please stay with me tonight. I want to be near you."

Laney thought for a minute. "Perhaps tomorrow night. Tonight, I want to be with Mother. She's been through so much."

"Blackberry is ready to come home. Can I bring her over to Maddy's tonight?"

Laney brightened. "That would be terrific. I miss her so."

The phone rang in the kitchen and Gray rushed to answer it.

"That was Gordon," Gray said when he returned. "Nick Owens has just been arrested for drug trafficking. A thirty-eight Smith and Wesson was found taped under the hood of his Mercedes. Police are doing a ballistics check to see if it was the gun used in Tony's murder. If it checks out, they'll add a charge of murder."

29

Late Sunday Evening, May 19

Laney sped over the stepping stones that snaked through the herb garden. The scent of the new growth of thyme filled her nostrils. As she passed behind the buggy house, she saw that the tiny blue buds of the vinca were closing in the deepening evening shadows. She missed Blackberry's white-tipped tail whipping ahead of her, but was comforted by the thought that they finally would be reunited tonight.

When she saw the gray walls of the springhouse ahead, Laney paused and pivoted to peer back up the hill at the buggy house. As the sun dipped behind the structure, a blazing corona flared around the slatted cupola. The weathervane was still, its arrow pointing north.

Down the path she trod, until she stood at the wooden door of the springhouse. A shiny new padlock was in place. One word to Jackson and it was done.

Jackson—his name evoked feelings of dread. What was she thinking of? She had promised Gray she would pack a few things and come directly to town. God, if he knew where she was heading.

She had gotten the idea when Jesse apologized to her that morning. "I can't imagine you doing anything like breaking into a house," she had said. Never in a million years would Jesse think her words would prove to be prophetic. But she needed more evidence—unquestionable proof that Jackson was somehow involved in the death of Cara and Tony. Now that Nick had been arrested, it seemed particularly critical.

She sped along the now familiar path, her long legs eating up the distance in great strides. Soon her face was damp with sweat. She regretted that she hadn't taken the Whooptie or bike down the black-top lane to the cottage, but Aaron was still at the barn, and she didn't want him to know where she was going. The shaggy bark of "Old Hickory" loomed ahead of her and she paused and languished a moment in its dark memories. Grabbing a clump of weeds for bal-ance, Laney knelt on the bank and dipped her hand into the quiet water and splashed its coolness on her face. Refreshed, she went on.

She knew what was ahead by the sound of crashing water and she kept her eyes focused on the trail, not wanting to see the dam again. But when she finally stood upon the millstone below the cottage, her eyes jerked to it like there was some mysterious magnet in the mam-moth pile of stones. The water wasn't high, but it rolled over the rim like a continuous sheet of gray-green foil to crumple below. Laney wrenched her eyes away and twisted her body around until she faced the cottage. As though the house was warning her to stay away, a sud-den surge of air swept down and chilled her. Fast moving shadows followed as the sun disappeared behind the hill.

Unnerved, she hung back, wavering.

The sound of beating wings brought Laney spinning around. There he was. The snakebird rose heavily from below the dam, his sodden wings glistening and flapping laboriously to gain altitude. His crude serpentine neck stretched forward and the white patches were visible with each thrash of his wings. Soon he was sailing above Stoney Creek, spiraling, soaring–free and powerful.

"Well, Laney, what's it going to be: cardinal or snakebird?" Ambivalent, she wondered what her sister would have done.

The words she heard in her head were as clear as if her sister had screamed them in her ear. "Go for it!"

Laney climbed the hill until she came to the steps of the porch. When she sneaked one last look behind her, she saw wispy mist rising from below the dam.

Stepping onto the porch was déjà vu. The canvas director's chair was back facing the creek. The wick of the citronella candle on the square table was still standing at attention where Jackson had pinched it out, and the wick of the other candle had melted into the dirty yel-low wax.

Crossing the porch, Laney tried the door. She was surprised when it opened with a twist of the doorknob. She stepped inside the sitting room. Why was she tiptoeing?

Everything in the room was unchanged. No pictures. No knick-knacks. Stark and barely functional. Laney hurried into the kitchen where Jackson had prepared her meal. The room was dim in the evening light. When she reached to her right and flipped the wall switch, a flashing fluorescent tube slowly heated up to cast its blinking light on faded green walls. Squinting from the eerie glare, she saw maple stained cabinets surrounding the room. The varnish had yellowed from age and a thick coating of grease. An antique butcher block clutched the center of the floor. On its scored surface, a ring of shriveled, dehydrated grapefruit lay next to what looked like a black, slimy head of lettuce. A cockroach moved crookedly out of an empty plastic bag then scurried back in. "Ugh," Laney shuddered.

Stepping to the sink, she peered out the window. By crouching, she could see Aaron leading a mare and foal to the horse barn beyond the grove of trees. It must be feeding time already, Laney thought.

The odor of garbage assaulted her nostrils and drew her eyes downward to the sink full of dishes. Her legs straightened with a jerk and her shoulders hunched to stop the sensation of cold fingers on her neck. The pot that had held the chowder that Jackson had prepared for their dinner was crusting away on top of the shattered soup bowls and plates that had held the "work of art" salads. Below the dishes, dried red wine stained the crystal shards of wine goblets. My God, these dishes have been thrown into the sink, Laney realized. Something happened here. It's like time stopped with that dinner. What kind of provocation would make Jackson do this? Could it have been my refusal of his marriage proposal?

Laney rushed from the kitchen, slapping at the light switch as she ran. When she got to the door to the porch, she pulled up. I've come this far. I've got to do this. I need proof that Jackson killed my sister.

She pivoted and rushed down a short hall that led past a bathroom and another room. Swinging the door open, Laney felt sure that she had found Jackson's bedroom. The bed was rumpled and clothes were scattered about the floor. This is so unlike Jackson, Laney thought.

She probed around in a small closet that was filled with fine sport jackets and pants. All the hangers were askew and much of the clothing lay in piles on the floor. By the looks of the disarray, Laney felt it was a recent peculiarity. When she opened the drawers to the dresser, the deep bottom two drawers containing Jackson's sweaters were neat with each sweater enclosed in a separate plastic bag. The upper drawers containing underwear and socks were in chaos. Socks were unmatched and hanging from the open drawer.

Nothing here. Laney dashed back into the hall and passed a narrow staircase. She could see the front door of the cottage down a short hall to the left of the steps. She ran up the creaky stairs two at a time. From the window on the landing, she saw that daylight was fading quickly. When she reached the top of the stairs, she turned left toward a door at the end of the short hall. When she turned the doorknob, the heavy paneled door suddenly lurched away as though the room were tilted away from her. It slammed against the wall. The jarring crash reverberated through the silent house like a crack of thunder.

As Laney's heart recovered its pounding beat, she peered into what was an office of sorts. A broken slat in a window blind provided the only dim light in the room. A cord, dangling from above, brushed Laney's cheek. When she gave it a quick yank, a yellow bulb swung recklessly, casting swaying shadows across the ceiling.

Quickly, she scanned the room. The only furnishings were a wooden student's desk, chair, and a four drawer filing cabinet.

Laney flew to the desk, frantically opening and closing the drawers. There was nothing but the usual paper clips, rubber bands, and assorted office supplies. Her eyes swept the desk top. It was bare except for an obsolete IBM typewriter.

She attacked the file cabinet. As soon as Laney pulled the first drawer open, she knew this was all together different. Unlike the chaos downstairs, Jackson's neatness and organization were evident. A group of green hanging files divided the folders.

The label on the first file staggered her: CARA MCVEY COLLINS. A file on her sister? As her eyes slid back to each succeeding folder tab, she felt a growing uneasiness: JOSEPH WILLIAM COLLINS, TONY RICHARDS. What was this?

Laney snatched her sister's file from the drawer and flipped it open. A typewritten sheet of paper lay on top of a legal document. As Laney's eyes scanned the words, she realized that she was holding a dossier on her sister: Cara's birth date, her mother and father's names, her own name listed as sister, Cara's wedding date, Karl and Maddy's wedding date. Every important family event and person in Cara's short life was listed. The personal record concluded with DATE OF

DEATH: APRIL 30, 1996. Attached to the sheet, a newspaper clipping from the *Hickory Herald* reported the canoe accident that claimed her sister's life. Lifting the dossier, she studied the legal document underneath. Across the top of the document, she read: THE LAST WILL AND TESTAMENT OF CARA MCVEY COLLINS.

"I knew it!" Laney shouted, "Jackson stole it."

Laying the file on the top of the cabinet, Laney grabbed the next folder: JOSEPH WILLIAM COLLINS. Inside, was a similar dossier on her late brother-in-law. Under the DATE OF DEATH was typed JANUARY 5, 1994, and clipped to the file was a newspaper obituary stating that the cause of death was a heart attack. It listed Cara as the only surviving relative. So, Jackson knew that Cara was to inherit everything. Laney placed the file on top of Cara's.

The *Lexington Post* article reporting the discovery of Tony's body in the freezer lay just inside TONY RICHARD'S file. His dossier listed his DATE OF DEATH as APRIL 28, 1996. Good God, Laney suddenly remembered, the police don't know the date of Tony's death. How would Jackson know when he died, unless . . . . Laney's face flamed and her rapid heartbeat and over-breathing left her dizzy. Licking her dry lips, she concentrated on breathing normally. I've got to take this to the police, Laney thought, tossing the folder on top of the others.

As she started to close the drawer, another file caught her eye: LANEY LEA MCVEY. She seized the file and swung it open. The folder was empty except for a large manila envelope. Her hands shook as she ripped the envelope open and dumped the contents on top of the other files. Her stomach abruptly plunged when she recognized the contents. A round trip ticket reservation to Baltimore lay on the manila folder. She slipped the ticket out of the USAir reservation packet quickly. The date of departure read May fifteenth. Laney's eyes riveted on the unused ticket festering in her damp shaking fingers like an ulcer.

"He's here," she choked. "Got to get out of here!"

As Laney scrambled to put the contents of the envelope together, the files slipped to the floor. She frantically gathered the contents of the folders into one haphazard pile and stuffed them into the manila envelope. After jamming the folders back into the file cabinet, she slammed the drawer and pulled the light cord. The room plunged into darkness.

Laney felt her way into the hall and when she peered out the landing window, a leaden shroud of fog obscured the black pine trees. She spun and stumbled down the stairs, hugging the folder close to her chest. Maybe Gray will believe me now, she thought. Reaching the bottom of the stairs she turned to her right. God, just let me get out of this house.

She was certain that Aaron had left the farm by now but she really didn't care if he saw her or not at this point. She just wanted to get off the farm as quickly as possible.

When she reached the door to the porch, she was shaken to see that the mist hugging the creek and bank was growing denser by the minute. She ran down the steps, turned and dashed to the front of the house. The blacktop drive began at the side of the house and swung between the pine tree grove to the horse barn, foaling barn and office. Laney clutched the folder tighter to her body and began the hike through the thickening fog.

Abruptly, she froze in her tracks. A pair of moving lights in the direction of the foaling barn filtered through the gloom. Jackson? Laney beat a retreat and stepped behind the house. The twin lights turned and faced the drive to the cottage. The fog was a ghostly cloud before the headlights. Laney didn't wait to see if they would follow the long drive to the cottage. She darted into the woods that ran along the creek.

As though pursued, she stumbled wildly along the path. The darkness had deepened and the encroaching fog was fast blanketing the trail ahead of her. The sound of water erupting below the dam identified where she was along the creek and its roar disguised any noises that would have indicated that Jackson was chasing her. Soon the crashing faded to a muffled rumble and Laney paused to catch her breath and look for signs that she was being followed. Nothing but chirping crickets penetrated the night. Maybe that had been Aaron leaving the barn to go home, she rationalized.

She had no idea when she passed "Old Hickory." By this time, the fog had shrouded all but the vaguest shapes of the closest trees as she struggled to stay on the dew slick pathway.

At last, the trail curved left and stepping stones replaced the path. Climbing the hillside, she found the wet rocks slippery and at some point near the springhouse, she lost her footing and fell forward onto the stones. With a crack, her knee hit the corner of a rock. She cried out with the pain and rolled onto her side clasping her knee. "Please . . . no," she cried.

Laney rolled from side to side, moaning, "Please don't let it be broken." Slowly, the knife-like throb lessened and she was able to sit upon the rock that had inflicted the agony. She flexed the limb stiffly, and groaning, she lifted herself upright. Balancing on her good leg, Laney shifted her weight tentatively to the injured one. Not broken, she determined. After a couple of small limping steps up the slope, Laney made out a black image through the fog. Almost home, she thought, as she reached out and touched the cold stone of the springhouse.

What was that? A faint sound reached her ears. It was muted, like an animal barking far away. At first, Laney thought maybe it was a neighbor's dog. Laney had often heard Jim Jason's beagle barking in the night. But no, this was closer, and it was a yelp punctuated with ruff-ruff-ruff. I know that bark, Laney thought, her heart jumping. "Blackberry!" Gray must have brought her home.

Laney picked up her pace, hardly giving her painful knee a thought. Thank God, they're here. She began to cry with relief and exhaustion as the buggy house loomed dark and shadowy in front of her. The fog was thinner on the top of the bank and she could barely see the cupola against the veiled sky. A few more steps and she was around the back of the buggy house and climbing onto level ground.

Blackberry yelped, the sound fading to a whimper. Laney stopped on the stepping stones in the kitchen herb garden, half way between the house and the buggy house. All was dark. No lights anywhere. Of course, Laney realized, Gray doesn't have a key. Where are they? "Gray?" she called. A muffled and distant whine answered her question, except it was in the direction of the buggy house.

Laney wheeled to her left and limped to the buggy house door. She grabbed the porcelain knob and in one quick thrust, shoved the door inward. "Blackberry . . . Gray . . . where are—" Laney never finished the question.

30

Sunday Night, May 19

Ping. Ping. Ping. Where was it coming from? Laney tried to move her hands to her head but they were so heavy. Why couldn't she stop the pain? Slowly, her eyes opened to a squint. The pinging merged with her heartbeat and the excruciating throb behind her eyes. She moaned and her eyes closed.

Somewhere far away, someone was talking. The words faded in and out of Laney's consciousness like a bad telephone connection.

She managed to form the word, "Who? . . . " The effort left her breathing hard. She thought she would vomit from the agony in her head.

Slowly, the connection cleared and the voice answered, "You know who this is, Laney."

Awareness returned–a whirling confusion of thoughts, sensations, recognition. She knew that voice. Oh God, the sickening fear. She turned her head and heaved. Oh God, that tiny movement. The pounding beat blinded her for a moment. She took a quivering breath and opened her eyes.

She was in the buggy house. She remembered now. She had opened the door and then something cold and hard cracked down on her skull. She focused on the form standing across from her. Jackson. Was it Jackson? It didn't look like him. But it was his voice–that cold emotionless voice. A lit kerosene lantern on the workbench cast a yellow-orange glow onto his face–an absurd jack-o-lantern, its wide mouth twisted into a freakish grin.

"God help me," Laney murmured.

The pumpkin face spoke, "Nothing can help you."

She sat on the planked floor, her body propped against the door to the kitchen garden. From the crack below the door, she felt the cool air upon her lower back and from somewhere below her, she heard a yelp.

"Blackberry," she whimpered. The dog answered with a series of barks.

The face smiled broader, the absurd toothpick moving to the corner of his mouth. Jackson held the point of a long blade against his left forefinger. As the fingers of his right hand twirled the handle, the long blade flashed in the eerie flickering light.

"Jackson, you didn't hurt her again?" Laney croaked through the pain.

In the unnatural light, Jackson's eyes were black with fiery reflections discharging like tiny explosions. "You came, Laney. I had to help her. I always help, don't I?"

"You do, Jackson. You're always there to help." Laney struggled to make herself sound sincere through her terror. "You'll help Blackberry again, won't you?" Her voice didn't belong to her.

The smile was gone. "No more."

Jackson's pupils alternately contracted and dilated as though bright lights flashed on and off in front of him. In horror, Laney watched while smoldering contempt distorted Jackson's face. She wasn't sure which was more terrifying–Jackson inflamed–or Jackson with no emotion at all. He appeared to be able to turn his emotions on and off at will.

"Why . . . why did you hurt Blackberry?"

"You said you would sell the farm."

"But I changed my mind. I told you." Laney took in his heavy growth of beard, the filthy clothes. Like a scarecrow, bits of straw were embedded in the expensive navy cable stitched sweater and the normally knife sharp creases in his slacks were stretched and baggy. Laney realized they were the same clothes he had worn for their dinner Monday night.

"You're just like Cara. Slut!"

"Like Cara?"

"She led me on. After all I did for her. I got rid of him for her."

"Wh . . . who?"

Jackson went on like he hadn't heard. "Stupid Jesse told me where he lived. Slut. You're all sluts."

Laney shrank against the door, listening with gruesome fascination to his words. She had to keep him talking. "How did you do it, Jackson?"

"It was so easy. I smiled at him. People like me when I smile at them. I said I wanted to see that runabout he was selling. He was so trusting . . . jumped right into my Rover and took me to the rental unit."

Laney slowly moved her legs until she was sitting on one knee. She raised her right foot and placed it on the wood floor. Pain shot through her injured knee. *If I can just keep him talking, maybe I can make a run for it.*

Jackson continued, seeming not to notice her change in position. "No one was around. No one heard. So easy to cram the body into the freezer. Locked up and came back to my farm. So easy."

Laney saw Jackson twirl the knife faster and faster. Drilling into his forefinger, the knife point began to draw blood and it dripped onto Jackson's pants. Just as Laney was ready to bolt, Jackson stopped its turning and pointed the knife at her and said deliberately, "Don't even think about it." His eyes were dark daggers of loathing.

Her heart sank. She didn't move.

From below, Blackberry whined. Laney ached to see her. Jackson went back to rotating the blade. He didn't seem to feel the pain. The blood dripped.

"The farm was almost mine." His mouth dissolved into an evil leer with the memory. "But I showed her."

"How?" Laney whispered.

"We had dinner that night . . . just like we did. The next morning, I met her at the springhouse. We took the canoe. She sat up front, her back to me. When I asked her to marry me, she laughed at me. She told me she would marry Tony. She kept laughing." His eyes temporarily glazed over, then abruptly focused back on Laney. "But it was my turn to laugh. I told her Tony was dead. She turned and looked at me just as I swung the paddle. She saw it coming. I saw the perfect O of her mouth as it hit her . . . heard the clean crack of the paddle. She fell into the bottom of the boat."

All through the grotesque narration, Laney watched the toothpick move about his mouth as though it had a life of its own.

"I went into the water just past the hickory tree," Jackson continued. "I gave the canoe a shove into the swift channel in the middle of the creek and watched Cara go over the dam with the canoe. It was so easy."

"The paddles . . . what happened to the paddles?" Laney asked, tears pouring down her cheeks as Jackson completed relating the last moments of her sister's life.

Jackson cocked his head as though he were remembering, blinking furiously. "The paddles? They flew into the creek when I hit her. I looked everywhere when I got back from the breeding shed, but I couldn't find them. Late that night, I stole one from Hickory Dock."

Jackson's orange face smirked with the pride of it all. To Laney, the beautiful dimple was now a pit into his deranged mind. Laney felt her whole body trembling with revulsion and a terrible rage. Like a craving, her body cried out for revenge for her sister's death. She wrung her hands together and felt her mouth salivate with the ache to grab him, to smash his pumpkin face in. Instead, forming two small fists with her hands, she breathed out through her nose with a frustrated whimper. She had to stall him. Someone would come to help her. They had to.

Her voice quavered, "Jackson, let us go?"

Another smile.

"Please," Laney pleaded.

Jackson lifted the knife with his right hand and with a quick downward stab, drove the blade into the workbench. Terrified, Laney cowered against the door.

Not taking his eyes from Laney, Jackson worked the handle back and forth, until the knife was released. "Another death, Laney? I'm so good at it, don't you think?"

"You won't get away with it this time," Laney threatened.

"But I will." Jackson spit out the nub of toothpick and popped another one from the pile on the workbench into his mouth. "They think Cara died in an accident and I planted the gun that I shot Prescott and Tony with in Nick's car."

"Gray?" Laney pretended surprise.

"Didn't I tell you? I killed your precious Prescott. Then, when I hid the gun in Nick's car today, I made sure the police got a little anonymous tip."

So, Jackson hadn't seen Gray at the farm today, Laney reasoned. He must have been in Lexington most of the day. She decided to keep the information that Gray was alive to herself. "Jackson, I thought you were in Maryland."

"That's what I wanted you to think. That's my alibi, you see. I'm good . . . really good."

Laney suddenly remembered the envelope with the dossiers and the unused round trip air tickets. Where was it, she asked herself. Mentally, she retraced her route back from the cottage. I fell. That's it! I must have dropped it when I fell. Then, when I heard Blackberry, I forgot all about it.

"Everyone will think I was in Maryland when you died." The comment jerked Laney back.

"Died?" Laney felt her heart stop for a moment.

"Laney, understand I've got to do this," Jackson said, taking a step toward her.

In one smooth move, Laney leaped to her feet, spun around and yanked at the doorknob. The door swung open but before she could run, Jackson's arm was around her body. The knife in his right hand lay cold against her throat, the blade poised to slice. Jackson dragged her backwards into the buggy house, his hand with the knife unwavering. She could feel his hard body against her back and could smell his foul breath from his lips pressed near her cheek.

"Don't do that again, Laney. I didn't plan it that way. I know a better way," Jackson breathed into her ear as he led her to the center of the floor. "Don't you want to see Blackberry?"

Feeling the knife press her skin every time she swallowed, Laney was afraid to speak.

Still holding the knife at Laney's throat, Jackson bent and with his bloody left hand, opened one of the double trapdoors to the icehouse. Laney felt a rush of cold dank air. Jackson grunted as he swung the door to the left and let it drop with a crash. There was a scurrying below in the inky hole and suddenly Blackberry's head appeared at the top of the steep stairs. Jackson swept her off the steps with single brutal thrust of his foot. She let out a series of yelps while she tumbled down the stairs.

"Go say goodbye to your precious dog," Jackson spat, as he released the arm that held her and gave her a vicious shove with his knife hand.

Laney's hands flew out in front of her and her scream reverberated off the stone walls as she pitched forward into the underground blackness of the icehouse.

Laney lay on her stomach at the foot of the rotting stairs. She thought she had lost consciousness, but the pain was too real. Her left forearm had taken most of the impact as she slammed against the steps and rolled the rest of the way down to the flagstone floor. Pulling her right arm under her, Laney rested her weight on her good elbow and turned onto her right side. She groaned as her left arm shifted position and rested on her left thigh. Sitting upright, she felt the arm gingerly with her right hand. Grunting and holding her breath, she felt for a compound fracture. She felt two distinct lumps, one just above the wrist and another about three inches further up her arm. Dizzy with the pain, she couldn't stop the tears that poured out of her. Above her, she heard Jackson walking over the thick oak planks. She strained her eyes to see around her but the blackness was absolute. Lifting her head, she could barely see faint cracks of lantern light between the floorboards.

A furry body touched her leg and she recoiled in fear. A whine and soft nudge against her thigh. "Blackberry!" Laney stretched out her good arm and gathered the warm body to her face. She felt the familiar licks on her wet cheeks. Moving her hand over the dog's body, she didn't feel Blackberry resist with pain. Her fingers touched the bare skin area where Gray had shaved the fur to remove the bullet, and she felt the puckered suture line. "Poor baby," she crooned, her tears wetting Blackberry's fur. Her tail wagged against her broken arm. "Easy girl," she said.

Jackson called down from above, "It's time, Laney."

Laney struggled to her feet. "My God, what's he doing?" She heard the slosh of liquid. A moment passed before she comprehended. When she did, she felt about with her foot until she found the first step. Holding her injured arm against her body with her right hand she staggered up the stairs. She pushed against one of the doors with her good arm. It wouldn't budge. Jackson had slid a board beneath the handles.

She smelled the fumes from the kerosene drifting down between the double trap doors.

"Jackson," she screamed, "Don't do this! I'll do anything you say!"

"I'll just set a little fire," Jackson laughed, the maniacal outcry of someone beyond reason.

"Jackson, they will know you did this," Laney cried.

"They will think you tripped and knocked over the kerosene lamp and bumped your head," Jackson said.

Laney couldn't believe his reasoning. Police would check the flight and find that he never boarded the plane. Wouldn't they? Remembering how Jackson had paid off the stallion manager, she wasn't so sure. But firemen would find the trapdoors barred shut and her and Blackberry below. But then she realized that once this old building was consumed in flames, the dry structure would most likely collapse into the icehouse.

She reeled down the stairs, her foot collapsing one of the rotten steps. She caught herself, only to almost fall again after tripping over Blackberry at the bottom. Holding her hand out in front of her, she began walking toward the circular rock walls. About two feet from the steps, her foot hit an obstacle that skipped and scraped on the flagstone surface. When she reached down with her right hand, she felt the smooth wooden surface of the canoe paddle. A lot of good it would do her now. Tears started anew. She thought of her mother . . . of Gray. Blackberry leaned against her legs, not understanding, her tail thumping with affection. From above, silence.

Then Laney heard the crackle, smelled the smoke, and through the cracks in the floor saw the first glow of fire.

31

Sunday Night, May 19

It had been a long day and the shower had felt wonderful. Gray slipped on his semi-dirty jeans, making a mental note to go to the laundromat tomorrow. In the clean clothes basket, he found a tee-shirt and a denim long sleeve shirt that wasn't too wrinkled. After dressing, he gave his wet hair a quick comb-through while two-stepping around the floor, trying to scoot his damp feet into his penny loafers.

Looking about his bedroom, he promised himself he would dig into the mess before Laney stayed tomorrow night. He recalled their conversation earlier and his heart lurched. He still couldn't believe she had said she loved him.

The past three weeks had certainly been grueling for both of them. He fingered the damp patch on his forehead and the rough scabs on his cheeks. Eyeing Puccini lying unfolded on his back with paws curled under, Gray was grateful no one had gotten killed. Puccini had suffered zip from his flying squirrel routine and his own injuries had proved minor. Poor Blackberry had received the most serious injury. Thank God that Nick, Karl, and Jake were all in jail. Maybe he and Laney could relax for a while. Ballistics testing of the gun found in Nick's car may finally solve the mystery of which one of them had shot at him, wounded Blackberry, and killed Tony.

Leaving Puccini purring loudly at the foot of his bed, Gray left the apartment and bounced down the steps to the clinic. The clinic was dark and quiet. He turned on the light in his office and checked his messages. No emergencies. Hallelujah! Only one call from Mary Jo Jenkins whose Persian cat, Jinx, had been operated on to remove a large tumor on Friday. Mary Jo would pick her up in the morning. Gray smiled. She had called at least ten times to check on her "precious."

Gray hooked his beeper to his belt and skipped out the back entrance to the line of dog runs. Blackberry had been the only other animal left at the clinic over the weekend. Most spaying and neutering procedures were done in the mornings during the week and the animals were sent home the next day.

The night was cool and foggy and Gray reminded himself to put on a jacket before he left for Maddy's. A large light lit up the runs in the back of the clinic. Gray loped along the path in front of the tall cyclone fencing until he came to the last run. He had put Blackberry in the largest pen. Special treatment, he admitted to himself.

When he got to the run, the gate was unlatched and ajar. The run was empty. "Blackberry," he called. She didn't come out of the shelter at the rear of the run. Maybe Laney had decided to pick up her dog herself, Gray thought. I hope I didn't forget to latch the gate this morning and she got out. Natine had been after him for ages to put padlocks on all the gates.

Gray ran back to the clinic and phoned Maddy. "Maddy, is Laney there yet?"

"Gray? No, is she supposed to be?" Maddy asked, a little concern in her voice.

"I saw her earlier and she said she was going to spend the night with you."

"That's news to me," Maddy said. "I haven't talked with her all day."

"Hmm. Guess she's still out at the farm. I'll give her a call."

"Ask her to call me. Okay?"

"Sure. Talk at you later." Gray pressed the button and dialed the farm. Laney's answering machine picked up after the third ring. "Damn," Gray said, uneasiness creeping into his gut. Hanging up the phone, he looked at his watch. Nine-thirty. We didn't set a time, but I thought she would be at Maddy's by now, Gray brooded. He recalled the debate they had this afternoon about Cara's death and how sure

Laney had been that Jackson had killed her. He ran over in his mind much that Laney had told him: Finding the canoe paddle, Jackson having a key to the house, Jackson arriving an hour late for the breeding and then apparently bribing the stallion manager. Was he taking all these clues too lightly? He had been so sure that Karl had been responsible for all the shootings. But now Nick had been arrested. But why would Nick shoot Blackberry, or at him, for that matter? What if Cara's death hadn't been an accident and Jackson wasn't as perfect as he appeared? Listen to me, Gray thought, I'm doing a real head trip about Jackson. He's one of the good guys.

Gray decided to go back outside and call Blackberry one more time, just in case he had forgotten to latch the gate.

Gray searched the hall tree in his office for his favorite wind breaker, but remembered it was in the hamper because of the blood stains from his accident. Gray slipped on a red sweatshirt with a Louisville Cardinal dunking a basketball, and ran out to the runs.

"Blackberry!" he called. Nothing. He had just about decided to go back inside to call Maddy again when something on the concrete in front of the run caught his eye. He stooped to get a better look, then lifted a sliver of light colored wood into the yellow glow of the sodium light. Gray stared at the chewed fragment, its stub a cluster of splinters. "Good God," Gray gasped, a ripple of cold fear rushing up his spine. "Jackson!"

"Damn it, Gray, why the hell didn't you tell me this before?" Gordon's voice boomed over the phone.

"Listen, Gordon, I didn't know about all this myself until Laney clued me in earlier today, and to be honest, I pooh-poohed it until I found this toothpick in front of the run. You don't think Jackson is back in town? He wasn't due back until tomorrow," Gray said.

"If he ever left at all," Gordon said sarcastically.

"I didn't think of that possibility–"

"Hold on. I have another call."

Gray paced around his office, waiting for Gordon to get back on the line. Anxiety chomped through his gut like an ulcer on the march. What if Laney was right about the guy. And why had Jackson picked up Blackberry?

The line clicked and Gordon's voice exploded over the line, "Listen, Gray. There's a fire out at Stoney Creek farm. The fire department's on their way. I'll meet you there." Click.

"God no," Gray cried, as he raced out the door to the parking lot. "Let Laney be all right." He was surprised to feel tears running down his face.

32

Sunday Night, May 19

Laney tried to remember everything she ever heard about surviving in a building fire. Stop, drop, and roll. No, that isn't it. Something about smoke rising and most oxygen is found close to the floor. She dropped to her knees and pain shot up the injured leg. God, how do I crawl with only one good arm, she sobbed, but managed to work her way over to the rock wall behind the stairs. She stood up and clutched at the cold walls of stone with her good hand. She began pulling at the rocks in a panic, like she could dig her way out of the underground prison. The stone wall was stacked without mortar and with every rip of her frantic fingers, rock chinking fell to the floor. When she discovered an old hay hook, its point crammed between the chinking, she grasped the wooden handle and scraped and clawed at the stones like a mad woman until she fell to the floor in exhaustion. Only then did she remember that the circular wall was built completely underground, the walls two feet thick to insulate the ice.

Blackberry snuggled at her face. "Blackberry," she cried. Laney could see the blaze flickering and snapping between gaps in the boards. She wondered how long she had before the smoke filtered down and flames penetrated the two inch thick floor above her.

"How is it, Laney?" Jackson called, from just above her at the trap door.

Good God, he's still here, Laney thought disbelievingly. "Jackson!

Please help me! Don't leave me here!"

"It's getting warm up here. I've got to go. I set the tobacco cottons hanging from the rafters first. The flames are shooting to the ceiling."

Laney thought hard–desperately. She had to get him to open the doors. Her leg hit the paddle. The paddle! Just maybe with his deranged reasoning, he might fall for it.

"Jackson," Laney called, "I found the paddle that you used to kill Cara. It's here . . . down here with me. I dropped it down here the day after you shot Blackberry."

Jackson laughed. "Good try, Laney."

"It's true, Jackson. Listen." She groped in the darkness until she grasped the wooden oar. She banged the paddle against the flagstone floor, then swung it about wildly until it bounced dully against the wooden stairs and flew from her hands and settled on the rocks with a clatter. "Hear that? The police will find it down here and know you killed Cara. I'll shield it with my body to keep it from burning completely." Laney was screaming the words to the ceiling as the smell of smoke became stronger. She heard Jackson cough.

"It was at the crossing. It washed down after the storm. Remember when I asked you to pick up my bike? I had put the paddle in the trunk of the Whooptie and later dropped it down here while you were with the farrier."

Jackson didn't answer. The only sound was the popping of the dry wood in the roof of the building.

Suddenly, she heard a grate and a thud. A creak. From behind the flight of stairs, Laney saw a blazing rectangle of light fall upon the steps. A billow of black smoke rolled and swirled around a dark shadow of a figure.

"Where is it, slut?" Jackson said, as he began to descend the stairs, his right hand holding out the flashing knife, the other covering his mouth with a cloth. He coughed. Through the open risers, Laney watched as Jackson's legs stepped down heavily upon each tread. She held her breath, afraid if she made the smallest sound, he would turn and see her. When his boot reached the rotted step, he stumbled forward, arms flailing until he caught himself, but not before Laney took the couple seconds of opportunity to reach out for the paddle. Instead, her hand found the hay hook. She stepped to the side of the stairs in the shadows, holding the handle between her first two fingers like a pirate hook. And when Jackson clomped down on the bottom tread, she lunged at him just as he cocked his head and spotted her. With all the force she could muster, she sank the hooked blade into his broad back. He let out a soft cry–almost a whimper–as he fell forward. Laney's hand, frozen to the handle, pulled and ripped downward.

Screaming, Laney pried her fingers from the handle of the hay hook and rolled off Jackson, not knowing whether he was still able to grab her. He didn't move. Moaning from the agony of her broken arm, Laney thought she would black out. Somewhere above her, she could hear sirens, but it was too late. Through the trap door opening, she saw the flames shooting up the walls and heard the sound of glass breaking. Black smoke poured through the opening and swirled about her head. Blackberry cowered in fear at her feet. With her good arm, Laney tried to lift her but her strength was gone. She pushed Blackberry to the stairs and shoved her ahead of her as she climbed. A roof rafter fell across the opening, scorched and smoldering. Choking from the smoke and fumes, Laney fell upon the stairs. Her last memory was reaching out for Blackberry.

33

Late Sunday Night, May 19

Gray thought he would never get to the farm. The fog lay like a fluffy white blanket at the bottom of every hill and he had to brake the Buick sharply to avoid going off the road. His fingers were frozen to the wheel, his eyes searching the sky to the east whenever he broke through the low lying fog.

"Laney, be all right," he mumbled over and over like a mantra. Why didn't I listen to her instead of discounting everything she said today? As he topped the final hill before the lane to the farm, he saw the glow in the sky, like a bright nebula above the trees. His brakes screeched and the Buick fishtailed as he managed the abrupt right turn into the blacktop lane.

Because of the higher elevation, only wispy tentacles of fog lay along the road to the house. Spooked, Unreasonable ran the fence line along the drive, the mare and Buick neck and neck to the end of the paddock. The trees blocked the sky, but ahead of him, Gray could see the flashing red, yellow, and blue lights of emergency vehicles long before his car swung through the stone abutments.

Before him, the night sky exploded into day. Flickering lights pulsated from the fire trucks and police cars scattered here and there about the yard. Water hoses snaked across the yard from two pump trucks and from a gaping cistern by an ancient maple tree. Dark figures dashed about like they knew their mission.

Gray leaped from his car and ran toward the blazing buggy house. Grabbing a fireman who was directing water from his fire hose onto the blaze, Gray screamed, "Where's Laney?" The sweaty black face of Warren Sullivan, Natine's husband, looked into Gray's stricken face.

"Say man, take it easy. We got her." He pointed to the ambulance just pulling out of the drive. Before Gray could move, the blazing skeleton of the buggy house drooped, hesitated, then buckled and collapsed in a shower of glittering sparks and flame. Gray ran, trying to catch the ambulance before it drove away, but someone grabbed his arm as he flew by a police car.

"Gray," Gordon yelled through the noise and confusion.

"Laney?" Gray cried, his eyes watching the ambulance fly down the road, sirens screaming, red lights oscillating.

"She'll be okay."

"I've got to go." Gray pulled from Gordon's grasp.

"No way you're driving. I'll take you." Gordon gave some last minute instructions to Freddie, and he hopped into the squad car where Gray was anxiously waiting for him.

"She breathed some smoke, Gray. She has a broken arm, maybe a concussion."

"Is she conscious?"

"Wasn't when they pulled her out of the buggy house but she came to after she got some oxygen."

The fog was growing thicker and was pulling up the hills. Gordon crept along. Gray wondered if the ambulance had arrived at the hospital.

"Jackson?"

"I don't know about him. If he was in there, it's all over. We barely got Laney out before the place was an inferno."

"Do you have any idea what happened in there?"

"We'll have to hear from Laney."

"Oh God, Blackberry! You see her?"

"She was with Laney when they found her. After they carried her out, she took off."

"Don't tell Laney she's missing," Gray said, as they finally pulled into the emergency entrance.

"Listen, Gray, I've got to get back to the farm," Gordon said, but Gray was already out of the car, dashing toward the double doors.

34

Early Monday Morning, May 20

The oxygen tube misted and cleared, misted and cleared. Gray couldn't drag his eyes away from it, as though Laney would stop breathing if he missed seeing one breath. Laney's swollen eyes were black and blue from a heavy blow she had sustained. The shoulder high cast on her left arm lay enormous and white on the blue blanket, her tiny white fingertips peeking from the gauze.

Laney had wakened briefly after the setting of her arm and smiled weakly at Gray before drifting back to sleep. Gray looked at his watch. Five-twenty. He sipped at the coffee that Maddy had brought him from the machine down the hall. He was nodding off when he heard Laney's barely audible whisper, "You're . . . wearing the wrong color." His eyes snapped open, but Laney's eyes were closed, the corners of her mouth curved slightly upwards. He stared down at his red Louisville Cardinal's sweatshirt and smiled. Now he knew she would be all right.

Stepping into the room, the night nurse checked Laney's pulse and pressure. Laney slept on. The nurse motioned for Gray to follow her out into the hallway. Closing the door behind her, she said, "Dr. Lyons wants to see you." She nodded toward the nurse's station.

Gray walked past several darkened rooms to a brightly lit area. Mark Lyons looked up and grinned at Gray. He replaced a metal chart in the cart and spoke. "Time you went home. Laney will recover. This experience may have more lasting emotional effects, so get some sleep so you will be fresh for her tomorrow."

"I want to stay."

"Damn, you're stubborn. Doctor's orders. Maddy listened to me and went home. I don't want to sic "Nurse Ratched" on you again," he said under his breath, eyes searching the hallway.

The elevator doors opened and Gordon stepped out. His face was smudged with carbon and his sooty mouth parentheses were typed in boldface.

"How's Laney?" he asked, as Dr. Lyons waved and stepped into the elevator. "Fill him in, Gray. I'm going back to bed." The doors closed.

Gray grasped Gordon's hand in both of his, pumped enthusiastically, then patted him affectionately on the shoulder. "Can't thank you enough for all you did. Mark said she'll be okay. Say pal, one more favor. Could you take me home? Left the car at the farm."

Gordon led the way to the exit stairs and they walked side by side, down one level to the parking lot.

"I drove your Buick back for you. You can drop me off. Freddie took the patrol car."

The sodium security lamps in the almost deserted parking lot cast vaporous halos in the heavy fog. The Buick appeared almost ethereal. Its chrome-draped tailfins were silvery wings poised to fly through the ground clouds.

"There'd have to be a pea soup fog before I would drive that thing," Gordon said, punching Gray's arm.

When they neared the car, through the haze, Gray thought he saw a woman with dark hair waiting in the passenger seat.

"Who's your friend?" he asked. Before Gordon could answer, Gray shouted, "Blackberry!"

Gray swung the door open and the dog jumped up into his face, practically bowling him over. "Where did you find her?" he managed between all the yips, rubs, and face washings.

"When I got into the car to drive it here, she was sitting in the front seat. You must have left the door open when you got to the farm and she jumped in. Don't know who shut it. Could have been anyone out there."

"Thank God. Laney couldn't have stood losing her." Gray let Blackberry stretch her legs and take a leak on a grassy strip dividing the parking lanes. She jumped back in the car.

"Can we go somewhere for coffee? I'm too wide awake for sleep,"

Gordon asked, nudging Blackberry over to the center of the front seat. She turned her soulful eyes on him like he really had some nerve.

Gray started the motor and looked at his watch. "Finish Line will be open in five minutes."

"Let's go," Gordon said, wrapping his arm around the dog.

Five minutes later, they were seated at Gray's favorite table in the corner. Gordon excused himself to wash up in the men's room. Several tables were already full with mostly retired gentlemen. Near the coffee machine, two tables pushed together were slowly filling with the morning regulars. "The Breakfast Club," they called themselves. There were usually at least seven at the table, plus or minus one or two guests that were invited to join them. All greeted and chatted with Gordon on his way back from the rest room and turned and waved at Gray. Jim Haley must have picked up the emergency call on his police scanner and it's already all over town, Gray thought. When Gordon returned to the table, Joni, a pretty girl who was Maury's daughter, brought hot coffee and took their order. Gordon ordered the western omelet. Gray was too wound up to eat.

"What'd you find, Gordon?" Gray asked, taking a gulp of the best coffee in town.

Gordon's face lit up with the thought of the story he was about to relate. He poured cream into his cup, stirred and leaned forward. "When it cooled down enough, we hit the icehouse. Amazing . . . the floor held. Warren said that most woods have a uniform char development of about 1.54 inches an hour. Those two inch boards kept the ceiling and walls from falling into the icehouse. The fire department did their job by ventilating as soon as they got there by breaking those six windows to let out the heat and smoke."

"Cut to the chase, Gordon. Did you find Jackson?" Gray asked.

"Yes, at the bottom of the stairs. Sure you want the details?"

"Go on," Gray said, not sure why he did.

Joni brought Gordon's omelet along with biscuits, grits, and home fries.

"He was lying on his stomach with a hay hook in his back. She ripped it down with a lot of force."

The visualization made Gray want to puke.

Gordon dug into his omelet. "It's not what killed him, though."

Gray swallowed another gulp of coffee. "Smoke inhalation?"

"When we turned him over, there was an eight inch butcher knife in his heart." Gordon took a bite of grits.

"Huh?" Gray's jaw dropped.

"The coroner was called when we found the body and he thinks when Laney got him with the hay hook, he fell forward on his knife. His hand was still on the handle when we turned him over. The autopsy will tell us more."

"Did you find the canoe paddle?"

"It was down there. Spooky place. Jackson must have shoved her down the stairs . . . probably how she broke her arm."

Gray felt like crying, thinking of the agony that Laney must have gone through. "I noticed that her right hand and nails are all cut and bruised. Think maybe when he started the fire, she panicked and tried to claw her way through the walls?"

Gordon paused in his junket through breakfast. He laid down his fork. "I think I've had enough."

"Why do you think Jackson did this?" Gray asked.

"I don't know for sure, but Freddie found something that may answer some questions."

"What's that?"

"When we were looking for Blackberry behind the icehouse, Freddie found an envelope containing some papers. I think they belonged to Jackson, and Laney must have dropped them earlier. A quick look over tells me it may be Jackson's personal account of a lot of people he knew . . . and hated. A couple who have since bit the dust. Cara's will was in there so Jackson knew that Laney would inherit. There's plenty of unanswered questions. I plan to talk to Laney tomorrow, if Doc Lyons will let me at her."

Dawn was creeping into the town and Gray knew the fog would lift with the warming sun.

"I'll take you home. Blackberry and I are going to try to get a couple hours of shut eye," Gray said, pushing out from the table and reaching for his wallet.

"I've got it," Gordon said, and yelled to Janie, "Put it on my tab." He dropped three bucks on the table and waved at the "Breakfast Club."

"Let's hurry before the fog lifts," Gordon said, as they headed for the pink Buick.

35

Monday, May 27–Memorial Day

"I really thought I'd be afraid to go out on the creek again, but this is wonderful," Laney said to Gray from the bow of the canoe. Blackberry sat facing her in the center of the boat, her ears perked and her nose twitching at the creek smells. The sun shone on her pretty black and white face. Behind the dog, Gray paddled, his oar alternating sides to keep the canoe steady in the center of the creek. Little beads of sweat lay on his upper lip and a curl of brown hair lay pasted to his shiny wet forehead.

"Sorry I can't help you with the paddling," Laney said, holding up the arm encased in plaster.

"I bet," Gray grunted, resting the paddle across his knees and letting the canoe drift. He stared at her with his brilliant turquoise eyes. "You look adorable, you know."

"I know," Laney said playfully, patting her orange life jacket with her arm in the sling.

"I mean it. Your bruises are about gone. I can see your freckles again."

"You trying to convince me?"

Gray smiled his wonderful smile. "You look like a Gibson girl with your hair up like that."

Laney tucked a wispy bright auburn tendril under her straw hat. "Mother fixed it for me. It's cool."

"A Victorian girl in a Victorian bed and breakfast. Think it will help you with your writing? . . . meeting new people?"

"That's what I'm hoping."

"When do you think you will open?"

"My arm has to have time to heal and I have to close up my apartment in Pittsburgh," Laney said. "And I promised some articles to John Bernard. Maybe by derby time next year, I can open up full time. First, I have to bone up on being an innkeeper."

"Will Maddy do the baking?" Gray asked, paddling again.

"You betcha." Laney looked down at her right hand. Her finger tips were still tender and her nails were short and uneven in spite of the manicure. She suddenly felt like crying again. She took a shaky breath and stared out at the sparkling water.

"You need to talk about it, Laney." Gray's brows knitted.

"I know. But it's so hard," she said, hot tears rolling from her eyes.

"Gordon said he told you what was in the rest of Jackson's folders at the cottage."

"He did."

"Tell me."

Laney squirmed in her seat. The canoe rocked slightly. "Jackson had always wanted the farm ever since he'd been a little boy. He adored his father, but the folder on his father showed that Cory only gave love and attention to Jackson when he was good, hence, all his self-esteem must have been solely based on being absolutely good. I've thought this through, Gray. I think he needed to see himself as good, even when he wasn't good at all."

"Must be why he was always doing good deeds for people. Practically everyone in this town has a story about something kind that Jackson did for them."

"And if you questioned his motives, his kindness made you feel guilty. Gordon remembers that seven years ago when Paul Carson decided to sell the farm, Jackson's father was going to make an offer on the farm. He had saved most of his life for it. But as luck would have it, he died suddenly. Cory Burns was hardly six feet under when Jackson's mother, Melby, ran off with the money. Cory's will had left her everything. Jackson's file on his mother really said it all. Jackson hated her. I think that hate transferred onto all women," Laney said, leaning over and trailing her right hand in the cool water. "Then, Joe Collins grabbed the farm up and married Cara. The rest is history."

Laney dried her hand on her jeans.

"No, Laney, there's more. Tell me all of it," Gray urged softly.

"I gave a statement to the police."

"You haven't told me how it was for you."

Her eyes filled again. "I told Gordon what Jackson related to me that night . . . that he killed Tony so Cara would marry him . . . so he could get the farm. When she refused him, he killed her. He already knew from the stolen will that I would inherit the farm, so he thought he had another chance. Marry me and get the farm. When I told him I was going to sell the farm, he shot Blackberry in a rage. When I changed my mind about selling the farm and told him I wouldn't marry him . . . he lost it. I think that was when he stabbed the doll. Later, he shot out your windshield and thought he had killed you. He planted the gun in Nick's car, thinking Nick would get blamed for both your and Tony's deaths. Finally, he decided to kill me and Blackberry, making it look like an accident."

"There are some things I don't understand. How did Jackson know about Nick and why kill you and me if it wouldn't get him the farm?"

"When Jesse told Jackson about the boat that Tony had for sale, she also added that Tony's partner, Nick, wanted Tony to sell the runabout. She also disclosed that the two of them didn't get along. Evidently, Jackson thought that might make Nick the number one suspect in Tony's murder."

"But why did Jackson want to kill us?"

"There was really no reason to do it, only pure revenge for the smoldering hatred that had built up in his mind. He struck out at those who hadn't responded to him in the way he wanted." Laney reached out and scratched Blackberry's nose. Her heart gave a lurch at the memory of Jackson kicking her down the stairs. "I loved Blackberry, so Jackson decided to include her in my torment."

"When did he pick up Blackberry?" Gray asked.

"It must have been on his way back from Lexington, after planting the gun in Nick's Mercedes. Being Sunday, Natine wasn't at the clinic. He thought he had killed you, anyway. He lucked out when he found Blackberry in a run in the back. He must have stayed in the front barn until dark."

Gray stopped paddling again. "Gordon said they found food and a sleeping bag in the tobacco barn. I shudder when I think of him being right here on the farm all the time we thought he was in Maryland."

"When he didn't find me at home, he must have dropped Blackberry into the icehouse, then hidden the Range Rover in the horse barn and walked back so I wouldn't know he was on the farm."

"Gordon told me that the murder charge against Nick has been dropped. But he, Karl and Jake Rudnik have quite a few other charges against them. All drug related," Gray said.

Laney didn't seem to hear. In her mind, she was still thinking about Jackson. Nothing was said for the longest time. A cloud obscured the sun for a couple of minutes and Laney felt goose bumps on her bare right arm.

"Laney, you still haven't told me," Gray persisted.

"What it was like down there?"

"Yes."

"I thought I was going to die. When he threw me down the stairs, I first was afraid of the rats and snakes. But when I smelled the smoke, I knew it was over. I came apart." She closed her eyes and felt the fear coming back. Suddenly, she exclaimed, "Gray, have you ever thought you were going to die?"

Gray gaped at her, his face reflecting his horror. Barely perceptibly, he shook his head.

"I remember trying to dig my way through the wall." Laney looked down again at her hand, upturned in her lap. "I don't remember much that went through my mind . . . just an overpowering terror."

"You must have come to your senses long enough to find a way to get Jackson to open the trap door."

"You know, the only thing I remember was when I realized that Jackson was still there, I had to use what wits I still had to get him to open it. I briefly remembered seeing a bluebird flying down the tunnel of trees in front of me when I had raced down the lane to help Mother the day before. I thought I would hit the bird with the Whooptie. Just before I did, he darted up and through an opening in the trees and escaped."

"He took advantage of an opportunity," Gray said.

"Yes. That's what I did, I guess. Anyway, when Jackson tripped on the rotten step, I made my move. Only my hand grabbed the hay hook instead of the paddle. How many times I've wondered if hitting him with the paddle would have allowed me time to escape." Tears were streaming down her cheeks with the thought of the night of terror. "Why did you want to know?" Laney suddenly asked.

"So I could apologize."

Laney was surprised at his words. "Why?"

"I blame myself for some of your pain. I discounted a lot of what you told me that afternoon. I should have believed what you had told me about Jackson."

"I'm one damn stubborn woman. I still would have gone to the cottage. Don't blame yourself, Gray."

"Penance, I guess."

"Don't self-flagellate." She smiled at him. "You're right though. Talking about that night has helped. You know how I tend to bury my head." Laney wiped her nose on her sling.

"Look Gray, 'Old Hickory!' " Laney pointed toward the west bank. The magnificent tree was outlined against the blue sky and the shaggy branches were covered thickly with green leaves.

"Laney, it's time," Gray said, nodding toward the fine blue-gray line in the distance. As soon as Laney saw the dam, she lifted the wreath from the bottom of the canoe. Blackberry sniffed at the herbs as it passed near her nose and snorted.

Laney laid the wreath in the water and watched the slow current carry it away. "Cara . . . for you. I'll never forget you."

The sun sank closer to the top of "Old Hickory" as Gray eased the canoe around and headed back to the springhouse. Laney watched until she saw the wreath slip over the top of the dam.

As the wreath wound its way downstream, the snakebird swung across the lower crossing and perched on a limb of a sycamore tree, just like it was any other evening on Stoney Creek.